THE
CARTEL
6

THE DEMISE

ASHLEY & JAQUAVIS

ST. MARTIN'S GRIFFIN 🐾 NEW YORK

THE CARTEL 6. Copyright © 2016 by Ashley & JaQuavis. All rights reserved. Printed in the United States of America. For information, address St. Martin's Press, 175 Fifth Avenue, New York, N.Y. 10010.

www.stmartins.com

Library of Congress Cataloging-in-Publication Data

Names: Ashley, 1985– author. | JaQuavis, author.
Title: The cartel 6 : the demise / Ashley & JaQuavis.
Description: New York : St. Martin's Griffin, 2016. | Series: The cartel ; 6
Identifiers: LCCN 2016001963| ISBN 978-1-250-06699-2 (paperback) |
    ISBN 978-1-4668-7490-9 (e-book)
Subjects: LCSH: Drug traffic—Fiction. | Urban fiction. | BISAC: FICTION /
    African American / Urban Life. | FICTION / Urban Life. | GSAFD: Romantic
    suspense fiction.
Classification: LCC PS3601.S543 C376 2016 | DDC 813/.6—dc23
LC record available at http://lccn.loc.gov/2016001963

Our books may be purchased in bulk for promotional, educational, or
business use. Please contact your local bookseller or the Macmillan Corporate and
Premium Sales Department at 1-800-221-7945, extension 5442, or by e-mail
at MacmillanSpecialMarkets@macmillan.com.

First Edition: July 2016

10 9

THE CARTEL

6

*This book is dedicated to Denard "G" Breland.
Without your hard work and support, none of this
would be possible. Thanks family.*

THE CARTEL
6

Chapter 1

Monroe leaned over the hospital bed, his fingers tented under his forehead as Carter lay before him. This was bad. The entire future of The Cartel was at jeopardy. War was imminent, and Monroe was very well aware they would be on the losing end. It was a numbers game, and in the grand scheme of things, Baraka was more powerful. He had a bigger motivation to win. He had lost his daughter at the hands of Carter's own wife. Baraka's shooters had the entire hospital surrounded, phone lines cut, cell service jammed, and Monroe was feeling like prey. Always he had been the hunter, the predator, the one with the most skin in the game, but on this day, the tables had turned.

"You think Fly made it out?" Monroe asked.

"I think Fly Boogie is the last mu'fucka we can count on," Carter replied. He didn't follow with an explanation. He could barely speak. The pierced lung made it hard for him to say any more than a few words before running out of breath. He was tired and cornered. Trapped, for the first time in his life, he felt hopeless. Carter wasn't naïve to the fact this could very well be the day he died. "This morphine they putting in my veins got me off, Money. I can barely get my thoughts together, let alone fend off Baraka's men. I'm floating, man."

Monroe could tell that Carter was on cloud nine. It was the only way for the doctors to decrease his pain, but Monroe needed Carter lucid. Their lives depended on it. He rushed around the bed to the IV and pulled it out, causing blood to trickle down Carter's forearm.

The monitor blared loudly, and a nurse rushed into the room at the sounds of alarm. "What are you doing?" she asked as she rushed over to bandage Carter's arm.

"We need to get out of here now," Monroe said.

"I'm sorry . . . I already told you . . . you can't take him tonight. . . ."

Monroe grabbed her upper arm and forcefully led her to the window. He pulled the drawstring for the blinds. "You see that?" he asked. The nurse's eyes widened in surprise at the men outside the hospital. They were cloaked in expensive *thobes,* which made them stand out immediately. Their Middle Eastern garb revealing their foreign roots.

"Those men are armed, and any minute now they are going to come in here after us. I need you to patch him up because with or without your permission, we've got to get him out of here," Monroe said honestly.

There were at least a hundred men outside. The nurse looked up at him, and Monroe could see the look of terror and uncertainty in her eyes. "I can call the police."

"By the time they get here, several lives will have already been lost," Monroe said.

The nurse walked over to Carter with shaky hands and sat him up. "He can't walk. You'll have to wheel him out. If he goes the entire night without a doctor, he'll die. So as soon as you get wherever you're going, find medical help. He still has morphine running through his veins, and once that wears off, there will be unbearable pain," she said as she wrapped additional gauze around Carter's already bandaged wound. "His bandages will soak through within the next few hours. They have to be changed to avoid infection," she urged. "I can lose my job. . . . I have four babies. I can't believe—"

"You won't," Monroe said. "You will be compensated for your willingness to help."

Carter grabbed her wrist and looked her in the eyes. "I'm good. Go home to your children. Leave right now," he said. Even in his weakest state, he oozed authority.

The nurse looked at him with tears in her eyes. She didn't know what was about to happen, or the exact severity of why it was happening. She couldn't even see the guns that Baraka's men had hidden under the folds of their long drapes, but somehow terror still filled her. She nodded and retreated from the room.

Before Carter or Monroe could follow, Baraka entered the room, flanked by two goons who didn't hide the pistols they held at their sides. Baraka stood in front of the men, the only one dressed in a tailored French suit.

"Going somewhere?" Baraka asked. He clasped his hands in front of his body as he looked directly at Carter. "You're not looking too well, my friend," he added. "Or can I even call you that anymore? Considering my only daughter has gone missing on your watch." His voiced turned sinister as he added, "Where is she? Her liaison hasn't seen her. She hasn't checked in. She knows my army crosses seas if she misses even one phone call to me, so she is habitual, almost down to the second with contacting me. It has been one week, and nothing. I'm going to give you sixty seconds to tell me what has happened."

"She's dead," Carter admitted. Even in his fragile state he wasn't one to mince words or back down.

The words seemed to suck the air out of Baraka's lungs. Baraka didn't flinch, but Carter noticed the change in the man's eyes. An extreme sorrow and anger swept over him.

"The last time she was seen, she had gotten a phone call from your wife to meet her," Baraka said, his voice searching for answers. "You lie here shot. You tell me my daughter is dead. Tell me who is responsible for this chain of events."

"I take full responsibility for what has happened here, Baraka. I am responsible. There is no one else to blame," Carter said, his breath so short that he could barely choke out the words. "I didn't directly cause this, but it is because of me."

"Who murdered my daughter?" Baraka's voice boomed this time, causing Money's finger to curl around the trigger of his gun. He raised it without thinking twice as Baraka's men raised their own.

"Lower your weapon, Money," Carter said. "This man's only child was murdered. I know the cost to pay for that."

Monroe frowned, but didn't move. "Money!" Carter barked as tension thickened the room.

"Old friend," Carter said as he stared Baraka in his eyes sincerely. "I know the cost to pay."

Baraka's eyes glistened with emotion as he replied, "You are too quick to admit your guilt. I know you did not directly harm my daughter. You're protecting someone, and if that is the case, I don't want you. I want to cut off the hands of the man who laid hands on my Yasmine. I want revenge. I deserve revenge. Who are you protecting? Tell me."

Carter stood firm. There was no way he was going to throw out Miamor's name.

"There are very few people a man will lay down his life for. . . ."

Carter could see Baraka putting the pieces to this complicated puzzle together in his head. "Your wife?"

Carter kept a stone face, but he knew Baraka's assumption wasn't a question. Had Miamor been any other woman, the notion wouldn't have even arisen, but her history made her different. She wasn't a homemaker. She didn't sit on the PTA or bake cookies. She wasn't like most women who played wifey but had no knowledge of their husband's street ties. Miamor was a Murder Mama, and her reputation preceded her. She had earned her own respect before she and Carter had even met. She was ruthless, and under different circumstances a man like Baraka would have retained her services, but today he found himself the victim of her hot head.

"I want her," Baraka said. "I want the woman who killed my little girl."

A look of bewilderment crossed Monroe's face, because he knew Baraka was asking for the one thing that Carter would refuse to give him. He contemplated shooting Baraka. Right then and there. *I could just end this shit right now,* he thought. *I could just . . .*

"Stand down, Monroe," Carter said sternly, holding up a hand as if reading his brother's mind.

Fuck, Monroe thought. *Ain't no time for honor right now.*

"I can't do that," Carter said to Baraka. They were at a point of no return. Too much had happened for them to ever coexist. Baraka had hung men from the streetlights in Saudi Arabia for even lusting after his precious Yasmine. The consequences for her death would be felt worldwide. There was no way Carter would hand Miamor over to Baraka. Yasmine was Baraka's princess, but Miamor was Carter's queen. He would protect her at all costs, right or wrong.

"I urge you to reconsider," Baraka said. His voice was calm, but anger danced in his eyes. Spit pooled in the corners of Baraka's mouth as he thought of how he would peel the meat from Miamor's bones. "Be very aware that what you do now will decide your fate for the next twenty years. Your children's fate, your grandchildren's fate. One sacrifice can stop this. No more have to die if you give up this one woman."

"I'm sorry it has come to this," Carter said sincerely.

Rage pulsed through Baraka, and Carter braced himself for a barrage of bullets that would end him right then and there. To his surprise, Baraka said, "War among great men has always been over unworthy women. Good luck to you, Carter."

With that, he was gone and Carter exhaled, realizing he had been holding his breath in anticipation.

War was about to erupt, and Carter knew that it was one they would lose. He just couldn't give her up. . . . Under any and all circumstances he had to hold her down. This time, everyone would pay for his loyalty to her. . . . Anyone associated with Miamor would feel Baraka's wrath; no one was off-limits.

* * *

"Why the fuck ain't she picking up?" Murder asked as he watched Fly Boogie call Miamor for the fourth time.

"Nigga, I told you I don't know. Wherever she is, she should be good until we find her. Carter probably got her and the kids tucked somewhere on the outskirts. This shit is all bad, though. Shit about to get real," Fly Boogie said as he stood to his feet.

"You mean to tell me you been out this mu'fucka kissing ass all this time and you don't where they would take her in an emergency?" Murder asked, a glint of anger behind his harsh stare.

"Nigga, this shit ain't no corner-boy operation. We got a hundred hideouts. She could be on a fucking plane to the middle of nowhere by now!" Fly Boogie stated angrily as he dialed her once again.

"'We,' huh?" Murder asked with a chuckle. "That mu'fucka Carter must got the gift of gab. He be seducing all you simpleminded mu'fuckas. You ain't Cartel, homie. You better remember that."

Fly knew that after Carter had discovered Miamor's name on his wrist, nothing could ever go back to being the same. He couldn't lie his way back into the inner circle. Fly Boogie's lust for Miamor had caused him to cross the line, and now his loyalty was questionable. Fly had taken a shot at Carter and missed . . . and although no one knew he was the man behind the gun, the tattoo had exposed him as snake. There was no coming back from that.

Over the years, he had forgotten about Murder's agenda and had developed one of his own. He had gotten so close to Carter that he respected him. It wasn't until the men had gone away to Saudi Arabia and Fly Boogie's feelings for Miamor grew that he developed malice for Carter. He wanted him out of the way, not for Murder's sake, but for his own. He had never thought twice about Murder catching up to him. Fly had thought Murder was somewhere rotting away in Miami, but when he reemerged in Las Vegas, Fly Boogie knew he had a debt to pay. He regretted the day that he had even agreed to infiltrate The Cartel, because now there was no taking it back.

CHAPTER 2

"We've got to get out of here." Panic was normally not a trait that Monroe Diamond possessed, but as he went to the door and peeked his head into the hall, an uneasiness took over the pit of his stomach. "Stay here," Monroe said as he eased into the hall. He walked swiftly until he spotted an idle wheelchair. He was so paranoid, sweat covered his forehead. His anxiety made it feel like someone had turned the thermostat up a hundred degrees. He half-expected Baraka's goons to come through the door at any moment. He rushed back to the room and helped Carter out of the hospital bed. "Come on, fam. We've got to move," Monroe said.

"Argh," Carter groaned as pain erupted through his body. He put his arm around Monroe's shoulder, bearing his weight down on him, unable to stand. "I can't feel my legs, bro. I'm in no condition to run, Money." He hadn't even made it to the hallway yet and already he was winded.

Carter was hurt . . . bad. . . . They both knew that in his condition, he was a liability. "Truth is, I wouldn't run if I could, fam. If this is what it's come to, then let it be. There is no reason why we both have to die tonight, Money. Miamor is my bitch. This is my debt. Get out of here, bro."

Monroe struggled to help Carter to the wheelchair at the foot of the bed. "Nah, bruh," he huffed as he carried Carter's dead weight. "Ain't no selfless sacrifice shit happening tonight. We both getting out of here." He adjusted Carter's feet and then took an anxious breath as he turned to retrieve the pistol from the hospital bed. "I know you fucked up right now, but that trigger finger still work, right?"

Carter grimaced, then answered, "Always."

Monroe passed the burner to Carter, who laid it in his lap . . . safety off. . . .

Carter placed a small towel over his lap to conceal the gun as Monroe rolled him out of the room.

Monroe's head might as well have been sitting on a swivel. He couldn't help but keep his eyes bouncing around as he and Carter made their way down the hall. Baraka was in the States, which meant an entire Arabian army had made the trip with him. The Cartel was on the brink of a war. They had barely survived the beef with the Haitians, and now this. With Carter severely injured and Zyir in the wind, Monroe knew it was only a matter of time before everything they had worked so hard to get back to crumbled.

Monroe stood over Carter, clasping the handles to the wheelchair, impatience torturing him as the elevator slowly rose up to their floor.

The gun holstered at his waistline gave him little assurance, because he knew that when Baraka came, he was coming with soldiers. Two guns against armed assassins would do nothing to protect them. He and Carter were sitting ducks in the hospital. The hairs on the back of his neck stood up as his internal alarm sounded. He was just waiting for someone to put a bullet in his back.

"You alright, bro?" he asked Carter.

"I'll be better when we're out of here," Carter replied, grunting in obvious pain.

"Just hold on," Monroe said as the elevator light finally illuminated. The doors opened, and Monroe hesitated when he saw two uniformed police officers standing inside. He hated pigs, but he stepped inside, easing the wheelchair in first. "Gentlemen," he greeted them.

They nodded, but didn't respond as Monroe pressed the lobby button. Tension made the air thick, and Monroe cleared his throat as silence filled the space. It didn't matter that they had done nothing wrong. They were the bad guys. The drug dealers. The kingpins. In the presence of the law they were always under a microscope. The elevator descended to a stop at the fifth floor, and Monroe clenched his jaw. *I just want to get out of this mu' fucka*, he thought, anxiety filling him. When the doors opened, his back stiffened as he stared into the eyes of two men. He knew right away they were Baraka-affiliated. It wasn't their black hair or their olive skin that gave them away. It wasn't even the traditional Middle Eastern cloaks they wore, but the look of vengeance in their eyes.

"Money, this is our floor," Carter said weakly, instantly recognizing the threat as well.

"Not quite, we're almost there," Monroe stated, refusing to get off the elevator. He knew the men couldn't pop off with the two officers around. The safest place to be was wherever those officers were . . . or so he thought. The Arab men stepped inside, stone-faced, and as soon as the doors, closed . . .

PSST! PSST!

Two silenced shots floored the officers before Monroe even had a chance to draw his pistol. Moments of life flashed before Monroe's eyes as he stared down the dark barrels of the gun. This was it. After reigning over Miami, transitioning to Vegas, prison, evading the law, surviving a coma . . . this was how it was going to end. The day of reckoning had arrived. He placed a firm hand on Carter's shoulder, who sat stoically. They weren't the type of men to beg . . . to fear. . . . They had lived their lives a certain way . . . followed the rules to a gangster's code. Now they had to die according to it, and even in the face of the devil, gangsters didn't fold. Monroe could feel his heart beating rapidly as he anticipated the final bullet.

"See you on the other side, brother," Carter said.

Suddenly the doors to the elevator slid open.

BOOM! BOOM!

Aries stood, gun smoking, still aimed as she breathed heavily from the adrenaline pumping through her veins. The hospital erupted into a frenzy. She hadn't hesitated. There had been no time to silence her weapon. If she had thought twice, Monroe and Carter would be dead. "You gon' get your asses out of the elevator or you gon' stand there looking crazy?" Aries asked urgently as she looked around. "Baraka's goons are everywhere. We've got an ambulance waiting in emergency. We have to go . . . NOW!"

Monroe had never been so happy to see Aries's murderous face in his life. "I could kiss you right now," he muttered as he followed her down the hall.

"Please don't," she shot back with a smirk.

She rounded the corner only to halt at the sight of Baraka's men entering the building. There was nothing incognito about them. They came in, guns drawn, as if they made the laws themselves. "This way," she said, turning around and running in the opposite direction. The lights suddenly went out, and chaos erupted. Gunfire exploded, and bullets flew their way. The Arabs were reckless in their assault. It didn't matter that they were in public, or that there were innocent bystanders all around. They had declared war on The Cartel. Aries ran as Monroe tried to maneuver Carter through the hospital while people ran for cover.

Monroe suddenly stopped running. "Fuck it. If it's gonna happen, I won't get clipped with a bullet to the back. Get him out of here. I'll cover you," he stated.

"Money, no," Carter whispered weakly as his head hung low, his chin touching his chest.

Aries knew if she had to make a choice, she would have to save Carter. Miamor would never forgive her if she let him die.

"Ain't no time for thinking. Go!" Money stated. He

reached down and grabbed the gun out of Carter's lap and then quickly unholstered his own. With a pistol in each hand he rounded the corner and popped off, firing bullets as he diverted the Arabs' attention. Monroe went left, going in the opposite direction as Aries hustled her ass out of there, pushing Carter swiftly down the hall. She burst through the emergency room doors. The ambulance they had hijacked was waiting there, engine running.

"Miamor!" she yelled. "Help me!" Aries rushed to the back of the vehicle and pulled the doors open. Her heart dropped when she found Miamor sitting at gunpoint at the hands of a hired Arabian goon.

"Shoot him!" Miamor shouted.

"واهن, ضعيف, أوطأ, أدنى!" The man shouted something in Arabic as he pointed his gun at Miamor's temple while holding her in a choke hold.

"Kill him, Aries! Shoot him! Now!" Miamor shouted.

"واهن, ضعيف, أوطأ, أدنى!" the man barked his orders, and although Aries didn't understand them, she clearly read the look of malice in his eyes. He was ready to commit murder. She had already lost so many of her friends. She didn't want to see Miamor get her brains blown out in front of her. She straightened her trigger finger and let the gun dangle from it as she raised both arms.

"Aries!" Miamor shouted. The man pointed his gun at Aries, and just as his finger curled on the trigger, Carter pulled the gun out of Aries's back waistline. He was weak, but he was always accurate. He fired.

BOOM!

The man's body jerked violently as a bullet to the forehead sent him flying onto his back. Miamor rushed to Carter's side, kneeling before him as she cupped his face, kissing him repeatedly. "I'm so sorry. I'm so sorry, Carter." The way that they nuzzled into each other's space reminded Aries of two lions. Each of them was powerful in their own right, but they were each other's weakness.

"Feels like I'm dying, ma," he whispered. His words sent a chill down her spine, and a tear fell down her cheek.

"I won't let that happen, baby, I swear," she said.

"Let's get him up here," Aries said, interrupting the moment, as the sounds of gunshots and police sirens broke through the air.

Miamor and Aries struggled to lift Carter into the ambulance without hurting him. "Agh! Fuck! Take it easy!" he shouted in pain as they managed to get him inside. Miamor climbed into the back of the ambulance as Aries rushed to the driver's seat.

"Money's still inside," Carter said as they pulled away from the curb. "Don't move this fucking ambulance without my brother!"

"We have to, Carter," Miamor whispered. "There are too many of them. If we go back in . . ."

Miamor stopped talking because they both knew what was happening. They were about to lose another Diamond. She gripped Carter's hand, and it didn't go unnoticed when he didn't squeeze hers back. Miamor was the cause of all of this. She knew it. So did he. Their entire empire was in jeopardy. This war was her fault.

* * *

Carter struggled to breathe as he attempted to stand up out of the wheelchair.

"No, Carter, you have to sit," Miamor urged as she steadied him just in the nick of time. He couldn't make it from the wheelchair to his desk. He was hurt bad and sweating profusely. "You're trying to do too much. Just tell me what you need."

"Call Monroe," he ordered.

"Okay, okay," Miamor replied as she immediately dialed the number.

Carter took three deep breaths and then managed to pull himself to his feet as he walked through the penthouse suite toward his office. It felt like he was running a marathon. His heart and lungs burned as if he were in full sprint.

"Carter! No!" Miamor said as she brought the wheelchair up behind him and he eased back into it. He was so weak; it was humbling and frustrating all at the same time. He wasn't running anything, not in his current state.

"Money isn't answering," Miamor said, her voice solemn, assuming his death.

Carter closed his eyes. Her words were like knives stabbing him as he thought of his brother's fate. Monroe was the only blood brother he had left. It had taken a lot for them to put their differences aside and band together as family. If anyone was supposed to sacrifice himself for the other, it was supposed to be Carter. He was the oldest. He was the strongest. It was his wife who had started this war. Monroe wasn't supposed to succumb to it. He didn't deserve to. Carter wanted to place blame, but it wouldn't help. They both knew the deaths to come in the days ahead were on Miamor's conscience.

Suddenly a rapid knock at the door interrupted them. Silence fell over them as they shot each other a paranoid glance. Carter put his fingers to his lips and then used his fingers like a gun, telling her to strap up. Baraka owned half the casino. Surely he knew where to find them. They would have to lock down the entire property in order to keep Baraka and his goons out. It would be damn near impossible to do that, so they needed to gather everyone, take what they needed, and find somewhere inconspicuous to gather their thoughts. Miamor grabbed her gun and headed toward the door.

"Mia, put down de' fucking gun and open de' door!" Aries hissed. She already knew the routine. Miamor was on edge, which meant she had an itchy trigger finger. It was only a matter of time before she popped off. It was what she did when her back was against the wall.

Miamor breathed a sigh of relief and snatched open the door. When she saw Monroe standing next to Aries, she couldn't stop the tears from welling in her eyes. They weren't necessarily the closest, but she had never been so happy to see him. She placed a hand over her heart in relief. If Money had been killed, Carter would have never forgiven her.

"Look who popped up," Aries said as Monroe walked inside.

"Good to see you, Money," Miamor stated.

"Good to be seen. There are fucking Arabs all over the place. I barely got out of that hospital. We've got to disappear for a while. Regroup," he stated as he rushed over to Carter.

Carter was hanging on by a thread as pain doubled him over in his chair. "Get Zyir on the line. I want to make sure he and Breeze are safe," he managed.

He was sweating profusely and grimacing in excruciation.

"Is he okay?" Aries asked.

Carter couldn't breathe, not deeply, not enough for him to think clearly. The room began to spin as a burning sensation seared through him, and he fell from the wheelchair.

"Carter!" Miamor whispered desperately as she knelt in front of him, holding his face in her hands. She looked up at Monroe, feeling empty as if she were watching the love of her life slip away. "Money, this is bad. We need a doctor here now!" She sat on the floor and laid Carter's head in her lap.

They had never seen Carter so incapacitated. They were in the middle of a war, and if they were going to survive, they needed their general. He had to pull through—not only for his sake, but for Miamor's as well.

CHAPTER 3

It was quiet; so quiet that thoughts of fear, of chaos, and of destruction thundered loudly inside her head. Ever since the men had disappeared to Saudi Arabia, Leena had questioned her loyalty to the street life. When they had returned, she had pushed her fears to the back of her mind, but she knew one day she would have to address them. Today was that day. Leena wasn't built for the warfare that came with the game. There was an uncertainty of survival every day that she woke up. She never knew what could happen, and the imminent danger that lurked in the shadows of her life terrified her. Although their hands were in the casino business now, she knew The Cartel would never truly be legit. They lived by the rules of the underworld, and Monroe would always be a part of the life. He had been born into it, and the moment she fell in love with him, she had committed to his lifestyle as well. It had its perks, but it was times like these that she remembered the flip side of things—the dangerous side. And now the tables had turned and they were cloaked in darkness from the storm Baraka was about to rain upon them. Leena had wanted to stay by Monroe's side, but instead he had her whisked away to safety. They all had responsibilities. She wasn't a shooter, she wasn't fearless, and she certainly wasn't a gangster, but she was a nurturer at heart. Therefore her job was to make sure that C.J. and Lil' Money knew nothing about the circumstances of duress. One of The Cartel's most trusted goons had been assigned to the task of keeping her and the boys out of harm's way. It wasn't enough to get them away from the casino. Monroe wanted them out of Nevada.

"Where are we going?" she asked as she looked out her window. They had been driving for almost two hours. The boys were asleep in the backseat, but she knew when they awoke they would have questions, and she needed to know what to say.

"Somewhere safe," he replied shortly. "You might want to get some sleep. Relax a bit. We have a little ways to go."

Leena settled into her seat, but her mind wouldn't rest. In the last war they had lost so much . . . so many of their loved ones. She couldn't help but wonder who would fall victim to Baraka. He was twice as deadly as Ma'tee. That fact scared her. The desert blurred outside her window as they drove top speed, heading west. She didn't sleep. She couldn't. Not with the knot twisting in her gut. She wondered: *Is Carter okay? What is Monroe going to do?*

There were too many unknowns, and they were filling

her with anxiety. She was grateful the boys were asleep the entire drive.

They pulled up to a house in Pasadena, California. "Whose house is this?" she asked, noticing a Cadillac sitting in the driveway.

"A friend's," he said as he exited the car.

Leena turned around and stirred C.J. and Lil' Money out of their sleep. "C.J., Mo, wake up," she said, putting on a fake smile. She didn't want them to sniff out her worries. "We're here."

She exited the car and ushered the boys out of the backseat as the goon got their bags from the trunk. When she turned toward the house and saw who had stepped onto the porch, she sighed in relief. "Polo," she whispered. She smiled as she placed her hands around the boys' shoulders.

He walked over to her and the boys. "It's like I stepped into a time machine right now. Aw, man," he said as he admired C.J. and Lil' Money.

"Mo. C.J. This is your uncle Polo," Leena introduced them.

Polo held out his hand, giving both boys a firm shake. "There's an Xbox in there. Why don't you go make yourselves comfortable," he said. The boys took off, racing inside.

Polo turned toward Leena. "Everything you need is inside. Groceries, clothes, whatever . . ."

Leena nodded. "Thank you," she replied sincerely. "From all of us."

Leena didn't want to say too much because she really

didn't know Polo well. She knew he had been Big Carter's right-hand man, but she had also heard rumors that he had cooperated with the feds. She knew Polo wasn't a threat to them. The fact that she was even in his presence meant Monroe trusted him. Still, she made sure not to say more than what was necessary.

Polo turned to the goon. "Keep your eyes open. Keep them inside. Keep a low profile."

Her newfound protection nodded, and Polo walked to his car. "Take care of yourself," he said. "And those boys. If Big Carter and I had done a better job, you all wouldn't be reliving the life that destroyed us. It's history repeating itself."

She saw emotion in his eyes. "Those boys inside will have a different story. I promise," she replied.

Polo nodded and sniffed away the emotion before getting in the car and driving away.

"We'd better get inside," the goon said as he carried her bags toward the door. Leena followed closely behind, feeling like she was walking into a cage.

Seeing Polo made her realize he had a lifetime of regret. She didn't want her son or her nephew to know this life.

As soon as Leena stepped inside, the boys came racing toward her.

"Ma! There's a hoop in the driveway. Can we get a game in?" Mo asked.

The goon stepped up. "Nah, that's not a good idea, lil' man."

"If we're going to be here, we aren't going to be cooped

up in this house. No one knows we're here. They should be fine in the driveway. Let them be kids," Leena interrupted.

"So we can go?" C.J. asked.

"Yeah, your ball is in the trunk," Leena said. The goon wanted to protest. She could see him getting ready to buck against her decision, but the piercing look she shot him silenced him instantly. "I'll go out and keep an eye on them," she said. "Let's get one thing clear. I know you're here to do a job and I appreciate your loyalty to my husband. Those boys don't need to know we're running. So don't lurk and you follow my orders, not the other way around." She grabbed a crossword puzzle and a pen off the table, then stepped out onto the porch. She took a seat on the swing as she watched the boys play a game of one-on-one. The goon kept his distance as he sat at the other end of the large porch and kept a keen eye on things.

A competitive spirit filled the air as Leena watched the cousins play. For a moment, no matter how brief, she felt peace. The gentle breeze hit her face, and she smiled at the boisterous nature of the boys. This was as close to normal as she would get. She yearned for a carefree existence such as this one.

"Foul!" C.J. called as Mo pushed him hard while powering toward the driveway hoop. C.J. fell hard to the ground. Easily tempered, he stood up and ran over to Monroe. "Foul, man!" he shouted as he pushed his big cousin back.

"Quit crying, pussy!" Mo barked back as he threw the ball at C.J.

Both boys were bred to be thorough, so neither backed

down. It didn't matter that Lil' Money was older and stronger; C.J. had heart. He charged his cousin, and the two began to tussle.

"Hey!" Leena shouted as she stood to her feet. The goon moved when she moved, but Leena motioned for him to stop. "I've got it."

Leena descended the porch steps and approached the fighting cousins. "Stop!" she said harshly as she pulled them apart. "You're family, and family don't lay hands on one another." The look on Mo's face reminded her of Mecca. Mo's temper was starting to become apparent, and the anger that brewed in his eyes was so familiar that it sent a chill up her spine. If she didn't know any better she would have thought that Lil' Monroe had come from Mecca's seed. "Monroe Diamond the second," she chastised. "Fix your face. You guys are cousins. You save the tough-guy act for the enemy. Don't ever fight one another, and watch your mouth." The musical sounds of an ice-cream truck distracted her. "Go cool off, hotheads," she said as she shook her head. "Get some ice cream." She looked up to the porch. "Can you grab my handbag from inside?" she asked the goon. He nodded, and she turned to follow the boys to the ice-cream truck. Just as quickly as the two had fought, they made up as they raced down the driveway, joking and clowning on one another. She smiled. They were thick as thieves, and she loved their bond. "These two are going to drive me nuts," she whispered to herself. She walked up to the truck and rubbed the back of their heads lovingly. "What do y'all want?" she asked. When she looked up at the driver, her heart sank. She could see the malice in his eyes without him ever having to say a word. Call it a mother's intuition. Butterflies fluttered as anxiety took ahold of her. Without thinking twice, she gripped the pen she had been using on her puzzle and jammed it into the man's eye. "Run!" she shouted to the boys.

"You stupid bitch!" the man shouted. Leena turned to flee, but before she could take one step, the back of the truck flew open as three men burst out. They grabbed C.J. first and then Leena. Mo was quicker and had made it out of arm's reach, but when he turned and saw one of the men placing a chloroform rag over his mother's mouth, he went back. He tried to fight the men, but he was no match. They grabbed him, too, and pulled him into the truck kicking and screaming. By the time their hired goon came back on the porch, they were speeding down the street.

"Oh, shit!" he yelled as he came up off his hip with a pistol. He dumped bullets in the direction of the truck, but he hit nothing. The truck bent the corner wildly, and the goon threw his hands up in the air as neighbors began to pour out of their homes. "Fuck!" he shouted as he swung at the air. He knew there would be hell to pay. He had one job and he had failed. Now he had to make the call to Monroe and tell him that his most prized possessions had been lost. Baraka had struck back.

* * *

"We have to get him to a hospital," the doctor said as he re-dressed Carter's chest wound.

"We've been to the hospital, Doc. We can't go back. I need you to fix my brother up right here," Monroe said.

"There is a lot of trauma from the gunshot. You should have never brought him here. He needs an IV. He needs medicine. Rest. Round-the-clock care. One doesn't simply walk away from a wound like this. There will be permanent damage. He can't catch his breath because one of his lungs has collapsed. He's lucky to even be alive," the doctor said.

"Y'all talking about me like I'm not in the room," Carter whispered in a weak tone. They had managed to get him to the master bedroom, and he was laid out atop of the king-sized bed.

"Save your strength, Mr. Jones. Just focus on breathing. I can't do anything for you in this room. There is no equipment, no staff, it's not sterile, it's—"

Miamor was fed up with the doctor's excuses. She walked up on him and put a pistol to his temple. Her pretty painted finger wrapped around the trigger. "You either turn this room into a hospital or I turn it into a morgue. Stop telling us what you can't do and help him," she ordered.

Monroe and Aries froze because they knew how close she was to making good on her promise. She was a ticking time bomb, and the one thing that could set her off was the thought of losing Carter.

The room was silent as the doctor worked with shaky hands. "I-I-I," he stuttered, and then closed his eyes. He took a deep breath and swallowed the lump in his throat. "I could work much better if you would please take the gun away from my head," he said nervously.

"Miamor," Carter managed to say. He lifted his hand for her to grab, and she lowered her gun. She knelt on the floor beside the bed as she held on tightly to him.

"I fucked up so bad this time," she cried remorsefully.

"Shh," he whispered. "Keep your head, ma. I need you calm. You can't be calculating if you're emotional. I'm okay." He grimaced as the doctor tried to sit him up against the headboard. "I'm down, but I'm not out. I'm right here," he whispered.

"If I don't start an antibiotic drip, you're likely to get an infection. I have to make a few calls to get the supplies I need brought here," the doctor informed him.

"Do what you need to," Monroe said.

They waited on pins and needles until finally the doctor's things arrived. By the time he was done with Carter, the bedroom of the suite looked like an intensive care unit.

"He's heavily sedated on pain medication and antibiotics. Change his bandages twice a day. Here is Vicodin for the pain." The doctor handed Miamor a prescription bottle. "Call me if he can't handle this."

Miamor placed a band of ten thousand dollars in his hand and said, "Thank you."

He made a hasty exit, bumping right into one of The Cartel's goons as he left.

Monroe rushed to the door when he saw his henchman enter the suite.

"You supposed to be three hundred miles away from here," he said, with concern. "Where's Leena?"

"We got to Cali and she insisted that I let the boys play

outside. An ice-cream truck pulled up. I turned my back for thirty seconds . . ."

"My wife and my son are gone? That's what you telling me? My nephew is gone? I trusted them to you and you coming in here to tell me they've been snatched?"

"I let off on the truck as soon as I realized what was happening. . . . I didn't—"

BOOM!

Monroe didn't hesitate to put a bullet in his head. There was a price to pay for this misstep, and it was a hefty one.

"Now how are you going to explain someone who walks into a public casino and hotel but doesn't ever walk out? De cameras place him here. How do you know no one heard de gunshot? You two are out here like de wild, wild fucking West!" Aries shouted.

"The floor is soundproof," Miamor answered. "Where are our kids, Monroe? I swear to God I am going to rip his heart out of his chest if anything happens to them," she threatened as her eyes swelled with tears. She trembled, she was so irate. "What do we do?" she asked.

Monroe hit the wall in frustration. "You killed his daughter! What do you think he is going to do to our sons?" he shouted. "You and your fucking hot head! This is your fault!"

"You think I don't know that?" Miamor shot back. "I know, Monroe! He's my son, too." Miamor didn't have many weaknesses, but C.J. and Carter were exceptions. At the moment, she was terrified for them both.

The phone to the penthouse rang as Miamor and Monroe continued to shout their frustrations at each other.

Aries went to answer the phone. "Somebody probably heard de fucking gunshot. Soundproof, my ass," she said, silencing them. She picked up the phone.

Silence filled the line.

"Hello? Who is this?" she asked. She frowned as she heard the sounds of cries in the background. She turned to Miamor and Monroe, shushing them. "One of you needs to take this," she said. The solemn look on Aries's face made Miamor rush to the phone.

"Is that him?" Miamor asked. She snatched the phone. "Baraka . . ."

She could hear muffled screams in the background . . . the cries of Leena, of her son, of Mo. "If you touch one hair . . ."

"I intend to do more than touch one hair, Miamor. I plan to rip his fucking head off his shoulders. You have forty-eight hours to turn yourself over to me and relinquish all shares of the casino to me. If not, I'll send your sons and this black bitch back to you piece by piece."

"Please . . . they're children. . . ."

"You took my child, I take yours," Baraka said. "Let me give you a little example of what will happen if you do anything other than what I've asked."

Miamor heard the sound of a chainsaw revving up.

"No! Please!!! Don't!!!"

It was Leena's screams. They were so shrill that Miamor closed her eyes and took her ear away from the phone as a tear slid down her face. Leena had become family to her. The sound of Baraka torturing her was gut-wrenching.

"There goes one hand," Baraka said.

"This is between me and you. Nobody else," Miamor reasoned. "She didn't do anything to you. She is someone's wife . . . mother. . . . You caught the easy fish because you couldn't catch me. I'll see you soon."

"Forty-eight hours," Baraka reiterated. "I'll text you a location."

The line went dead, and Miamor looked up at Monroe. "I have to give myself up in order to get them back."

"Carter's going to veto that, you know that," Aries said.

"He has our son. There is no other option," Miamor replied solemnly.

Monroe's nostrils flared. His eyes were red from rage as he stormed out.

"What do you need me to do?" Aries asked.

Miamor looked at her with regret-filled eyes. "Pray for me."

Aries and Miamor hugged long and hard because they both knew this was the end. They had started on this journey together as young girls. It had been five of them at the beginning. Death and destruction had dwindled their number to just two. This was a loss they had felt before, but despite that, it still hurt. "You're going to be the last Murder Mama standing, Aries," Miamor whispered as she grew emotional. They had been in this game side by side for years. They were best friends, sisters, and confidants. The memories of the capers they had pulled, the murders they had gotten away with, flooded them. Neither of them expected to die a peaceful death. Their karma wasn't set up that way, but Aries and Miamor had never expected it all to come down to this.

"Me feel like me should do something," Aries said. "You know me will go all out with you, Mia."

Miamor stood back and grabbed both of Aries's hands. There had never been a friend more loyal. Aries was the most stand-up person she knew. Miamor gripped her friend's hands tightly and smiled weakly. "This is what I need you to do, Aries. Get out of this game. Disappear and keep your son safe. Move on with your life and bury your memories of the Murder Mamas when you put me in the ground. Don't end up like me, Aries. I love you, Murder Mama. This is good-bye."

"Me love you, too, Mia," Aries whispered, a tear falling from her eyes. This was heartbreak for her. The Murder Mamas had been Aries's first family. She was about to lose that forever, and that fact was digging a hole in her heart. "Save a spot for me up there."

Miamor laughed and nodded as she wiped the tears from her face. "Sure thing," she said. They both knew she wasn't going to heaven and that they would see each other again . . . but when they met, it wouldn't be in the clouds. It would be in the fires of hell.

* * *

When Carter came to, he found that the pain was still there but he could now breathe easier. He looked over at Miamor, who was cuddled into him, sleeping peacefully with dried tearstains on her face. He nudged her awake and as soon as she opened her eyes, he peered into her soul.

"What happened?" he asked, clearing his dry throat. He sat up, grimacing as he moved slowly.

Miamor climbed out of bed and walked around to the nightstand to pour him a glass of water. She grabbed the pitcher, stalling for time as she tried to decide how to tell him what had gone down.

She raised the cup to his lips and he drank, grateful for every drop.

"Sit down and tell me whatever it is you're trying to figure out how to say," he said, knowing his woman. Carter had always been well-versed in the book of Miamor.

"Baraka has C.J. and Leena and Mo," she whispered. "He wants me to give myself up in exchange for them."

"I'mma kill him," Carter whispered. "I'm going to fucking kill that mu'fucka."

Carter could feel his world crashing. This was an impossible choice. His wife or his son. "He can have me," he said as he clenched his jaw.

"He doesn't want you," Miamor replied. "We both know I have to be the one to die. He's our son. He is the product of our love. . . . He is proof that what me and you had was real," she said. She was emotional . . . weak . . . torn up over the fact that she had caused this to happen. "Somehow we got lost. Life tore us apart, but C.J. is the evidence that we were extraordinary together. Our love was real. Right?" She was crying, and it was the most peaceful cry Carter had ever seen. Tears fell out of her eyes like rain from the sky, but her face was serene like a beautiful summer day. She had accepted her fate.

"It is the realest thing I've ever felt, ma," Carter replied.

"We have thirty-six hours left. Can I spend my last day with you?" she asked.

Carter pulled her into him and kissed her forehead as he held back his own tears. He didn't want to show her his fear. He was terrified for her. He was terrified for himself. Life was not worth living without her. There were no wins in this predicament. By saving C.J., he was sacrificing Miamor. C.J. was the only soul on Earth he would do that for. He felt like he was dying. The reality of the dire situation was eating him alive. "I wouldn't have it any other way, Miamor," he replied.

"Are you in pain?" she asked.

"Not the kind that you're thinking of. . . . My heart hurts more than any bullet could ever cause," Carter admitted.

* * *

Miamor showered and styled her hair just the way Carter liked it. She put on his favorite dress. She wore his favorite scent. She put on her makeup flawlessly. This would be the last time Carter would ever see her alive and she wanted to give him something to remember. When she stepped out of the bathroom, she was surprised to see him out of bed. "What are you doing?" she asked in concern as she rushed to his side, noticing he had taken the IV out of his arm.

"You should be resting." She grabbed some gauze and tape before approaching him.

"I'm good," he assured her. She could tell that it was taking all of his strength just to stay on his feet, but she didn't protest. He knew his limits. She didn't want to waste time arguing.

"Here, just let me put this on your arm so it doesn't bleed where the IV was," she said. She bandaged him, all the while feeling his eyes on her.

"You're beautiful," he complimented her.

She blushed as he caressed her face, staring so intently that she knew he was trying to commit every inch of her to memory.

"You've made me a better man, Miamor," he said. Even wounded and weak, he was the strongest man she knew. She smiled. "You taught me how to love. You taught me forgiveness. You taught me how to appreciate someone while I can, because you never know when they will disappear from your life. I love you. You're the only woman I have ever said that to. C.J. will know you and the sacrifice you made. I'll make sure of it. There will never be another woman who can fill the void you're leaving in my life, ma. This divorce shit, it got out of hand. I never wanted this, and now it's too late to take it back. Just know that I love you, Miamor. I've never stopped. I never will. Every breath that I take, I'll take for both of us. You're in me, ma, and I'm in you. So you'll live as long as I live. That's my word."

Miamor's stomach felt hollow. He was saying good-bye. This was it and it hurt. This long prelude to her death was torture. She would have much preferred the unexpected bullet instead of this long walk toward the grim reaper's door. "You won't forget me?" she asked.

"Never. Every second of every day you'll be in the back of my mind," he said. "Every part of me wants to go to war over you. I don't want to give you over to him."

She could see Carter's temple flexing in anger. He was so powerful that being powerless in this situation made him feel less than a man.

"Not even God can stop this," she said. "You don't have to feel bad. If there was any way you could save me, I know you would. You can't." She paused as she took a deep breath. The feeling of air moving in and out of her lungs was one she savored. Her breaths were now numbered. She exhaled. "Not this time."

She walked over to the nightstand and opened it. A 9mm pistol sat inside. She had always lived by the gun, so she wasn't afraid to die by it. It was Baraka's unknown intentions that terrified her. If she left it up to him, he would slowly seep the life out of her. He wanted to inflict pain. She reached inside and pulled out the weapon, palming it. She ran her hands against the steel as tears came to her eyes.

"What are you doing?" Carter asked.

"I'm going to die, Carter," Miamor said. "If I have to go, I want it to be at your hands. I don't want Baraka to take my life. I'm scared."

"I can't do that, ma," Carter responded. "You're the one person I've never been able to curl a trigger on."

"You have to," Miamor whispered, her voice full of

sorrow. "I don't want to see what Baraka has in store. You can do it here. Peacefully. One shot and it'll be over. Baraka will accept that. He will return C.J. after you show him my body." She reached inside the nightstand and pulled out a silencer. She began to screw it onto the gun.

Carter grimaced as she placed the gun in his hands. "I can't," he said as he looked at the gun and then intently into her eyes. "I won't."

"You will," she said as she kissed his lips. He wiped her tears. "Because we both know what will happen if you don't."

Carter pulled her close and she sobbed into his shoulder. She cried in a way she had never done before. He held her, but his mind was spinning as he tried to think of a way out of this. His son or his wife? His wife or his son? Why couldn't he just give his own life to save them both?

"Lay with me," he said as he pulled her to the bed. The pain of his injuries paled in comparison to the ailments of his heart. They lay side by side, facing each other as they held hands. Her tears fell onto the white pillows as she stared into his eyes.

"Close your eyes, Miamor," he said.

She trembled as she lowered her lids. She had to bite her lip to stop herself from crying aloud.

"Pray," he whispered. "Our Father, who art in heaven, hallowed be thy name . . ."

Memories of the last time she had said that prayer flooded her mind. Mecca had locked her in a basement . . . had tortured her . . . and she had prayed to God. She had been much tougher then. She hadn't feared anything on that day, but on this one, she feared it all. Loving Carter, having his child—it had changed her. She had become vulnerable in a way she had never expected. It wasn't the thought of it all ending that frightened her. It was the thought of never seeing Carter and C.J. again. Leaving them . . . abandoning them. Facing her karma at the hands of a man whose child she had killed. It all overwhelmed her.

"Thy kingdom come," she joined him. "Thy will be done. On Earth as it is in heaven," they said together.

Carter took a pillow and placed it over her face, then pointed the gun at it. He knew he wouldn't shoot if he had to look at her. He never stopped praying. "Give us this day our daily bread," he continued. His hand was shaking so bad that he thought he might miss. He gritted his teeth as his finger settled on the trigger. "And forgive us our trespasses as we forgive those who trespass against us."

Miamor stopped and said, "Just do it."

"Grrr!" Carter yelled as he pulled the trigger.

The sound of the gun bullet whistling past her head almost gave her a heart attack.

"Why didn't you just do it!" she shouted. "You're gonna give me cardiac arrest! Jesus, Carter!" She turned on her back and looked at the ceiling as she panted.

"I can't," he whispered, tormented as he threw the pillow and pulled her into him. The weight of her crushed him, sending bolts of pain through his body. He didn't care, though. He just wanted to hold her. To feel her. To keep her. He stood to his feet.

"Where are you going?" she asked.

"To call Monroe," Carter replied. "I can't give you up, and I'm not losing my son. There's only one way to make this go away."

"What's that?" she asked.

"To kill him before you have to turn yourself in," Carter replied.

"You're hurt. You almost died, Carter. You're in no condition to do anything," Miamor said.

"I can't just do nothing," he replied. He quickly grabbed one of his designer shirts out of the closet. He could barely put it on by himself, but he fought through the pain.

"Carter, stop," Miamor whispered, but he was determined. He stepped into a pair of Versace slacks. The effort that it took to dress himself caused sweat to form on his forehead. His body was too weak. He had lost too much blood. He was still so fragile. The room started to spin.

He reached out and gripped the post of the king-sized bed. Miamor rushed to his side. "Carter," she said with a sigh. "Please just lay down. I'll call Monroe. I'll get him over here so you can two can figure it out."

Carter gripped the back of her neck and placed his forehead on hers. "On my life, I'm going to fix this."

"I know," she replied. "I know." She helped him back onto the bed. "Let me get you some tea. It'll relax you until Monroe arrives."

She slyly palmed the Vicodin in her hand before easing out of the room. Miamor couldn't let Carter intervene. It would do no good for him to take a stand against Baraka.

She had to turn herself over to him. It was the only way to guarantee C.J.'s safety. She quickly made him a cup of hot tea and took three pills out of the bottle. She ground them up fine and then mixed them into Carter's drink. It was enough to knock him out for hours. He drank it without question. It wasn't long before he began to feel his head cloud.

"What did you do, ma?" he asked as she sat on the edge of the bed.

"What I had to," she replied. "I'm not letting you jump into another war over me. I love you, Carter. Good-bye, handsome." She leaned down and kissed his lips one last time. She didn't even look back as she made her exit because she knew if she did, she would never walk away. *This is the right thing to do,* she told herself. *It's the only way to make this right.* When she made it to her car, Miamor picked up her phone and called Baraka. As soon as he answered, she said, "I don't need any more time. I'm ready to meet today. I need your word. If I give myself up, you'll let Leena and the boys go."

Baraka simply responded, "Meet me where you buried my daughter. One hour."

* * *

Miamor took her time heading out to the desert. Baraka would wait. His need for revenge would make him stay there until she arrived. She sat on the side of the highway, splitting a dutch. She rolled down her window and emptied the contents, then pulled out a Baggie to empty the Kush weed

inside. It had been a habit she had given up when she had
her son, but in this moment she gave herself a pass. *Thank
God for Aries,* she thought, chuckling slightly at the fact
that she was smoking the small stash her friend had left in
her car.

She rolled up like an expert, as if she had never stopped.
She sat and smoked patiently, silently, as she watched the
minutes of the clock run down. *Thirty-six minutes,* she
thought. It was the amount of time she had left on this
Earth. Her life of tyranny had come down to this. She had
left bodies on top of bodies in her wake. She wasn't naïve.
She knew that this day would come. She was surprised it
hadn't come sooner. She wasn't a good person. She didn't
deserve to grow old. She knew exactly what sins she had
committed to deserve this fate. That's why she took her time
and savored the blunt. She was stalling. When she had finished her smoke, she flicked it out of the car and sped off
down the highway route, headed to the middle of nowhere.

She saw the headlights coming up in her rearview and
they were coming at her fast. She frowned as the car passed
her. It swerved in front of her, forcing her to hit her brakes
to avoid a collision. The windows were tinted, and Miamor
couldn't see inside, but she was sure it was one of Baraka's
goons. She reached for the pistol that sat in her passenger
seat, but then halted. She would go willingly. It was instinct
for her to fight, but this time she had to concede defeat. The
doors of the vehicle popped open, and two masked men
hopped out. She opened her door and stepped out. She kept

her hands by her side, palms out, so they could see she wasn't carrying a gun. "What is this?" she asked.

The two men rushed her, and she immediately noticed their hands. They weren't Baraka's men. They were black. "Did Monroe send you?" She instantly began to regret getting out of the car without her gun.

They said nothing and approached her with guns drawn. "Why would he do this? Do you know what's at stake?!" she shouted. One of the men grabbed her, and she snatched away from him. "No! Don't do this!" she said as he grabbed her waist. *Why is Monroe stopping me? Why would he do this?* she thought as she kicked and screamed as she was pulled toward their car. Miamor fought with all of her might to break free, but when they slipped a rag over her mouth, she knew it was useless. The familiar smell of chloroform overwhelmed her, and within seconds everything around her faded to black.

* * *

The sun shined brightly through Monroe's window, awakening him before he had the chance to recover from the bottle of cognac he had consumed the night before. He didn't even want to turn toward the window. He squeezed his eyes closed, pulling the cover over his head as he groaned. Drowning his sorrows away had brought him no relief. The only thing that would make this right was Miamor's sacrifice. Monroe had already decided he was handing Miamor over to Baraka, whether Carter agreed or not. This was bigger than a woman. This was about family. Miamor was affiliated by association; she didn't have Diamond blood flowing through her veins. That fact alone made her expendable. He knew he would be at odds with Carter for years to come over the decision that had been made without him, but Monroe didn't care. His only concern at that moment in time was his wife, nephew, and son. Monroe knew it would take some time for Carter to accept this. He only hoped Carter could see that this was the only way to put an end to things. He grabbed his phone and called Carter, but when he didn't receive an answer, he decided this was a conversation best had in person. Monroe stood and quickly dressed before heading out. When he made it to his car he noticed his trunk was slightly ajar. He frowned as he approached it. "What the fuck?" he mumbled. When he pulled it open, the sight before him ripped him apart.

"Leena, no baby, no," he cried as he looked at her bloody, naked body. Her eyes were still open as she stared off into space. There were burn marks all over her, her hand was missing, and her face was swollen to the point where it was unrecognizable. If it had not been for her wedding ring, he might have doubted her identity. "No!" Monroe sobbed as he pulled her from the trunk. He fell to the ground with her in his arms. Blood was everywhere. "Somebody help me! Please!" he shouted. He had never been so wounded— even when his parents had died or Mecca had been murdered. This was a different emotion. This was the woman he loved. She would have never been a part of this life if it had not been for him. She was a victim of circumstance;

another tragic love story. He was devastated. It felt like his heart was made of glass and had been shattered into a thousand pieces. He knew that the only thing Leena had done wrong in her life was to love him. A gangster and a good girl were never a wise mix. The dead body in his arms was evidence of that. He had known that she wanted him out of the game. If he had just heeded the signs Leena had given him, she would still be alive. This felt like his fault. Somebody had to feel his wrath. There would be hell to pay for this loss. He would drop a body for every tear that slid down his face.

CHAPTER 4

Miamor awoke to the distinct smell of him. She recognized it instantly. It was ingrained in her memory. She knew his scent. She knew him and as she realized she was in his clutches, it all began to make sense. He was the only person in the world who could catch her slipping. He had taught her the game, and the student never surpassed the teacher. Murder. He was her first love, but love was a tricky emotion. When handled correctly it was a beautiful thing, but where matters of the heart were concerned it could quickly spiral out of control. Murder's love for her had become an obsession. She didn't know if he loved her or if he just wanted to say that she belonged to him. Between them, things were always so complicated. It was a constant cycle of cat and mouse and once again he had caught up to her. Her head was cloudy. She had been chloroformed, and it would take some time to shake the haze that incapacitated her. She wasn't at her best. She couldn't fight him. Not now, and if she was being honest with herself, not ever. He was better than her at killing; probably the only person whose heart was colder than hers since Mecca Diamond. She sat up, weakly, hanging her head as she leaned against the headboard of the bed. Her movements were limited and she gritted her teeth as she yanked at the handcuffs that bound one of her wrists to the bed frame.

"I thought I killed you," she said maliciously as she leaned against the headboard in defeat.

"I thought you did, too," Murder replied as he puffed on the Kush-filled blunt. "You did a nigga cold, Miamor," he continued as he moved from the chair across the room to the bed. He sat directly next to her and stroked her hair. "You look like you need this more than I do." He held the blunt up to her mouth, and Miamor closed her eyes as she took it between her lips. She inhaled and then blew it out slowly.

"What have you done, Murder?" she asked as a tear rolled down her face. "Do you know what the fuck you have done?!" Her voice raised to a holler as she stared at him, enraged.

"I saved your fucking life, Miamor! That's what I did! I'mma always choose you! That pussy ass nigga Carter was just going to hand you over if I didn't step in!" Murder shouted.

"There is no saving me, Murder! When will you get that through your fucking obsessed head? I don't need saving!" she screamed. She broke into sobs as she thought of the repercussions of Murder's interference. Her thoughts of his interference wrecked her. "I killed the daughter of a very powerful man. I'm a dead woman walking regardless. He took our son, Murder! He was going to give him back if I gave myself up. He was going to give him back—" She tilted her head back, hitting it against the wood as she cried. "All you had to do was let me do that. He's dead, thanks to you. They're going to kill my baby." She whispered the last words . . . not wanting to hear them.

"I didn't know, Miamor. The nigga Fly didn't say anything about a kid," Murder stated.

Miamor sniffed as she stared at him in disbelief. The narrow slits of her eyes were like daggers as anger pulsed through her. "Fly Boogie? He was a part of this? He's working with you?" she asked. She had trusted Fly. She had leaned on him for support and friendship. "Why? Why can't you ever just let go of me, Murder?"

"Because you're mine," he replied. "You might not remember how much we meant to each other. Carter might have you blinded by this Cartel bullshit, but I remember, Mia." He leaned his face into her as he tried to kiss her, but she turned her face defiantly.

"I don't remember," she whispered as her lip trembled at the thought of her child.

"You remember," he insisted as he kissed her cheek sensually, then her ear, and her neck. He was intoxicated by her scent, and she cringed at his touch. "You remember me busting that pussy open, you remember me putting my tongue on it. I can still hear you calling my name, Miamor, begging me for it. I know you ain't forget that. You said it was mine. I got locked up and left you out here, to survive on your own. I know you're pissed about that. You latched on to another nigga so that these streets didn't eat you alive. I get it, but it's time we got back to what we used to be. Before you switched up." He pulled back and mushed her head hard. "You hear me?"

Miamor gritted her teeth to stop herself from getting slick at the mouth. She didn't know what Murder was capable of. Not anymore. The last time they had faced off she was pregnant and defenseless. She had seen a side of him that was so psychotic, she knew he wasn't above killing her. He would rather see her buried six feet deep than back in Carter's arms. She would have to play this carefully. A knock at the door caused Murder to rise off the bed and she sighed in relief. She didn't fear Murder. She didn't fear anyone, but she did fear for the fate of her son. He was just a kid. He wasn't supposed to pay for her sins.

Murder snatched open the door to the bedroom, and Fly Boogie walked inside. In his hands he carried brown paper bags of food. He looked at Miamor. She looked away. "Miamor," he said.

Miamor didn't respond. Confusion plagued her as a million things ran through her mind. *What is he doing here? How does he know Murder?* she thought.

"Did I tell you to talk to her?" Murder asked. "Don't overstep, young." It was a subtle warning.

"What, nigga?" Fly Boogie asked, challenging him.

Miamor realized Fly Boogie was in over his head. He had no idea what a man like Murder was capable of. She needed him to tread lightly, so she spoke up. "Baraka has C.J.," she told him. "The longer I'm here, the worse things will get. He's probably killing him right now."

Fly Boogie cleared his throat as he looked at her sympathetically. "You've been out for a couple days, Miamor. It's too late, ma. Baraka killed Leena and the kids," Fly informed her. "The memorial is today."

It was like she had been slapped in the face by his words. They stunned her as her heart immediately felt hollow. It was like all the love that she had collected in her life had drained out of her in that moment. It hurt. Like nothing she had ever felt before; her soul burned like the fires of hell were scorching her. "No," she said as she shook her head in denial. "No!" she screamed. "He's my blood. My only son. You have to let me go. I can't . . . be . . . here." She spoke passionately, pleadingly, desperately as she pulled at the handcuff. "No—oo." She sounded wounded, as if she were being tortured slowly. What they didn't know was this was her worst fear. This was a nightmare. Neither man had ever seen her so distraught.

Murder rushed over to her side. "Miamor, stop," he said. She was pulling at the handcuffs with such force that he thought she would break her wrists. The entire bed shook as she lost control.

"I'm going to fucking murder this motherfucka!" she shouted. She snapped. Like a shark out for blood, her instincts clicked on. "Get these fucking handcuffs off of me." She sneered. Her resolve was so strong that he could see the malice in her stare. "This isn't about Carter, Murder.

This ain't about me and you. It's about my seed. If you keep me here, I will never forgive you. I will never love you. I will never see you the same again. You won't want me because you won't be able to trust me. You won't be able to close your eyes around me. I swear to God. I will kill you if you keep me here. My son's funeral is today! I have to be there! I have to see him! His mother has to be there," she pleaded.

"Look what they did to you, Mia. Look how vulnerable they made you. You wouldn't be like this if you had stayed with me. I would have protected you," Murder stated.

"I know . . ." she cried. "I know. I remember. I remember you as the man who would do anything for me, so be that guy right now. Do this. . . ."

Against his better judgment, he dug in his pocket to retrieve the key to the cuffs. He released her and then gripped her face tightly. "Don't play me, Miamor. You know what happens when I have to come find you. You do what you have to do with your kid, but you know where home is. Don't make me come snatch your pretty ass out of that casino."

She nodded and scrambled from the bed before he changed his mind. "Take her back," Murder said to Fly Boogie.

"And my money?" he asked.

"I'll get your money, nigga. You think she's in any state to get to the casino account right now? I'mma pay you. For now, make sure she comes back," Murder insisted.

Miamor and Fly Boogie walked in silence out of the hotel suite. It wasn't until they were in the elevator that

Miamor spoke. "What did you do?!" she shouted as she pushed him hard in the chest. She was livid, and although she was the more deadly of the two when she was armed, unstrapped she had no wins against his strength. He pinned her against the wall, pressing the weight of his body against hers.

"Calm down, ma," he said as he stopped the elevator.

"How could you work with him? How do you even know him? How could you do this?" she cried. She was hysterical at the thought of her child. How had he died? Had Baraka been cruel? Had he tortured her son the way she had tortured Yasmine? "This is all my fault. My baby boy. Nooo," she said, coming undone as her knees buckled. "He needed me!"

"Shhh," Fly Boogie soothed her as he held her up, steadying her while placing his forehead against hers. "Look at me, Miamor."

"I can't . . . I just can't." Her heart ached so badly.

"I didn't know. I didn't know about the kidnapping. I had love for Leena and for your son . . . for Money's son, too. You know I wouldn't have made that type of move had I known what was up. But giving yourself up was the wrong play, ma. Men like Baraka don't hand out pardons. He lost his daughter. Your blood ain't enough. He wants Carter to feel the loss of his legacy. He would have killed your son whether he had you or not. I wasn't about to sit on the sidelines and let anything happen to you. It ain't in me," Fly Boogie said. His face was so close to hers that when she spoke, their lips touched.

"Why are you here with Murder?" Miamor asked.

"Shit is complicated," Fly Boogie said.

"Uncomplicate it," she shot back.

Fly Boogie swept a hand over his face. "I met Murder years ago in Miami. He paid me to infiltrate The Cartel," he admitted. He left out the part about knocking off Carter. "I got sucked in. I got close to Carter and then Carter went away and I got close to you. I left Miami and said, 'Fuck Murder.' I didn't look back. He showed up here a few days ago. I helped him snatch you."

Miamor shook her head in disgust. "So all this time you were just his bitch? You were his spy? His flunky? Reporting my every move to him? What was the endgame? Huh, Fly? Were you going to kill me? Or was bringing me back to him the plan the entire time?" she asked.

"Hell no, I wasn't going to kill you, ma!" Fly Boogie defended himself. "I wanted you for myself. I started feeling you. You know that. The shit between me and you got heavy. I would have never—"

"Yeah whatever," she said, cutting him off. "I just need to go back. I need Carter," she whispered.

"It always goes back to him," Fly Boogie scoffed as he stepped back. "You literally have niggas waiting in line for you, ma. Niggas that will go to war for you . . . and you keep crawling back to the one who fucked you over. You're worth more than that, but whatever, ma. It's your world."

He stepped back, giving her space, and smashed his finger into the elevator button to allow them to descend. In her heart she knew it was too late to save her son, but until she heard the words fall off Carter's lips, she would hold on to the little hope she had left. *God please just give me a miracle. Please let Baraka spare my baby,* she thought. As if Fly Boogie could read her mind, he said, "Your son is gone, Miamor. I'm not saying that to hurt you. I just want you to be prepared for what you're going back to. I don't want anyone else to see your breakdown. So process it now . . . feel it now so that when you walk into the church, they won't witness you fall apart. You're a queen, ma. Can't let that crown fall."

* * *

The cemetery was peaceful on that day. The birds chirped, and a faint breeze blew over them as Carter, Monroe, Breeze, and Zyir gathered in front of Leena's solid gold casket. Three framed pictures sat behind it. Carter couldn't even bring himself to look at them. Leena's smiling face along with C.J.'s and Mo's were lined up next to one another. Only Leena's body had been recovered. Baraka had never had the courtesy of burying his daughter, so he didn't extend the opportunity to Carter and Monroe. They were forced to memorialize their children instead. Carter kept hoping this was a nightmare that he would eventually wake up from. The finality of his reality was too much to deal with. His son was gone. His nephew gone. Leena gone. Their deaths marked a change in him. He was gone. His soul was so damaged that it felt as if he would never be the same again. The cadence of his heartbeat had changed. Everything hurt. Even the thoughts that ran through his mind caused him unbelievable pain. He just wanted it all to end. Carter had been living wrong. He had thrived on power, on money, on prestige. What he wouldn't give to be a regular Joe at that moment. Regular Joes didn't usually bury their kids. They lived a comfortable, routine day-to-day life without even realizing how lucky they were. Carter's kingpin lifestyle had brought him riches, but the things he had lost in that pursuit were priceless. This was a blow he would never recover from. The sound of an approaching vehicle caused everyone to turn their heads in its direction. It was a private service. No one knew they were there. Not even Leena's parents had accepted their invitation to attend. They had written her off long ago, when she had chosen that lifestyle.

"Fuck is she doing here?" Monroe asked as he saw Miamor roll down the passenger window.

"Money," Breeze whispered. "Please. Not today."

* * *

Miamor wasn't ready for this. "I can't breathe," she whispered as her chest tightened. She sat in the passenger seat of Fly Boogie's F-150 as she watched the small ceremony take place in the middle of the cemetery. It was intimate, only family attended, but still she felt unwelcome. She was on the outside looking in. Her guilt had ostracized her. "You can go, Fly," she whispered as she reached for the door handle.

"I ain't going anywhere. I'll be right here," he replied as he watched her exit the vehicle.

She walked across the grass, closing the distance between her and the people she had once called family. She halted a few yards away. Pictures of the children had been enlarged and framed. Leena's casket was the only one present. Tears accumulated in Miamor's eyes. Breeze was the first one to react. She watched as Breeze knelt down to whisper in Carter's ear. He looked up at her and when their eyes met, she knew . . . it was true. Their prince was gone. Monroe could no longer contain his anger as he stormed over to her.

"Give me one reason why I shouldn't put a bullet between your eyes," Monroe said as he snatched Miamor by her neck, flinging her against an oak tree as if she were weightless.

She wasn't afraid to die. She didn't even flinch as she stared at Monroe. "Shoot me, Money. Just do it," she whispered to him. She was broken. Nothing he could do to her could be worse than what she already felt.

"Money!" Carter barked, but there wasn't much he could do. He sat confined by the wheelchair. He would never move the same way again, let alone run to her rescue. "Monroe!" he called.

Zyir walked up behind Monroe. "This won't solve anything, bro," he said.

"That's my life in that box over there!" Monroe shouted as he pressed his gun point-blank against Miamor's head. "My wife! And now my son is dead because of you. . . . He was a little boy and he was taken from me because of you." She could practically see fire dancing in his eyes, he was so heated. She didn't blame him and she would deserve her fate if he chose to pull the trigger. She would have if she were the one holding the gun.

"She knows, Money," Zyir stated, his tone mellow. The last thing he wanted to do was incite Monroe. "We all know. We don't need more bloodshed. We all feel this hurt."

Monroe pulled back the hammer of his gun and gripped the trigger. He wanted so bad to end her. Staring into her eyes, he saw nothing. It was as if she were gone.

Mentally she had been depleted; emotionally she was damaged for life. It was as if she were already dead. Guilt had pushed her to the point of no return. Someone had to be held accountable for this. The lives of their babies had been taken. Her dear friend Leena had been taken. She deserved to die at the hands of Monroe. She silently wished that he would just pull the trigger, because death would be easier than carrying the grief of this around for the rest of her life.

"I don't blame you. This is my fault. Just do it. Do it, Money! Do it!" she screamed. She saw how bad he wanted to. In his rage he was the spitting image of Mecca. If she didn't know any better, she would have sworn that Mecca was the one threatening her life. Goose bumps formed on the back of her neck, and despite the Nevada heat, she shivered.

Breeze finally managed to roll Carter's wheelchair through the grass over to the heated scene. "Take a walk, Monroe," Carter stated. He might have been out of commission, but his tone of voice was strong and it was clear. He wouldn't stand by and allow anyone to gun her down . . . not right in front of him.

"After all this, you still defending this bitch?" Monroe said through gritted teeth. His nostrils flared as he lowered his gun and stormed off, completely livid.

Breeze rushed after him as Zyir lingered. "You a'ight?" Zyir asked.

"Yeah, give me a minute, Zy," Carter replied, conflicted.

Carter looked up at Miamor. He was a shell of the man she was used to seeing. She could see that he hadn't slept. His red-rimmed eyes and the bags beneath his lids gave away his restless nights. He seemed to have aged overnight. The burden of a dead child weighed on him heavily. The bullets in his chest had penetrated so deep that one had nicked his spine, rendering him to a wheelchair temporarily. It would take months of healing before he could walk without pain, but he could deal with that. It was the inner battle he was fighting that made life feel unbearable.

"You played this shit all wrong, Miamor," he said. He could barely look at her. "You drugged me and tried to handle this by yourself, and you got our son killed."

"I planned to turn myself in—"

"He was our son, Miamor!" Carter yelled, interrupting her. His voice held so much judgment, so much contempt. He held up his hands and looked at them with tear-filled eyes. "All I see is blood on my hands. I thought I wouldn't be able to choose between you and C.J., but we both understood what had to happen. I knew you were selfish, but I never thought you would put yourself over our son."

"I didn't," she shot back. "I would trade my life for his in a heartbeat, Carter. You have to believe me. You must know me better than that by now. I loved our son. I wouldn't have fucked up the exchange. I was taken. It was Murder. He's alive and he—"

Zyir walked back up as Carter interrupted her. "I'm done, Miamor. My son . . . was the most innocent person I've ever met. His soul was pure, and he was killed because of something you did. I can't say it is all on you. I played my part. I chose this life. I chose you. I knew what type of person you were, and I still tested your gangster. I cheated. You retaliated the only way you know how—with murder, with torture. We both caused this. But it's over now," he said. "Baraka has placed a million-dollar bounty on your head. I'd advise you to go far away from here."

"I can't live without you, Carter. You're all I have left," she whispered. Tears clung to her thick eyelashes, threatening a downpour of emotion.

"I'm done with you. Done with all this shit. There is no us. There is no Cartel. Y'all can have this shit . . . all of it. I'm out," he said.

Zyir gripped the handle of the wheelchair and looked at Miamor sympathetically as she fell to her knees. She placed a hand over her heart just to make sure it was still there . . . still beating. It felt like he had ripped it right out of her chest. She wanted to say that she was the type of queen Fly Boogie spoke of, but she wasn't, and as she watched Carter being wheeled away, she broke down. Her pride wouldn't let her beg him to stay. The farther he got from her, the more it hurt. She leaned her back against the tree and pulled her knees into her chest as she cried her eyes out. Carter didn't want her. Her son had paid the ultimate price for her actions. She had nowhere to go but right back where she had come from . . . right back where she had spent years trying to escape. Murder had been right all along. He would always represent home to her. He was the only one who would put up with her treacherous ways, because he had taught them to her.

She heard sticks breaking under the weight of approaching footsteps.

She knew it was Fly Boogie. He wanted to be her knight in shining armor. He was determined to rescue the damsel in distress. What he didn't know was that she was the wicked witch in the story. Everything she touched seemed to rot. If he wasn't careful, she would curse him, too.

"Let's go, ma," he said as he knelt down in front of her. "There's nothing left for you here."

She stood up. "Take me back to Murder," she said in a tone so low that he almost didn't catch it.

"Why would you want to go back to that nigga? What's so bad about staying with me? I'm not Carter. My pockets aren't as heavy as his. I know I can't compete with what y'all got, but Murder?" Fly Boogie stated.

"I don't want to hurt you, Fly Boogie. I like you. You're loyal, you're handsome, you have heart—but you're young. You need a nice, fresh chick . . . someone like Breeze. You don't want me. You just like what I represent," she said.

"Why Murder?" Fly Boogie pressed, perplexed.

"Because he will kill anybody who tries to lay a hand on me, and I need protection. Baraka has money on my head," she revealed. "How much did Murder promise you to play this game? To get inside The Cartel . . . to get close to me?" she asked.

He shifted uncomfortably. "It stopped being about the bread a long time ago," he replied.

"How much?" she insisted.

"Fifty bands," he replied.

"I'll wire the money to an account for you. I want you to leave Vegas. Murder was never going to pay you. Once he was done and you were of no use to him, he would have killed you," Miamor said.

"I'm not leaving Vegas without you, ma," Fly Boogie said.

"Fly! You're not hearing me. Get lost. I'm trying to spare your feelings, lil' nigga. You never had a chance with me. I like big boys," Miamor said. Her words were so abrasive that she cringed on the inside, but she had to make a point. She had to bruise his ego, wound his pride so that he would finally turn his back on her. She didn't want anyone else around her to die.

He nodded his head defensively as his mug twisted into a scowl. "Yeah, a'ight, Miamor," he said, feeling burned. He swaggered off in the direction of his truck, and she backpedaled in the opposite direction. Their good-bye was a silent one as she lowered her head and made her way back to the hotel . . . back to Murder.

* * *

The musty mixture of rotting food, body odor, and alcohol filled the hotel room. It bitch-smacked Murder as soon as he entered. His lip curled in disgust as he spotted Miamor's silhouette across the dark room. She was still lying there . . . in the same spot that she had been in for two weeks. "Nah, nah, you can't keep doing this, baby girl. You've got to get up, Miamor. Snap out of it," he said as he made his way across the room. He snatched open the curtains, allowing light to flood the space, revealing an ugly sight. Miamor's hair was matted and nappy. Her clothes were dirty, she reeked, and her eyes were bloodshot. All she did was cry. He had witnessed death many times and had never seen grief in this form. Miamor's pain was raw. She didn't care about anything, not even herself—and the razor scars on her thighs were proof of that. Blood dripped out of the open wounds, and Murder sauntered to her side. He looked at her as she still gripped the razor in her hand. She was holding it so tightly that it was cutting her fingertips. "What the fuck is wrong with you?" he asked her, exasperated. He was at a loss. He didn't know what to do. This woman before him was a shell of the woman he once knew. She was weak. Her normal fire had been snuffed out the moment she found out her son's fate. He snatched her wrist and applied pressure to it, causing her to drop the razor. "Why are you doing this to yourself? The fuck is this gon' solve?" he asked.

Her eyes were spaced out as she stared past him. She was in a daze as she responded. "It's the only way to let the pain out." She tilted her head back as she closed her eyes. "Just let it all bleed out," she whispered.

Without warning, Murder slapped fire from her, snapping her out of her funk and filling her with rage. "You want to feel something? Feel that!" he chastised her as she lunged at him.

"Fuck you! Fuck. You," she screamed as she beat his chest.

He hemmed her up as she struggled to swing on him, but he overpowered her, restricting her movements as if she were in a straitjacket. "Snap the fuck out of this shit, Miamor! I know you lost your kid, but how many kids have you left motherless? Or fatherless? How many of them little mu'fuckas have you bodied?!"

She keeled over, bawling, as the harsh reality of karma slapped her in the face. It was a far mightier blow than the one Murder had served.

Murder had fought so hard to get to her. She had damn near killed him back in Miami when he had tried to take her away from The Cartel the first time. Still, he pursued her. He wanted her. He had to have her and now that he got her, time had changed her. She wore her grief like a heavy cloak. It weighed her down. There was no life behind her vacant stare. Her teary gaze was filled with nothingness, and it was hard to stomach. He felt like he was babysitting. Where was his ride-or-die? *A nigga ain't beat for this shit,* he thought. His heart beat intensely. He was overwhelmed by anger and disappointment. This wasn't how it was supposed to be when they reunited. The sulking, the depression, the insanity . . . he couldn't understand her logic. Sure, he sympathized, but he was ready to get back to reality. Miamor was stuck in her grief. She was frozen.

"I need my Murder Mama back," he said as he bent down to help her stand. "That's who you are, Miamor." He motioned to her, waving his hand up and down her body. "This . . . this chick ain't you. Bring my Murder Mama back. Murking something always made you feel better."

Miamor looked him in the eyes and blinked slowly. It took so much effort to do everything. All she really wanted to do was sleep. . . . If she could sleep forever she would be happy. In her dreams was the only place where she could see her son. "You would do anything for me, wouldn't you?" she asked.

A little patience crept into Murder's heart as he replied, "You know that. Just tell me what you need."

"I need you to let me go," she said. In one swift movement Miamor pulled Murder's gun from his waistline.

He chuckled as she pointed it at him. It was instincts like that—her murderous nature, her quick draw—that turned him on. It was over gunplay that they had connected and over gunplay that they would reconnect. He was sure of it. "That shit is in your blood, ma. I love this shit. This is the bitch I know . . . but I know you well enough to know you not gon' curl that trigger on me," Murder said. His hands were at his sides. He was relaxed and unmoved by her theatrics. He knew when Miamor was out for blood, and now was not one of those times.

"No, I'm not . . . not on you," she said. His eyes bulged

in horror as she turned the gun on herself and without pausing to think twice . . .

CLICK.

She didn't even flinch at the gunshot that should have ended her life. Instead, disappointment filled her face as she realized that Murder had emptied the chamber and popped out the clip upon entering the room. She had been ready to end it all, but the unloaded pistol only revealed how deeply her psychosis had settled in. "No, no, no!"

CLICK. CLICK. CLICK.

She pulled the trigger over and over again, aiming at her temple, wishing that she would just die already, until finally Murder rushed her. "Get your ass in here," he screamed at her as he dragged her across the room, kicking and screaming. "Have you lost your fucking mind? Do you know what you would have done had that shit been loaded, ma? You can't take that back! You can't undo suicide . . . once it's over, it's over."

"Just leave me the fuck alone! Just go! I don't want to be here! Don't you get that! It hurts. Unlike anything I have ever felt . . . it hurts," she shouted, snot and tears mixing on her face as he manhandled her.

He gripped her shoulders and shook her hard, hoping to shake some sense into her. "I can't trust you. You're not thinking straight. I know what will clear your mind," he whispered more to himself than to her. He flung open the closet door and pushed her inside and then barricaded the door so she couldn't get out.

He heaved in exhaustion as he rested his forehead against the door. "Hold tight, Miamor. I'll be back. I know something that will help you get through this. I just need you to stay still. You can't hurt yourself in there. I'm sorry," Murder whispered, winded from their struggle. "Crazy bitch."

Murder grabbed his gun and snatched his keys off the table as he stormed out. He was determined to get Miamor back. . . . He had her physically in his clutches, but he needed her mentally to be strong. He needed her, and he knew just the type of therapy to get her to come back to him.

* * *

Murder sat in the smoke-filled bar, shoulders hunched, a beer gripped between his hands as thoughts of Miamor cluttered his brain. He turned in his chair as the loud music blared throughout the hole in the wall. Drunken frat boys and college girls made up the crowd. He turned in his barstool and faced the dance floor as his eyes scanned the room until he set his gaze on a pretty, young girl. Her caramel skin, bare midriff, and short pixie cut appealed to him. She was what he needed. She was the perfect distraction, and he nodded his head, greeting her as he lifted his beer bottle to his lips.

She flashed her pretty smile before walking over to him. "You don't look like the college-boy type," the girl said.

He wasn't thirsty. He simply turned back toward the bar when she sat in the seat next to him. He wasn't with kicking game, not for what he intended. . . . It wasn't necessary.

"I'm Alisha," she introduced herself. There was curiosity in her eyes. She was young and reckless; the thought of a new adventure with this obvious bad boy was an exciting notion. In a room full of clean-cut college boys, his grown-man swagger stuck out like a sore thumb. He was just the type of guy she wanted to take home for the night. There was something about those bad boys that made a good girl swoon.

Murder motioned for the bartender. "Scotch . . . neat. And whatever she's drinking," he said.

She smiled. "So do you have a name?" she asked.

"You're drunk," Murder observed. "You're standing there with your ass hanging out the bottom of your shorts, your titties on display, your shirt half-ripped, and cheap six-inch heels on. I'm a hood nigga with a big dick and loaded pockets." He paused as the bartender delivered both drinks. "Does my name really matter, or you ready to get out of here?"

He was crass, direct, a bit rude, but she loved it. The girl took her drink and tossed it back before replying, "You've got a room?"

Murder left a fifty-dollar bill on the bar and walked out. He didn't look back because he knew the college girl would be right behind him.

She smirked, feeling herself, as she took a deep breath. She looked back at her friends, who were preoccupied on the dance floor. She thought about telling them she was leaving . . . thought about telling them who she was leaving with, but instead she hustled out of the bar. *I'll catch up with them later.*

She walked out of the door and looked left, then right, as her heart raced in anxiety.

"You ready?" Murder asked, startling her as he leaned against the side of the building, hidden in the shadows as he blew smoke from a cigarette. She turned around, smiling, as she walked up on him. He pulled her in, gripping her firm behind as he pressed his manhood against her. The thought of the night to come had him ready.

"Feels like you're more ready than I am," she flirted. He flicked the cigarette and then grabbed her hand. "Let's get out of here."

He led her to his car, which was parked down the block, in a darkened alley, and then opened the door for her.

She eased into the car and then he ran around the front to enter from his side.

As soon as he sat down she grabbed him, caressing the print that had formed in his pants. He sat back as he pulled out into traffic and then with one hand on the wheel and one hand behind her neck he guided her mouth down onto him. "Show me what you got, lil' mama. Who knows—if you do it good enough, I just may have a reason to keep you around," he said.

* * *

Miamor had stopped fighting. She had stopped banging . . . stopped screaming. There was no point. No one was coming to her rescue. She wasn't getting out of the closet until Murder felt like letting her out, so she sat, stoically recounting all the ways she had caused her current circumstance. It had been her hot head, her inability to rationalize her anger without the help of her gun, and her quick trigger, that had brought her here. She knew Carter hated her. Hell, she hated herself. He was the only person who could heal her heart and he wanted nothing to do with her, so instead she accepted Murder as a consolation prize. She didn't love him, but he loved her and because of that, she would be protected.

She heard the door to the suite open and she waited until the closet door was pulled open. She was curled up against the wall, knees to her chest, as she looked up at him.

"Get up," Murder said.

Miamor reluctantly climbed to her feet and ambled out of the tiny space. Murder tossed some clothes at her roughly. "Put these on. I've got something to make you feel better," he stated. There was no compassion in his tone, only annoyance. He was determined to snap her out of this depression. There was nothing attractive about her current state and the longer she dwelled in it, the more he could feel himself pulling away.

Miamor sneered at him as she stepped into the jeans and shrugged on the jacket. Her hair was a mess, her eyes swollen and red, but she didn't care.

He shook his head as he grabbed her elbow and led her out of the room.

"Where are we going?" she whispered. "I can't be seen anywhere around town. You're going to get me killed."

"Shut up and walk," he said.

He escorted her to the trunk of his car. "I've got something for you," he said as he stood behind her. He kissed the nape of her neck and handed her the key. "Open it."

She rolled her eyes, but snatched the key and inserted it. She turned it and lifted the trunk.

When Miamor saw the young girl, gagged and bound in the trunk, her heart dropped. The terror shined in the girl's eyes. Miamor quickly closed the trunk and turned to Murder. "What the fuck is wrong with you?" Miamor asked.

"What's wrong with you?" Murder shot back. "This is who you are, Mia. This is what we do," he spoke through gritted teeth, his frustration rearing its ugly head.

"This girl can't be older than twenty-one, Murder. You don't know her. She hasn't done anything wrong to you. She hasn't crossed you," Miamor reasoned. "She's innocent. This isn't my game."

"What are you talking about, ma? You've gone soft! You know the rules. Anybody—"

"Can get it," Miamor said, finishing his sentence. "I know the rules, Murder. I remember. I just can't be a part of it anymore. This shit right here," she stated, motioning to the trunk. "This type of shit is the reason why my karma is so bad. This is the reason why I lost my son."

Murder stood toe-to-toe with her as he pointed his finger in her face. "No, that bitch nigga Carter is the reason you lost your son. He was too pussy to protect his family. You chose him. You chose wrong," Murder said. "Now you want lil' mama in the car to die your way or my way? Either way, she gotta get it. She's seen my face."

Miamor wanted to leave the girl hanging. She wanted to tell Murder to kiss her ass and to do what he had to do, but she couldn't. She knew the type of death he would deliver. He had a thing for inflicting pain. If he killed this girl, it would be slow, torturous. Murder had an itch to scratch. He wanted to wring Miamor's neck, and she knew it. He wished he had the balls to body her . . . to punish her for choosing Carter over him. He had years of resentment built up toward her, but they both knew he wouldn't act on it. He couldn't hurt Miamor even on her worst day. *He wants to kill me. Instead, he's going to take it out on her,* she thought grimly. There was a time that she wouldn't have cared. She was once a girl who didn't care who was on the other end of the barrel of her gun, but now it mattered. After all of this strife she had learned the ultimate lesson: Life has value. She had grown.

"Murder, please," she whispered. "Just let her go."

"I'm not letting her go. The way she dies is up to you. By your hands or mine," he threatened. He thought he was giving her what she needed. He was trying to fulfill her bloodlust, but that craving—the craving to murder some-one when she was upset—had passed. . . . It had died with C.J. Still, Murder had forced her hand. He knew the beast that had retreated inside of her and he was determined to unlock it.

"You're the devil," she stated in disgust.

"In the flesh, baby," he replied. He kissed her, forcing his tongue into her mouth as she pushed against him.

"Get off of me!" she shouted, infuriated at his arrogance. He chuckled, finding humor in her discomfort. He slid his hand into his waistline and came out with a 9mm pistol. He screwed a silencer on the end. Her eyes burned holes through him as she stared in contempt.

"You might not want to put a gun in my hand right now. I just might shoot you with it," she said snidely.

He handed it to her. "We both know that's a lie, lil' mama," he said. "I'm all you've got." It was a sad truth that kept her linked to him.

Miamor popped the trunk and looked at the girl. For the first time ever, Miamor was afraid to pull the trigger. Her soul was on the line. Tears accumulated in her eyes. Her emotions were unstable. Murdering this innocent girl was the furthest thing from her mind.

"Do it," Murder stated. He knew Miamor was like a pit bull. Once she was back in the swing of things, she would go all out. He would have his old Murder Mama back. "You do it or I can."

She pointed the gun into the trunk as the girl began to plead. The duct tape muffled her, but Miamor knew exactly what she was saying. She had heard it time and time again.

Please, don't kill me. Please. Just let me go, Miamor spoke the words in her mind. She had played executioner so many times that she knew this script verbatim. All of her victims had always used the same lines. Their last words were always the same. Even the hardest man had turned to putty when staring into the black hole of her gun. This was the only time she felt differently, though.

Her aim was steady, but her heart wavered, quivered, shook with uncertainty. "I'm not doing this," she whispered. She turned to Murder. "I've had enough bloodshed. Enough is enough, Murder. You want to know why I always choose Carter over you? Why I am so pulled in by him? Because he's a good man. He has blood on his hands, but he has never hurt anybody who didn't hurt him first. He isn't a monster."

Murder took the gun from her hands and, without even moving his eyes from Miamor's, he fired into the trunk. The gun whispered five shots as he continuously pulled the trigger, ending the girl's life without remorse.

Miamor didn't flinch. Death didn't scare her or move her. At this point, it disgusted her. Murder disgusted her, but his callousness is also what would protect her. He would body anyone who threatened her existence. "I'm going back up to the room," she said.

As she walked away he shouted over to her, "We're the same, Miamor! I know you! I see you! You the one hiding from yourself!"

If she weren't so afraid of Baraka and his goons, she would leave Murder, but the Arabs put a fear in her that she had never known existed. So as long as she had to put up with Murder, she would—at least until she could figure out a plan B.

CHAPTER 5

It felt good to be back home. Miami had treated him well, but there was nothing like having his own kingdom. Flint was where he was bred, and as Zyir cruised the city blocks, he realized he never wanted to leave. He felt the buzz of his cell phone and when he looked at the screen, Breeze's name appeared. He sighed and sent her to voice mail. He had to stay focused. He was about to sell ten bricks to a first-time customer and he needed to be aware. Distractions were deadly in this game, and Breeze's unhappiness was the biggest one. She wasn't adjusting well to her new surroundings. After Leena's murder, she was paranoid all the time and she wanted him at her side 24/7. He loved her, but he wasn't in the babysitting business. He had to move around. He had jumped onto Flint's drug scene full force, and it was important that he make his presence known. Hustling in Miami and hustling at home were two different feelings. In Flint, he was king. He tried to stay busy to keep himself from dwelling on the fact that The Cartel had fallen apart. They'd all dispersed. Carter was tucked away in the mountains in Colorado, and Monroe had gone back to Miami. Zyir was holding things down in Flint, but there was no one around he could trust.

He pulled up to a neighborhood park. It was deserted. Nightfall and the freezing winter hawk ensured that not a soul was in sight. Zyir peered out his window and checked his rearview as he slid his burner in his waist. He shined his headlights and spotted a black Camaro. His buyer stepped out of the car. Stepping out into the night, he pulled the collar to his Moncler jacket up and tried to duck his head low to escape the biting wind. It was so cold that white clouds floated from his mouth with every breath he took. Adrenaline coursed through him—not from fear, but from caution. Each time he made a drop, he knew what was at stake. This wasn't Miami. He was back in the murder capital, and in Flint, Michigan, good niggas died young every day.

"What up, man, you got your paper together?" Zyir asked.

"Yeah, how many you got?" the dude replied as he tucked his hands in his pockets.

"I got the ten you asked for. Fuck you mean? Where the bread?" Zyir responded, all business as he looked left, then right, before focusing his gaze back onto the man before him.

"I'm saying . . . I might want more if the quality on point. We can go to your spot real quick. I'm trying to spend, heavy. You got a nigga out here freezing his balls off. I can give you the money for the ten and then we can ride to get the other ones and do business right there. I want thirty now," the guy said.

"Go to my spot?" Zyir scoffed. Zyir had been around the block a time or two. This dude had no intention of buying anything. He was trying to find out where his stash was. Zyir had a low tolerance for games. He smelled a setup. "You want thirty?" Zyir asked. He stepped closer to the man casually until . . . suddenly . . . shit wasn't so casual. "Nigga, do I look like a fucking clown-ass nigga out here?" Zyir asked as he grabbed the man by his neck and drew his pistol in one swift motion.

The dude's hand shot up in defense, and Zyir instantly curled his trigger finger.

BOOM!

He blew a nickel-sized hole through his palm. "Agh!" the man hollered as he instantly gripped his hand in pain.

"Don't fucking play with me. You quarter-ounce buying ass, nigga. Now all of a sudden you tryna cop weight? You never seen thirty your whole life," Zyir chastised as he hit the man brutally with the butt of his gun, splitting his nose wide open.

"Nah, big homie, it ain't like that," the man pleaded, but Zyir followed up with another vicious blow. This hit sent him to the ground.

"Don't 'big homie' me. You older than me, nigga," Zyir shot with a smirk. He leaned over and grabbed the man by his collar and placed the gun at point-blank range against his forehead. "Who else is in on it?" Zyir knew that the dude couldn't have had the balls to rob him on his own. There had to be another snake lurking in his grass.

"It ain't like that, I swear, fam!" the man hollered. Zyir could see the fear in the man's eyes, but he had no sympathy. In Miami he had love, respect. They had their enemies, no doubt, but he never had to worry about getting robbed by someone he did business with down there. His hometown was an entirely different ball game. It was a city full of wolves and they were starving. A come-up was a come-up. It didn't matter if a nigga had to kill his man in order to sit at the table. Niggas just wanted to eat. If the opportunity was lucrative enough, even the best of friend could turn foe. Zyir threw him back to the ground. He was a pleading, bleeding, blubbering mess because they both knew what Zyir had to do.

"Niggas always forcing my hand," Zyir said to himself. He aimed his pistol and fired. Two to the chest.

He wiped the fingerprints off the gun with his shirt and then retreated to his car, pulling away from the scene. He'd have to make an extra stop to Devil's Lake in order to toss the gun. It was infamous for its depth—most said it was bottomless—but he was sure there were plenty of dirty burners and bottoms somewhere down there. He was simply adding to the pile.

* * *

Sweat beaded on Breeze's forehead as she threw up in the toilet. "Oh my God," she whispered as she laid her cheek flat on the seat in desperation. The queasiness that had taken over her was unbearable. She couldn't hold down anything. She was miserable. "What the hell is wrong with me?" she whined. *I was fine last night. We ate dinner . . . we made love . . .* Her thoughts stopped abruptly, and she sat up. She gasped as she placed her hand over her mouth. Struggling to her feet she rushed into the master bedroom and grabbed her phone off the bed. She quickly opened her calendar and when she realized what date it was, her mouth fell agape. "Oh my God," she said again, this time in disbelief. *Am I pregnant?* she thought. Her heart sank into her stomach. She didn't know how to feel. She felt the obvious elation, but so many other emotions coursed through her. *Is this real? Is this what I want? Is this what he wants? Are we ready? Do I want to bring children into this mafia lifestyle?* She had all questions, no answers. She loved Zyir with everything in her, but she had come up in The Cartel. She had witnessed both of her parents' lives being taken at the hands of The Cartel's enemies. Would history repeat itself? The last thing she wanted was to bring children into destruction, but Lord knew she loved Zyir. The thought of his seed growing inside her womb brought tears to her eyes. She was overwhelmed. For the first time, she was grateful that Zyir hadn't come home all night. She wanted to be sure she was pregnant before she got him excited for nothing. *I need to get a test,* she thought. *And find a doctor here and get a prenatal vitamin. I hope I don't miscarry. I think you aren't supposed to tell anyone until twenty weeks. Or is it twelve?* "One step at a time, B," she whispered to herself. She was the type to get worked up. She already had nursery themes floating around in her head. "First, let's make sure there is even a baby cooking in here," she said aloud as she placed her hand on her flat stomach. Breeze went into the bathroom and gargled before grabbing her handbag to head out the door. She was halfway down to her car when she realized she had misplaced her keys.

"Damn it," she whispered. She rifled through her purse in frustration, to no avail. Zyir pulled up behind her, and she smiled. *Don't even say anything until you have a positive test in your hands,* she reminded herself.

When he stepped out of the car, she smiled and ran up to him. Wrapping her arms around his neck, she leaned her back to study his stern features. He was tense . . . stressed . . . and her smile faded as she asked, "What's wrong?"

"Nothing to worry your pretty head about, B," he replied. "My bad on staying out all night. I wasn't on no fuck shit. It was necessary."

She placed a finger to his lips to silence him. "I don't need an explanation, Zy. I trust you. If you could have made it home to me, I know you would have."

She could see her love easing him, soothing him. She prided herself on being the solace away from the streets . . . especially these Flint streets. They were different . . . colder . . . more ruthless than sunny Miami.

"I was about to make a quick run. You know me. I can never find my keys," she said with a shrug.

Zyir held up his own. He had the extra to her car on his ring. She grabbed them. His cell phone rang and he answered it. "Money, what's good?" he said as he held up a finger to halt her momentarily and began to walk toward the house.

"You've got to let me out. . . ." she whispered, but he kept walking. She blew out an exasperated breath. "I just need to pee on a stick," she said with a laugh. She eyed Zyir's shiny, foreign car—the one he never let her drive—and she smiled wickedly. "I'll just take his."

She hopped in the car and peeled off. She drove for ten minutes before he even figured out she was gone. She smiled when she heard her cell phone ring. She reached over with one hand and rummaged through her bag, taking her eyes off the road momentarily. She swerved just as she wrapped her hand around her phone. The honk of a car horn caused her to fishtail slightly until she straightened her wheel.

She answered the phone, but the red and blue lights flashing in her rearview mirror caused her to frown. If it had been one squad car behind her she wouldn't have been alarmed, but the five unmarked black SUVs that trailed her let her know they were the feds.

"Zyir," she whispered. "There are five unmarked cars behind me."

"Where are you?" he asked frantically.

"I'm a few miles from the house. On Saginaw Street. I was headed to the pharmacy," she said. "Zyir. Should I pull over?" she asked.

"Yes. I'm coming, B. Ask for your attorney, don't say shit else," he instructed.

"My attorney? Zyir, what's happening right now?" she asked.

"Just listen to me, Breeze. Pull over. Don't resist, baby. I'm on my way."

CLICK.

* * *

Zyir located Breeze's keys with ease, picking them up out of the same spot she always "misplaced" them in. He found himself doing 100 mph until he saw the federal agents pulling Breeze from the car. It was now a scene. There were agents in blue jackets in addition to local police. He was enraged. They had Breeze's face pushed into the trunk of one of the squad cars, manhandling her.

He pulled up recklessly and barely threw the car into park before hopping out.

"Sir, back away . . . you can't—"

"That's my fucking wife!" Zyir shouted as he pushed past the officer.

"Zyir!" Breeze shouted, hearing his voice. "Agh!" she hollered as they put the cuffs on too tight.

"Don't touch her!" Zyir shouted with a look of malice in his eyes. "I will kill you." Zyir never lost his cool, but seeing his wife being roughhoused had him seeing red.

"Mr. Rich," one of the monkeys in suits called out. "You're under arrest, for the intent to distribute narcotics, for possession of narcotics. You have the right to remain silent . . ."

Zyir stood toe-to-toe with the agent reading him his

rights as another officer put him in metal bracelets. He gritted his teeth as his jaw flexed and his nostrils flared. "You sure you want to play it like this?" he asked.

"Mr. Rich, I'm playing it by the law," the agent said. The agent turned toward the police car that was pulling away with a stoic Breeze inside. "This is a warrant to search the vehicle your wife was driving. We both know what we're going to find. As a matter of fact, let's go take a look."

They led Zyir to the trunk of his car. The world seemed to be moving in slow motion as they popped it. *Damn,* Zyir thought. His stomach was in knots, but his face was unrevealing. He had made a monumental mistake.

They were the same bricks that he was supposed to trade off the night before. He hadn't meant for Breeze to take off in his car before he had taken them out.

"I can take that time. It's nothing. Do whatever you have to do," Zyir said arrogantly.

"Oh, I believe you," the agent replied. "But the question is, can your dainty little wife do the time for your crimes? That's who we're going after. Daughter of the infamous Miami kingpin, Carter Diamond, found with drugs in the car. The jury will convict off of her family history alone."

Zyir shot a venomous look at the agent.

"Get him out of here."

The cop dragged him by his elbow to his awaiting squad car. Zyir remained collected on the outside, but appearances could be deceiving. The inner turmoil he felt crippled him. The last thing he wanted was for Breeze to take the fall behind his actions. He couldn't let her. He wouldn't let her.

How could I be so stupid? he thought. He knew better. Riding around with product in the car. In Miami he had people for that. He never even touched it down there, but he didn't have his crew around him. Every shooter he had on deck now felt foreign. He trusted no one, which meant he was playing all roles in order to build his own organization. Zyir had overextended himself. He had been sloppy, and now Breeze was wrapped up in the consequences of it all.

* * *

"I want my lawyer," Breeze stated, trying to stay strong as the officer on duty passed by the cell. She had told herself that she wouldn't say anything—not one word—but that was forty-eight hours ago. She had been locked up in the county bull pen for two days and she didn't know how much more of this she could take. She hadn't slept and she'd refused to eat the stale bread and moldy meat sandwiches the officers passed out once a day. Breeze felt like her world was ending. *Where is Zyir? Where is my lawyer? Why am I still in here?* she wondered. The officer continued to walk by the cell, blatantly ignoring her. "Hey! I know you hear me. What is happening? I have rights. I want my attorney now," she shouted.

"Sit down and be quiet," the officer said sternly as he pointed through the unbreakable glass toward the dirty concrete slabs.

Breeze turned reluctantly as she peered around at the women snickering behind her. It was clear she didn't belong there. Even rushing out in her haste she had thrown on an ensemble worth almost a thousand dollars. She looked privileged, sheltered—spoiled, even. The women looked at her like fresh meat, but little did they know her affiliation alone was more gangster than their entire street résumé.

She walked over to the nearest seat and removed her Gucci poncho and placed it down before sitting.

She leaned over and placed her face in her hands as she willed the tears that burned her eyes not to fall.

Minutes felt like hours; hours, like days. The daunting wait was torture in itself. She had no idea what she was even waiting for. What was she being charged with? What did they think they had on her that warranted this type of detainment. Was this about Zyir? Her brothers? Where the hell were they? Why was she, the most innocent of them all, sitting in a jail right now. She sat up and swept her hair out of her face, blowing out an exasperated breath. Before she could find answers to her questions, the same asshole officer who had been ignoring her for days stepped inside.

"Breeze Rich. Let's go," he announced.

"About time," she muttered as she snatched up her poncho and followed the officer out of the bull pen. She was greeted by a Spanish beauty. She was carrying a Chanel briefcase to match her Chanel ensemble. Her hair was pinned to the back in sophistication. "Hello, Mrs. Rich. I'm Cynthia Sanchez. I'm your attorney."

"My attorney?" Breeze questioned.

"Your husband, Zyir, retained my services," she explained. "He's waiting for you outside. You can collect your things and I'll take you to him."

Breeze's mind spun as she signed paperwork.

The police officer returned her handbag and driver's license. "You're free to go," he said gruffly.

"That's all?" she asked, looking at her new beauty of an attorney. "Just like that?"

"Just like that," Ms. Sanchez replied.

Breeze walked out of the building, stunned but grateful to be going home. Zyir sat curbside, leaning against a black SUV, arms folded across his chest. When she saw him, she couldn't help but to run toward him. He stepped away from the car and picked her up as she threw her arms around him.

"I'm so sorry, B," he whispered as he appreciated her presence. Even after two days of rotting in a cell, she had her own lovely scent. His strong arms around her waist made all of her worries melt away. In the safety of his embrace she finally let her tears rain down.

"What's going on, Zy?" she asked.

"Nothing I can't handle, Mrs. Rich," the woman interrupted. "I'm the best defense attorney in the Midwest. Apparently local and federal entities have high incentive to bring down you and your affiliates. It's my job to see that they fail."

"Don't worry, Breeze. I got us. I got you. This will all blow over. Let me take you home," he said.

She nodded and slid into the car as he opened the door for her.

Zyir turned to Sanchez.

"She will be okay, Mr. Rich. So will you. Just let me do my job," she assured.

Zyir was solemn, serious, tormented as he nodded his head before running his hand over his face. He knew that getting them out of this wouldn't be as easy as Ms. Sanchez tried to make it seem. He had gotten them in hot water; now he had to go to great lengths to get them out. He had to go see Carter, whether he liked it or not. He'd have to sacrifice his pride, his code, his manhood in order to right this wrong. It was the only way to save Breeze.

CHAPTER 6

Carter sat. He sat so still that even he questioned whether his heart was still beating, but the steady pulse in his own ear told him he was still here. Still alive. Still breathing. Still existing. He counted his breaths. He had never really marveled at the wonder of life before. He had never realized how blessed he was to take each breath, because before, they didn't hurt. Now, as he sat, staring into the burning fire, he felt the pain of every single inhale and every single exhale. That ominous, empty feeling that came from losing his only son. It was unbearable. It ripped through him like bullets, and every time he breathed, he thought of how C.J. no longer could. The empty bottle of Louis that sat at his feet wasn't enough to mask his torment. If anything, it intensified it. He wasn't a man who liked to lose control. He didn't normally drink in excess or smoke or hinder his mental in any way, but he was searching for any relief from the agony.

He was angry and he wanted to point the blame solely at
Miamor, but he had to accept responsibility for his actions
as well. They both had led to this. He hated her and loved
her at the same time. He couldn't imagine her hurt. He
couldn't consider her because he was drowning in his own
emotions. Carter wasn't naïve to the fact that he loved her.
He always would. . . . He knew that if she were here with
him, grieving with him, going through the motions with
him, that it would be easier. He didn't deserve easy; however, neither did she. They had to feel the magnitude of this
time in their lives. They had to survive it without the intensity that their love would bring to the moment. They had to
hurt. It was the punishment for not protecting their seed.
Now they could never be. He couldn't even look at her. The
line between love and hate was so faint that he would cross
it without trying.

The gun that he gripped in his palm was the only thing
he could rely on to end his suffering. He had been holding
it so tightly that his fingers felt numb. He felt his jaw quiver
from the flood of sorrow that overwhelmed him and he
clenched his teeth to stop himself from losing it. He hadn't
cried. He had fought the urge to. He was supposed to be
strong. He was supposed to stand tall. He had survived so
much: The death of his mother. The streets. The Haitians.
Miamor's disappearance from his life years ago. All of these
things had formed the fire that he was forged from. He was
boss. He was untouchable . . . only he *had* been touched. He
had given his enemies a way to touch him as soon as he had
planted his seed inside of the woman he loved. If he was

truthful with himself, he had developed a weakness the day he had met Miamor. To create a little person who was made up of him plus her was perfection. It was love in its purest form, and losing that had destroyed him. These breaths that ached in his soul no longer felt worth it. He lifted the gun slightly and then placed it back on his thigh, his hand never leaving it. He gritted his teeth, lifted the gun, tears filling his eyes. He didn't blink as he brought the weapon to his temple. Those painful breaths had stopped. He realized he was holding it. The weight of the decision he had just made caused his shoulders to hang as his finger curled around the trigger.

Life wasn't supposed to feel like this. He wasn't afraid to die. His worst fear had already come to fruition. Every story had an ending. There wasn't another man alive who could do what he was about to. End him. He was all G. Men of men. King of kings. If he wanted this all to end today, then he would have to do it himself because no other man had been successful at taking him out of the game. His demise would be at his own hands and then he could finally reunite with his son. "God save my soul," he whispered.

KNOCK! KNOCK! KNOCK!

The unexpected sound at his door saved him from curling his finger on the trigger. He looked up, confused. No one knew where he was. He had purchased a magnificent chalet in the mountains of Colorado. It was secluded on all sides by dense forest, and his nearest neighbor was a mile down the only road that led into the mountains.

He went to the door, opening it cautiously.

Zyir stood, cupping his hands in front of his face, blowing hot air into them as he shifted from foot to foot.

"What up, Carter? What's going on in here, G?" Zyir asked, immediately noticing the mist in Carter's eyes and the gun in his hand. Carter's scruffy appearance threw Zyir. He was usually clean-cut and shaven, but today he was rough, the makings of a thick five-o'clock shadow coming in. His clothes were wrinkled as if he hadn't changed in days. His eyes were dark, with circles underneath.

Carter retreated into the cabin, and Zyir followed him, looking around the immaculate home. His brow creased in concern when he saw the empty cognac bottle. "Where the gunfight?" Zyir asked, treading lightly with his words.

"No fight, fam. Done fighting," Carter replied. The sadness in his voice and the double entendre behind his words told a story all their own. "You know what it's for," Carter admitted as he walked over to his bar and took another bottle of brown down. This time he opted for a glass. He tossed one to Zyir, who caught it out of midair with ease.

"Nah, it ain't for that," Zyir replied. "We built stronger than that, fam. I'mma have this drink with you, though, so you can work that shit out, but I'm your friend, Carter. I ain't too comfortable with the way you looking. I'd be more comfortable if you put the gun up."

"How did you find me?" Carter asked, respecting the request. He kept the gun tucked in his waistline.

"You talked for years about retiring in a big cabin in the mountains. This was the dream, bruh. Now it looks like it's become your nightmare," Zyir admitted.

"Hmm," Carter replied. He walked up to Zyir and poured his drink before pouring his own and taking a seat. He was defeated. They both knew it. He wore his heart on his sleeve. His eyes couldn't conceal his torment.

"I just got to end this shit, Zy. I ain't never felt no shit like this," Carter whispered. This time he knew it was useless. His pain rolled down his face in clear liquid pools of emotion.

He leaned over, his elbows resting on his thighs as his head hung low. Zyir's stomach twisted. Carter was breathing, but he wasn't living. He was stagnant. Buried under unresolved grief. In all their years of friendship, Zyir had never seen Carter weak. Zyir's conscience weighed heavily on him. He was bringing trouble to Carter's door and he already had enough of his own.

"Time heals, big homie," Zyir said. "You've got to just endure."

"Time won't heal this wound, Zy," Carter replied. "There's only one person in the world who can relate to this weight I'm carrying."

"Have you talked to her?" Zyir asked, knowing that he was speaking of Miamor.

"I can't talk to her," Carter said. "That's over." The finality in his tone was shocking. He knew he was half a man without Miamor. It was another thing that plagued his heart. She was his Eve. His curse. She could talk Carter into biting the forbidden apple on her worst day. No, she brought destruction to his life. He couldn't lean on her for support. He never knew how much he had until it was no longer. He envied the working man with the average family. That man got to go home to his wife and his child every night. The type of man he had chosen to be dug early graves for the ones he loved. Being the king was a gift and a curse.

"I know it's—"

"No offense, Zyir, but you don't know shit," Carter said.

If Zyir had seen it coming, he would have reacted faster. He would have taken the gun, but it had all happened so fast. It was like a light clicked off in Carter's eyes and Zyir watched as Carter brought the gun from his waistline. Zyir lunged, tackling Carter, but the loud bang in his ear let him know he hadn't stopped anything.

Red. Blood. On his hands, on the floor.

"No!" Zyir shouted. "What did you do?! Fuck!" Carter's eyes were still open, but blood covered one side of his face. He groaned. "Bro, stay with me, Carter! You gon' be good, baby. You gon' be good." Zyir pulled his phone out of his pocket and dialed 911. Before the operator could even ask him his emergency he shouted, "I need an ambulance. Now!" He kept the call connected so the operator could trace their location. He realized his face was wet and wiped his face with the back of his hand to find that it was his own tears. "Just hold on, fam. They coming for you, man. They coming. They coming."

* * *

Zyir sat in the waiting room, rubbing his hands together anxiously as he leaned over in his seat. He hadn't called anyone. Not Miamor, not Monroe, not even Breeze. He didn't know how to tell them what he had just witnessed. Never in his life did he feel such stress. He was sick. Carter had tried to end his own life. Damn. Shit was bad. He had been waiting for hours. Carter's blood had dried to a dirty brown on his clothes, but he didn't care. He wasn't leaving until he knew his friend would be okay. It wasn't until this night that he realized how deep their bond ran. They were brothers—not by blood, but the love was just as strong, and to lose Carter would be like losing a piece of himself. Carter was the one who had taught him how to be a man. He taught him how to get money and how to weed out the snakes. He ingrained in him that family came first. *Damn, big homie,* Zyir thought as he shook his head in disgrace.

Carter's doctor walked into the room, and Zyir tried to read his expression. Was it grim, hopeful? Zyir couldn't tell. He stood. "Is he . . ."

"The bullet grazed his left temple. It's a pretty deep graze, but the bullet didn't penetrate," the doctor explained.

"Why was there so much blood?" Zyir questioned.

"Any gunshot wound is going to give you profuse bleeding. He lost quite a bit, but we gave him a transfusion and treated the wound."

"So he's good?" Zyir asked in disbelief. He'd seen the blood with his own eyes. He'd heard the shot.

"He will be. He is very lucky. A fraction of an inch to the right and it would have killed him," the doctor said.

Zyir watched the doctor begin to walk away and stopped

him. "Doc, I want to make sure something like this doesn't happen again."

"We have a counselor set up to speak with Mr. Jones as soon as he is awake," the doctor informed him.

"Nah, we need a little bit more than that," Zyir admitted, his chest feeling hollow as he thought, devastated by the night's circumstance.

"What did you have in mind?"

* * *

The world came into focus as Carter's eyes opened. He grimaced as he felt an intense pressure in his head. "Hmm," he groaned as he attempted to sit up. He tried to turn on his side, but was halted when he felt his left wrist jerk in restraint. For the first time he noticed that he was bound to the bed. His right arm was free, but his left kept him in place. He pulled hard against it and then looked around the sterile room. *I'm in the hospital,* he thought. He reached up and felt his bandaged head. The previous night came rushing back to him.

The door opened, and Carter saw Zyir walk in. For the first time, he didn't know what to do or say. All the power, all the influence, all the money meant nothing. He was just a man with a broken soul. "What is this?" Carter asked, referencing the restraints.

"I saw something last night that I never thought I'd see," Zyir said. "You just need some time to regroup. Get your head right."

"Where am I?" Carter asked.

"This is the psychiatric ward of the hospital. I had you committed under suicide watch," Zyir said.

Carter's jaw clenched, and anger danced in his eyes. "You just need a little time, my G. A little rest," Zyir said. "I didn't call nobody. I'm the only one who knows you're here."

For that fact, Carter was grateful. "I'm good, Zy. Shit got out of hand last night, but I can handle it. Come on. Get the fucking doctor and take this shit off. This feeling too much like handcuffs for me," Carter reasoned.

"You can't leave here until I sign you out, Carter," Zyir said. "And I'm not signing anything until I'm sure you've had time to clear your mind. Last night wasn't you. I understand the pressure. It don't feel right going back to Flint thinking you gon' do something reckless again."

Carter looked at Zyir proudly. It was a full-circle moment. Zyir had absorbed Carter's philosophy like a sponge and now he was the one standing strong while Carter was buckling in grief. "I'm back, I'm fine. The alcohol and the silence. It . . ."

"No explanation needed, fam. I was there with you. I know what you lost . . . what we all lost," Zyir said in a low tone as his eyes drifted off in thought momentarily. "I'm only signing you out if you agree to get help. Someone live-in. A therapist or a cleaning lady—hell, a stripper . . ."

Carter chuckled at that one. Zyir continued, "Anybody to keep an eye out on you."

Carter nodded. "You have my word."

"Let me go get one of the doctors to come and check you

out . . . move you off this floor," Zyir stated. He turned to the door.

"Yo, Zyir," Carter called. Zyir turned. "Why were you in Colorado, anyway? You didn't come to my door to peel me off the floor. You need something?"

Zyir remembered what had brought him to Carter's door in the first place and he was filled with sorrow. "Nah. I'm good. Everything's smooth. Just wanted to see how you were holding up," he said. "Glad I got there when I did." Carter knew him well enough to know that he was lying, but respected him too much to call him out on it.

"Yeah, me too," Carter replied. Carter watched Zyir walk out of the room and then lay back on the bed, closing his eyes.

The physical pain he was in was excruciating, but he was grateful for it. It served as a distraction from the emotional war that was waging within him. He didn't know how to feel. He was angry that Zyir had interfered, but filled with regret for taking the actions in the first place. Carter knew that if Zyir let him stay in the seclusion of the mountains, eventually the depression he felt would surmount to the point where he put himself out of his misery, and next time he wouldn't miss. He hated to admit it, but therapy was essential to him right now. He needed to hear someone tell him that it was okay to keep living. He knew he wouldn't divulge all the details, but just having another person around him daily would make it easier to cope.

Carter didn't sleep that night. He stayed up, mind racing, heart pounding, head banging as he gazed out of the hospital window. The amber-and-orange hues that appeared with the rising sun captivated him. He had never taken the time to truly appreciate the marvel of it, and he realized he would have missed it had Zyir not shown up at his door. His heart and soul had never been so conflicted. His grief was tormenting him. At that very moment he just wanted to hold his wife. He wanted to touch her, to smell her, to hear her voice. *Damn, I miss you, ma,* he thought. He couldn't help but wonder where she was. Was she hurting? How was she doing with it all? Did she need him?

A rap at the door interrupted his thoughts, and he turned to find Zyir entering with a woman. Her brown skin was flawless and accentuated only by the faintest shade of pink blush. Her long hair was pulled back in a sleek ponytail that fell down her back. She was thin, with a model's frame. Her beauty spoke for her before she ever opened her lips, and Carter appreciated it as a fine work of art. In all her splendor he couldn't help but notice her eyes. They were plain, just a dark shade of brown, but the smile that hid behind them took his breath away.

"Carter, this is Samantha Dean," Zyir said, introducing him.

"Hello, Carter," she said with a smile as she crossed the room. "I'm in psychiatric care. I wanted to meet you. Zyir says you have some things you need help with sorting out. I'd be more than happy to help you with—"

"Psychiatric care?" Carter questioned. "I'm not—"

"Crazy?" Samantha finished for him. "Well, good, because I can be sometimes." She chuckled. "One of us should have a level head, no?"

He smirked at her wit. "Look, Ms. Dean."

"My friends call me Sam," she replied.

"We're friends?" Carter questioned with an amused look on his face.

"We could be. I'm a good listener," she said. She walked closer to him, invading his space with her Chanel perfume. She reached up, smiling at him with her eyes as she checked the bandage on his head. "You're in pain," she whispered.

"It's okay," he replied.

"I wasn't talking about the gunshot wound," she said. She removed the dressing and retrieved a new one from the cabinet in his room. She quickly tended to his injury, then continued. "Let me help you."

"I'm not into all that psycho shit, ma. I'm good. I had a moment. . . ."

"Psychiatry isn't always about being crazy. Sometimes life just becomes too much. You lost your child. That could eat away at any man, especially a good one. I'm here if you need anything. Even if you don't want to talk about that. Maybe you need someone to talk to about the weather."

A deeper laugh escaped him this time. "The weather?"

"The weather," she confirmed. She went into her white jacket and came out with a card. "You can call me anytime. Day or night."

Carter didn't respond, but he accepted the card and

watched as she walked out of the room. When she was gone, he looked at Zyir. "You couldn't bring her to the house, my nigga? Got me in here, ass-out in a hospital gown," Carter said.

Zyir chuckled. "My fault," he replied.

"You know how to pick 'em, don't you?" Carter said. "No man can be that close to a woman like that and think about anything other than living."

"I figured you would appreciate the aesthetic," Zyir shot back with an amused smirk. "Let's get out of this mu'fucka."

* * *

"It was good to see you, Zy. Real good," Carter said as they locked hands and pulled each other in to show love. It was an unspoken thank-you, an unneeded appreciation that he extended for Zyir saving his life.

"Always, bruh, always," Zyir responded. He turned to see Sam's car pulling up to the cabin. He felt uneasiness in the pit of his stomach. He wished he could turn back the hands of time to fix things before they ever got so out of control, but life didn't work that way. "I'm out of here. Keep your head," he said.

Sam walked up the stairs carrying a box of her things, bypassing Zyir. "See you around, Mr. Rich," she said.

He didn't respond, and she made her way up the walkway to Carter. "You never said the job required me to live here," she said with a bright smile. She looked around at the massive, snow-covered chalet. "I could get used to this."

"Come on in," he said. "I'll show you to your room."

* * *

Breeze walked into the hospital, her heart beating out of her chest. *Something's not right,* she thought. She was indeed pregnant. She had peed on ten different sticks to confirm it. It was times like this she wished she still had her mother. Why couldn't she just be a regular girl? With a regular life? With a regular man and parents who were alive and well? Breeze was terrified. She was with child and she was bleeding. That didn't quite add up, and she had no one to call for guidance. She had contacted her doctor and he had told her there was most likely no need to worry. A little implantation bleeding, he had said, but Breeze's intuition was telling her otherwise. She hadn't told Zyir yet, so she couldn't call him. Besides, he was off visiting Carter, anyway. He couldn't get to her right now, even if he wanted to. So she did the only thing she could think of and went to the emergency room.

With every step she took, she could feel the bleeding get worse. It was like life was slipping out of her.

"Excuse me. I need to see someone. I'm pregnant and I'm having some bleeding," Breeze said. Her mouth felt like cotton, and she was hot . . . so hot. Even in the dead of winter she was burning up. "I'm sorry . . . I just need to sit . . . for a min—"

Breeze turned to find a chair, but before she could even take one step, everything went black.

She awoke on an ultrasound table. A nurse stood on one side while a man in a white lab coat and scrubs sat in a chair on the other. "Welcome back," the man said. "I'm Adam. I'm an ultrasound tech. We're going to have a look at your baby. The nurse is going to jot down some information so we can actually get you checked into our system. Okay?"

Breeze nodded, slightly dazed.

"What's your name?" the technician asked.

"Breeze Rich," she whispered. "Is my baby okay? I noticed blood. . . ."

"Well, let me take a look while you give the nurse all your info," he said. He sounded happy, optimistic, confident. *That's a good thing, right?* she wondered. The calmness of his voice soothed her. He took out a cold, clear gel and applied it to her lower abdomen as Breeze gave the woman the details she needed.

Breeze was so nervous, she held her breath as the ultrasound technician placed a scanner on her stomach. He rolled it all over the gel as the image of the inside of her uterus appeared on the screen. Breeze gripped the sides of the table she lay on. Tension filled her body.

"Okay, we're going to do a vaginal ultrasound—okay, Breeze?" he said suddenly.

"Is something wrong?" she asked.

"I just need to get a better view," he said.

He put her feet in stirrups and spread her legs as he stuck a long wand into her womb. "Just relax. Try to stay still," he coached.

Doom filled her body. Although the tech kept telling her everything was fine, she just sensed that something was wrong.

"Do you see anything?" she asked, her voice cracking as a tear escaped her.

The wand slid out. Silence.

"Could you go get the doctor?" the tech said to the nurse. There was no alarm in his voice, yet still, Breeze's stomach was in knots.

A woman came in and washed her hands. She was moving so slowly that Breeze thought, *It can't be anything bad. She would be rushing. She would be moving faster if something was wrong.*

"Hello, Breeze. I'm going to take another peek," she said. Breeze nodded because she was unable to speak. Fear seized her. The doctor put on a pair of gloves, wrapped a plastic covering over the wand, and put it back inside of Breeze. No matter how gentle they were, each time they invaded her, it hurt.

Minutes felt like hours until finally the doctor pulled it out and snapped off her gloves. "Breeze, you're experiencing an ectopic pregnancy. There is no heartbeat. The fetus is stuck in one of your fallopian tubes. We have to remove it or it may rupture."

Remove "it." Fetus. No heartbeat. It wasn't an "it." This was her baby. This was supposed to be her and Zyir's first child. "Are there any other options? Is there any way to save my baby? This is a baby you're talking about. You talk like it's a thing. . . . It's a person. It's my little person," she said, becoming emotional.

"I'm sorry. This is the only option. If we don't operate, it will rupture and you will bleed out," the doctor said. "Call the OR and let them know I need a room, stat."

Everything was happening so fast. She was being stripped, put into a hospital gown, her hair was covered, all while she cried. Before she knew it, she was on her back being rushed down the hospital halls.

1, 2, 3, 4, 5, 6. . . . She counted the passing ceiling lights as they rushed to the operating room. The chill of the room when they entered immediately made the hair stand on her arms. Her teeth chattered. They lifted her onto a metal table. The room smelled. . . . It smelled so much like nothing that it reeked. A mask went over her face.

"Okay, Breeze. Count down for me from ten," the doctor instructed her. Breeze wanted to slap the woman's smiling face. What the hell was she smiling about? This was a tragedy. She was about to close her eyes with a baby in her womb but wake up without one. *This isn't right,* she thought, but before she could even protest, the anesthetic put her to sleep.

* * *

When Breeze awoke, she felt an emptiness that she had never experienced.

"You're going to be fine. Your surgery went very well. We removed your left fallopian tube," she heard the doctor say. She felt the woman putting the blood-pressure jacket on her arm.

"What are my chances of getting pregnant again?" she asked.

It was then that the doctor's friendly expression changed. Breeze saw the look of hesitation . . . the look of uncertainty . . . the look of fear. "What are my chances?" Breeze demanded. She didn't know why she was angry at the doctor. This wasn't her fault.

"About fifteen percent," the doctor replied. "But there are options. We are coming out with new technology every day. . . ."

"Leave," Breeze said as she turned her head to stare out of the window.

"Mrs. Rich—"

"Get out!" she shouted.

The doctor and the nurse retreated from the room, leaving her to have one good, long cry.

She knew she had to get it all out of her system. Zyir would be home in a couple days. He couldn't know about this. She wasn't going to tell him that he had chosen a defective wife. She was so glad she hadn't told him about the pregnancy yet. He didn't deserve this type of disappointment. The pain she felt was suffocating. No. She would shoulder this burden alone and by the time he returned, she would put on that same smile that the doctor had given to her. She was going to lock this secret deep down inside and pray for a miracle.

CHAPTER 7

His hands on her body caused the hairs on the back of her neck to stand up. He knew her body. He was its conductor, and the sounds of her moans, the musical score. "I love the shit out of you, ma," Carter whispered in her ear.

"Oh my God," she screamed, animalistic as she threw it back at him, matching his gusto, taking his passion just the way he liked it. "I love you so much," she whispered. "What are you doing to me?" She couldn't silence herself. He was making her feel too good. He slow-stroked her from behind, the girth and length of him hitting the back of her, teasing her. Her back arched, deeply. Sweat pooled in the small of her toned back. Every time he rocked inside of her, he gave a mixture of pleasure and pain. It was so good that tears came to her eyes.

She knew his rhythm and felt him pulsing inside of her. He was at his peak. After bringing her love down three times, he was ready for his pleasure. Suddenly he withdrew, disconnecting their bodies. The few seconds that it took for him to travel south of her navel were sweet torture, but when he placed his mouth on her, she gasped in utter ecstasy. He ate on her as if she were a sweet summer peach on a hot Atlanta day, not letting a drop of her nectar escape his wanting tongue. With his thumb on her pleasure knob and two fingers exploring the middle, she felt her climax building and building and building . . .

"Yeah, mama, give me that."

She frowned. She heard the voice, but it didn't match his face.

Miamor opened her eyes, shattering the orgasmic dream as she looked down at Murder between her legs. "Get. Off. Of. Me," she shouted as she scrambled out of his grasp. She looked around, wondering how he had undressed her from the waist down without her even awaking. She clutched the bedsheet to her chest, covering her body.

He chuckled. "I don't know what you're covering up for. I done seen all of that, plenty of times before," he said as he licked his fingers that had just been coated in her juices.

A flash of anger blazed in her eyes, and she was across the room in seconds. "You ever touch me again without my permission and I will kill you," she said.

"You loved it," he said, licking his tongue out at her mannishly.

SLAP!

Her hand crossed his face so swiftly that he didn't see it coming. This was what he loved about her. Their chemistry was volatile and raw. He brought out the worst in her and he had a thing for bad girls.

He grabbed her neck and pushed her against the wall, causing her head to hit it so hard that pieces of plaster crumbled off.

"I love this shit, lil' mama," Murder whispered. "But don't forget who taught you all that rah-rah shit you popping."

If I didn't need him to keep me safe from Baraka, I would put a bullet in his head while he sleeps, she thought bitterly.

Miamor hawked up as much spit as she could muster and let it fly onto his face.

Murder slapped her so hard that she fell to the ground, stars appearing before her eyes. "You better get with the program real quick, Miamor," Murder said as he looked at her with malice while wiping the glob of spit from his face. "You don't want to become more trouble to me than you're worth."

"You threatening me?" she asked. "Save that shit for someone who believes you, nigga. I gave you a whiff of this pussy damn near ten years ago and you been chasing after me like a pathetic little lost dog ever since." She got to her feet and stood toe-to-toe with him arrogantly. "You can't kill me, Murder, because it would be like killing yourself. Let's be clear. If I could go home to my nigga, I would. You got me by default. Fate is not on your side. We aren't meant to be. . . . I'm here because I have nowhere else to be. Baraka will kill me if and when he finds me. This isn't about you. There is no us."

"All that and I'm still the only nigga willing to protect you . . . fucked-up ways and all. I ride for you, Miamor. I don't see that bitch-ass nigga you praising nowhere in sight.

He left you for dead. I'm all you got," Murder reminded her. She wouldn't have been so pissed if he hadn't been right.

"I gave you time to get your head together, Miamor, but all you do is pop these and sleep," Murder said sternly as he picked up the Xanax bottle that sat on the nightstand of the hotel room. He threw the bottle across the room. "It's time to shake this fucking city. You need to empty them casino accounts and sell your shares so we can take that bread and disappear. I can settle up with the nigga Fly and then we can blow this joint."

He whispered the last part, knowing he had considered killing Fly and making off with all the money. Miamor could see the treachery in his eyes. She pulled herself up from the floor, her face still stinging slightly from the force behind his blow. "Call Fly," she said. "I need to go see the Italian about the casino shares. If you want a quick sale, then he is the one to go to," she informed him. "Otherwise a deal like this could take months. I can't afford to hang around here that long." The thought of what Baraka would do if he ever caught up with her caused her face to pale. For the first time in her life she feared another man.

"The fuck you need that little nigga for? I can handle it," Murder said, offended. He had noticed Fly's affection for Miamor. The way he looked at her. Murder had taken Miamor's cell phone in an attempt to keep her from reaching out to Carter. Fly Boogie had frequently hit her up, and it didn't go unnoticed. He couldn't read the full text messages, but each time Fly's name popped up on her screen, Murder felt a type of way. Murder was sure of the chemistry he noticed whenever Fly was around Miamor, and it had him vexed.

"Salerno ain't taking no meeting with you by my side. He doesn't know you. Every single time I've met with him, Fly has been with me. Salerno's comfortable with him. This is the Italian mafia I'm getting in bed with!" Miamor exclaimed. "I'm not going in solo or with a new nigga just to soothe your ego. We do it my way or not at all. So call Fly Boogie."

* * *

Miamor sat, flawlessly put together on the outside. A Fendi jumpsuit clung to her flawless body, and snakeskin stilettos graced her feet. It was the first time she had put on clothes in weeks. Her mood didn't match her Manolos, but she had to make a move. Sitting in the hotel room, rotting away, was making her an easy target. Moving targets were harder to hit so it was time for her to get out of dodge. She had close to a million dollars put up in her bank account, but she was too afraid to withdraw it, thinking it would make her easier to find. As long as Baraka was hunting her, she would have to think about each move before she made it. If she sold the shares at a discount and then had Salerno pay her in cash, he would play ball.

The knock at the door caused Murder to emerge from the second bedroom of the suite as he went to answer. Fly Boogie stood on the other side.

"What up, lil' nigga?" Murder greeted.

"You can kill all that 'lil' nigga' shit," Fly replied. Fly had stepped into the big leagues years ago when he became Miamor's go-to while Carter was locked up. He had earned his stripes, and if he hadn't been so in love with Miamor, he would have moved up steadily in his position with The Cartel. His own admiration had turned him into a foe of Carter, but even still he would always ride for Miamor. Whenever she called, he would answer.

The tension in the room was so thick that Miamor could hardly breathe. "Let's just get this over with," she said as she stood and walked out.

As she passed Murder, he grabbed her arm. "Right back," he said.

She snatched away, glaring at him as she and Fly made their exit. They didn't speak until they were inside his car. Miamor stared out of her window, arms folded across her chest. She was deep in thought. "You gonna drive or what?" she asked, when she realized they hadn't moved.

"I've been calling you. You can't answer the phone for me now, ma?" Fly Boogie asked.

"I don't have my phone," she replied.

"Are you okay, Miamor? Why are you even doing any of this shit? You staying with this nigga like you some fragile little girl. I know your résumé. You don't need that nigga. We can pull away right now and not look back," he said.

"And then what? Stay with you? Be with you?" Miamor asked.

"Maybe," he said directly. "I can do everything that nigga doing for you. I can keep you safe, Miamor."

"Difference is, I can't keep you safe, Fly. Being attached

to me is a death sentence right now. I don't care if Murder catches it behind me. I can't have you on my conscience, too. I know you have this image of me and you're attracted to that, but the pedestal you have me on is too high, Fly. You're my friend, and in another lifetime I could even see you being more, but in this lifetime I was loved by a man named Carter and it's something I'm loyal to, even when we're not together. You don't want half a woman, Fly. You deserve a whole woman, every part of a woman. I can't give you that. My heart is too invested elsewhere, and since C.J., it doesn't even beat the same."

Fly turned her chin toward him because she was talking at the window as tears glided effortlessly down her face. Her hurt was so palpable that it took over the car.

"I don't give a damn about any of them niggas, Miamor. I want what I want, and that's you," Fly said.

"Let's just handle this business, Fly," she said, wiping her face. Miamor just wasn't the same. Her soul didn't feel the same. She felt . . . so . . . so . . . vulnerable, and that was something she had never allowed herself to experience . . . not truly, not 100 percent. Even with Carter she had been tough, but after losing their child, all guards had been stripped away. She had nothing but pent-up, raw emotion, waiting to explode.

Finally Fly drove away from the hotel. "You strapped?" she asked.

"You know it," he replied. He reached under the seat and came out with a .38 handgun, knowing it was her preference. He passed it to her. She smirked, took the pistol off

safety, and then placed it in her handbag. Each switched
their focus to the task at hand, knowing it would require
all of their attention.

* * *

Benito Salerno sat in the greasy booth of the strip club,
spread out like a pig as a young little piece put on a show
before him. Exotic dancers were his guilty pleasure. The old
man, with his big belly and his half-functioning penis, had
no business frequenting an establishment as such. He was a
family man—he had a wife and adult children at home. In
fact, he had a daughter the same age as some of these girls,
but he still had a thing for tasting young snatch. He tipped
well and had no problem paying for extras, so he was a favorite among the girls in this particular joint. It was far
removed from Vegas; in fact, it was a hole-in-the-wall just
outside of Reno. It was important that his extracurricular
activities didn't get back to his wife. He respected her, but
she no longer held his interests sexually. She was from the
old country and lived in a demure way. He was looking for
a girl with no morals, and this had been his secret for years.
He made the drive once a week.

The dancer in front of him climbed on the couch and
positioned herself directly over his mouth. Salerno could
practically smell her through the fabric of her thong. The
mixture of her womanly juices, perfume, and sweat made
him groan in anticipation. He slid her panties to the side and
trailed his tongue from the bottom of her slit all the way to
her clit and slurped loudly. He was in heaven as he buried

his face in her. All of a sudden he felt the cold kiss of steel against the back of his head.

His eyes flew open as he saw the girl collect her things and accept payment from Miamor. "You dirty bitch," he said to the stripper. The girl fled the room, unbothered.

"Relax, Salerno. I come in peace," Miamor stated.

"Some peace," he scoffed. "There is a gun at the back of my head."

Miamor nodded to Fly Boogie, who lowered the weapon. Miamor thought about sitting, but decided against it as she looked around the disgusting room.

Salerno was visibly disturbed. He was so livid that his skin flushed a bright red. "What is this about? Have I ever brought trouble to you, Miamor? If you wanted my attention, a phone call would have sufficed. I invite you into my city, I help you acquire your casino, and this is the thanks I get?" he huffed.

She didn't want to let him know she was running from anyone, so she didn't explain her extreme attempt to have a private meeting.

"My apologies," she said. "I'm here to offer you something." She didn't leave him time to guess her intentions as she continued. "I'm getting out of the casino business. I plan to sell my shares. I thought it proper if I offered them to you first."

Salerno's entire disposition changed. She had piqued his interests.

"I don't want a public sale. I'd prefer to do this in private," she paused.

"How much?" he asked.

"Twenty-five million," she said. "You can wire the funds to a Swiss account."

He laughed heartily as if she had told the world's biggest joke.

Miamor didn't flinch.

"The way I see it, the only reason you would want an untraceable wire is if you're in a bind," Salerno said, reading the situation. She knew he was about to stick it to her.

"I'll give you five million," he said. "Best I can do." He waved his hand dismissively as if the deal were done.

It was Miamor's turn to laugh. "The shares are worth close to seventy-five, maybe more," she countered. "I was giving you a deal the first time."

"Yeah, well, the bounty on your head would cost me nothing. I could easily make a better deal with the Saudi that you're running from," Salerno threatened.

Miamor could see the satisfaction shining behind his eyes. His fat, greasy face was smug, as if he had the upper hand. She was shaken, but didn't show it. "You see, I thought you might say that," Miamor said. "It's unfortunate that we have to take this route."

"Take a look at this, big man," Fly Boogie said as he reached around Salerno with a phone in his hand. He flipped through pictures on his phone, and Salerno's eyes turned big and his face turned white. "While you out here tricking, you leaving your family exposed." Pictures of his daughter and wife, sleeping soundly in their beds made him jump up in alarm. Fly Boogie put a firm hand on his shoulder. "Sit your ass down."

"Like I said," Miamor started, "this could have been an amicable deal. I didn't want to force your hand."

"I don't have that type of money on hand," he said.

"You've been shaking down every business owner in Vegas for years. You don't think I know the type of paper you're getting?" Miamor replied. "The casino is a good investment. I'm a businesswoman. I'm giving you a great deal. You'll make the twenty-five million back within three months."

Salerno wanted to say no. He was usually the terrorist; he had never met anyone, especially a woman, who'd had the moxie to shake him down. He had made a mistake by underestimating her pretty face.

"Make the call," she said sternly. "Before I lose my patience."

"It's two in the morning! Who am I supposed to call at this hour?!" he said in a panic.

Miamor checked her watch and nodded. "You're right," she said. Fly Boogie hit Salerno over the head with the butt of the gun. "Get your ass up. You're coming with us."

Miamor led the way as Fly Boogie walked Salerno out of the club. When they were outside, Fly pushed him into the trunk. "Guess you'll have to stick by my side until morning," she said before slamming it closed.

* * *

By morning, Miamor had the money in a Swiss account and had left Salerno stranded in the middle of the desert.

As Fly Boogie sped down the highway, he glanced over at Miamor. "You sure you want to go back?" he asked. "I can take you anywhere you want to go."

She knew that wherever she went, Murder would eventually follow. Despite her disdain for him, she trusted him with her life. "No, I'm going back, but I want you to leave. I want you to take half a million dollars from this money and go somewhere else, start somewhere new. Murder says he's going to pay you for what you did. For infiltrating The Cartel for him . . . but I know him. He's going to kill you," she admitted.

"I ain't never ran from a nigga in my life," he said. "And what I look like? Taking your paper, ma? That's your money. I've got my own."

Miamor turned in her seat so that she was facing him. "Just go somewhere and start over. I'm no good for you. Leave Vegas in your rearview, Fly. Start your life. You're the right type of man for the right type of woman . . . that's not me," she said. "Pull over right here."

He did as she asked, stopping in a small hick town. She opened her door and got out. "What are you doing, Miamor? Get in and close the door," he said.

"Drive away, Fly," she stated.

"Where will you go? You can't stay in Vegas," Fly stated.

Miamor shrugged. "I don't know. Maybe I'll take this money and buy a little beach bar in the Bahamas," she joked. Fly could see a bit of truth behind her words. "I just want to leave everything behind. All of it. It's too painful." She nodded as she began to choke on her emotions. Sniffing back the tears, she finished. "Actually, that plan is sounding kind of nice."

He got out of the car and stood, looking it over as he rested one hand on the roof. He was conflicted, and she knew it. He wanted to be her man, but she couldn't allow that. She had already let the lines between them blur a little too much. They were more than friends, but not lovers. Fly's emotions ran deeper than hers ever could for him. Her heart was already taken, so she was letting him go.

"I'll be okay. . . . Go," she insisted.

He bit his lip sexily, clearly troubled by her request. He was handsome, suave, and so fresh that it was ridiculous. She smiled. "You're going to make one of these young girls very happy," she said. "Take care of yourself, a'ight?"

He nodded. "You, too, Miamor."

She watched Fly Boogie lean back into the car and drive away. She sighed deeply in relief, knowing that she had just saved his life. Sticking around for her would lead to nothing but his demise. She didn't want that. She would rather let him fly free. Miamor pulled out a bottle of Xanax and opened the top. She popped three and swallowed them down with water. Placing her hands on her hips, she looked around. *Now what?* she thought, knowing that she was a long way from Las Vegas. For a moment, she actually considered leaving Murder, but Miamor had never been alone. She had gone from her sister to the Murder Mamas, to Murder, then to Carter. . . . She didn't want to be on the run alone, and if the day came that she did have to face Baraka, she would need Murder on her team. She went to the road and stuck out her thumb, ready to hitchhike the long way back to Vegas.

CHAPTER 8

"Over the past three years, you and I have done a lot of business together. I haven't seen anyone move like you since the passing of my own son."

Fly Boogie looked out of the window of the helicopter as the City of Angels illuminated beneath him. His connect's voice boomed through the headset he wore. He looked over at Baron Montgomery. He was the connect's connect. The end-all, be-all in the Los Angeles drug trade. He had been a Midwest player before coming to L.A. to take over a new territory. Fly had been personally invited to attend the annual Gentlemen's Ball. It was his first time being in Baron's presence. When Fly first left Vegas he acquired a Mexican connect, Josiah, who supplied him with enough pills to start a pharmacy. Fly had moved so much that Baron had insisted he meet the young hustler. Today was that meeting, and Fly was thrown off that Baron was being so open.

"I'm sorry. I don't have kids, but I couldn't imagine," Fly offered.

"No worries," Baron said. "So tell me. How is it that you move more than Josiah? It seems like I have the wrong man in position. Perhaps it's time I shift some things around."

"Nah," Fly Boogie replied. "I'm more than okay with getting this low-key money. I don't need the title."

Baron knew that Fly Boogie was being modest. He had built a fine empire of his own in the past three years. He was major and very sharp.

The pilot landed on a helicopter pad on top of L.A.'s finest hotel. The entire property had been rented out; every single room and ballroom was reserved for the highly exclusive event. It was invitation only, and all the heavy hitters in the game would be there.

"Tonight will blow your mind, young. I still remember my first ball," Baron chuckled. "It'll be the best night of your life besides the day you marry your girl or see your kids born. It plays a close third."

Fly smirked, allowing the corners of his mouth to turn up in amusement. When the two men stepped out of the beast of a flying machine, they were quickly greeted by two Brazilian beauties.

"Hello, Mr. Montgomery. Welcome to the Gentlemen's Ball. Here are your masks. You and your guest can follow us this way," one of them greeted them. Fly couldn't help but take in her essence. Her rear was poking out of a fitted Herve Leger gown. She had curves that should have come with a warning sign. He held the masquerade mask in his hands.

"We playing dress up?" he asked.

"You want your identity concealed. You never know what might happen to you tonight. It's best if no one bears witness to these festivities. The cameras throughout the building have also been shut off for the private function," Baron informed.

Damn, Fly thought as he put on his mask without further question. He had no idea what he was getting himself into. Fly followed Baron down into one of the ballrooms. No expense had been spared. The finest of everything— linens, liquor, decorations, women, food. . . . It had all been arranged with first-class elegance.

"You enjoy the night and when you're ready to leave, drivers are awaiting you out front to take you wherever you need to go," Baron said. "Let's circulate."

Fly Boogie had checked in his normal fresh threads and was clad in a more mature look. Ralph Lauren suit, personally tailored with diamond cuff links, and Prada shoes made him look like money. His fresh fade and diamond Bezel Rolex rounded out the presidential look. Fly had always wondered why Carter, Zyir, and Money walked around in suits, but as Baron had told him, "When you look like money, you attract money. Everyone in here is somebody.

Not all are drug dealers. Some are politicians, moguls, but everyone has achieved a level of power that is respected across the board." Fly got it now.

Fly moved through the room taking in the vibes as Baron introduced him to player after player. Not one person in the room was a slouch. They were all major. He realized he was being inducted into the big leagues. He wasn't beat for crowds, and he tried to hide his discomfort as he kept his eyes moving around the room.

"Relax, kid, Baron schooled. "You're good here. Everybody checks their weapons at the door. Any existing beef is off-limits inside these walls."

Fly nodded, but still his neck was on a swivel. He couldn't believe that in just a few years he had worked his way to the top. He was on. He dibbled and dabbled in cocaine, but prescription pills were the new-school hustle. He had been skeptical to try his hand at it, but once he did, he was hooked. There was a drought in L.A.'s cocaine trade, but his pockets had adjusted to the new flip nicely.

Just when he had taken the tension out of his shoulders and begun to relax, a young boy crashed into him, spilling champagne all over Fly Boogie's jacket. Fly pulled out his handkerchief and brushed off his jacket. "Yo' fuck is this, a day care? Little homie, watch where you . . ." He didn't finish his sentence. When he looked down at the young boy, his words stopped in his throat.

"Mo?" Fly Boogie whispered in disbelief. It was as if he had seen a ghost. He was staring at Monroe's son, a boy whose memory they had buried.

Mo's eyes flickered in recognition, but before he could respond, Baron came walking up with a smiling Baraka at his side. Baraka held a pretty Asian girl's hand. "Take care of him, sweetheart," Baraka said, handing Mo off to the girl, who looked to be no older than sixteen herself. Mo walked away with the girl, looking back only once at Fly before proceeding to be led away. Fly Boogie's heart stopped in his chest when he noticed Miamor and Carter's son trailing behind Baraka. Mo and C.J. were the only faces in the ball uncovered. Fly had never interacted with Baraka, so Baraka had no idea of his Cartel affiliation.

"I see my young boy has ruined your suit. My sincerest apologies," Baraka said. "These boys are like sons to me. I try to bring them here to get their first peek, and they turn into a ball of nerves."

Baron's laugh was deep and genuine as he made the formal introduction. "Fly, this is Baraka. Baraka, this is Fly Boogie," Baraka said.

"Interesting name," Baraka said.

"Interesting plus ones," Fly replied, referring to C.J. and Mo, who were clearly out of place.

Seeing Miamor's son brought back the feelings he had suppressed since leaving Las Vegas. He hadn't thought of her in years, but just now in this moment his loyalty to her resurfaced as if it had never left him. He had witnessed the strongest woman he knew break down over the loss of her son. Yet this very boy was standing here in front of him alive and, from the looks of it, well. He knew she didn't know. She couldn't have. Miamor would have left a trail of bodies behind her as she searched for her son if she had even a whim that C.J. was still alive. Both he and Mo had been missing from their families for three years. Everyone thought they were dead. Fly Boogie wanted to tell himself that it wasn't his business. He wanted to walk away because they weren't really his problem, only they were. The love he had for Miamor wouldn't allow him to just pretend he hadn't discovered this.

"Oddly enough they were the sons of the men responsible for my daughter's death," Baraka offered freely. "When I took them, I intended them harm, but I couldn't bring myself to do it. . . ."

They all knew what "it" was. He couldn't murder them without the soul of a dead child weighing him down.

"So instead, I turned them into my sons. The sons I never had, and my enemies will mourn them forever at the mere thought of them being gone," Baraka finished.

"Mental warfare," Baron commented, indifferent to the entire situation.

"Muscle wins battles, mental wins wars," Baraka insisted.

"Indeed," Fly stated. He stopped a waitress who passed with an empty tray. He grabbed her gently and whispered in her ear. "Louis neat . . . two of them . . . and water, no ice," he ordered. "And keep them coming." Only she heard his order. He turned to Baron and Baraka. In no time the waitress was back with their drinks and Fly Boogie passed the cognac to the gentlemen and kept the water for himself.

"Good choice," Baraka said as he smelled his cognac. He

nodded toward Fly's cup. "Vodka is a young man's drink." He laughed as if shaking off memories. "I couldn't even get that down."

Fly smirked and replied, "It's all preference." He lifted the glass. "To a good evening and potential business."

The men downed their cognac, and Fly took in the water, wincing slightly.

The waitress was back with another in no time.

Baron placed a hand over his heart. "None for me, sweetheart. I'll leave you gentlemen to it," he said.

Fly and Baraka toasted again. Fly Boogie made small talk, passing the time, as the waitress brought the third round, then the fourth, and finally the fifth, before Baraka conceded, "I'm done, son. My tolerance isn't what it used to be."

Fly laughed lightly. "Understandable," he said, completely unfazed. "Enjoy your night." He watched as Baraka walked away to network with the other guests. He didn't miss the fact that he couldn't walk a straight line and that the dapper businessman had begun to sweat. The liquor was throwing him off. Fly scanned the room until his eyes rested on C.J. and Mo, who were seated at Baraka's table. A million thoughts ran through his mind. He was trying to talk himself out of interfering, but he knew he wasn't leaving the ball without those boys. They didn't seem to be in danger. They weren't being tortured, or paying for their mother's sins, but this was not where they belonged. Miamor deserved to be reunited with her son. Fly hugged the bar, this time getting himself a real drink to take off the edge. He

was in a building full of powerful players and about to do
the unthinkable. Fly discreetly reached down across the bar
and grabbed a visible corkscrew, sliding it up his jacket
sleeve.

"Gentlemen, the auction is about to begin. Please make
your way to ballroom B," an announcer said. Fly watched
as most of the men began to shift from their places. The
auction was the main event of the night. His eyes followed
Baraka as he beelined for the restroom. C.J. and Mo stood
outside the door while Baraka went inside.

Fly hadn't wanted them to witness what he was about
to do, but it was now or never. He made his way over to
them.

"You remember me?" he asked as he pulled off his mask.

"You used to work for my family," Mo said. "Are they
here? Did they come for us?"

"Nah, they not here, man. I'm going to take you home,
though, a'ight," he said. "Go to the lobby and wait for me."

"But Baraka said—" C.J. began to speak, but Fly interrupted him.

"I don't give a fuck about what Baraka said," Fly shot
back.

"He's going to kill them if we ever try to leave. He said
he would kill everybody we love," Mo insisted.

"I won't let that happen, homie. Go now. Wait for me
in the lobby," Fly urged. He walked into the bathroom
where Baraka was using the urinal.

"One too many drinks," Baraka chuckled as he concealed himself and then began adjusting his clothes.

"I hear you," Fly said casually as he walked by to get to the next urinal. He slid the corkscrew down his sleeve and gripped it tightly in his hand. Baraka never even anticipated Fly's treachery. Fly jammed the corkscrew into his neck so deep that it felt like his head would pop off.

"Aghh," Baraka cried, his eyes bulging out of his head as Fly Boogie held him up by his collar.

"Miamor sends her love," Fly stated as he removed the corkscrew and stuck it into his body, stabbing him up quickly.

Baraka stumbled as he grasped his neck, trying to stop the profuse bleeding. Fly Boogie grabbed the man's head and snapped his neck. He had so much aggression and a look of pure evil in his eyes as he ended Baraka's life. He had put his murder game down before, but this time it had been personal. He had just touched the untouchable and by doing so, he had freed Miamor from her self-induced seclusion.

He pulled Baraka into the last stall and then walked out. It was time to shake before anyone saw his bloodstained suit.

Finding C.J. and Mo waiting anxiously for him, he ushered them toward the exit.

They stood, shocked and afraid as he hightailed it toward the door.

"Where are we going?" C.J. asked as he tried to keep up.

"Home, C.J. I'm taking you both home."

CHAPTER 9

Miamor held the broom in her hands, sweeping as the sounds of the ocean crashing onto the shore soothed her soul. She hated the silence. It left her with too much room to think and whenever she got into her emotions, the past would come back to haunt her. Now she understood how Aries could leave it all behind. When her best friend had moved to suburbia and established a new identity, Miamor had judged her. Now, here she was, years later, doing the exact same thing. Living a lie, a beautiful lie, where she was a bar owner named Lisa, married to a man named Brandon. Miamor and Murder had become two regular people, living in paradise, under false pretenses. Nobody knew that their marriage was fabricated. It was forged with fake documents, fake identities. Nobody knew that they barely spoke. Nobody knew that they slept in separate beds. All people saw was what Miamor wanted them to see. They were ordinary and far removed from the violent path of bodies that they had left in their wake. Miamor had thought of leaving Murder, but the security that he provided was priceless. She wasn't afraid. She wasn't paranoid. After fleeing the country and buying a little piece of property on a beach in the Bahamas, her nerves had settled. She and Murder were ready for Baraka. Whenever he decided to get revenge, they would be prepared. Two guns were better than one. They were partners and she respected him for sticking by her side, despite the fact that she didn't love him. She had to admit that he was loyal.

The sound of heavy footsteps behind her didn't raise the hairs on the back of her neck. She knew it was Murder, coming to take her home after a busy day at the bar.

"Give me one minute, Murder. I just have to finish cleaning," she said without even turning to look his way.

"You take all the time you need, ma, but when you're done, I'm taking you home."

She froze at the sound of his voice and then spun around in shock. Fly Boogie stood before her. He had changed. He had grown. He was still fly as ever and carried the same charming smile. "How did you find me?" she asked, now worried that she wasn't as low-key as she thought.

"It doesn't matter," he said. He didn't want to tell her that he had committed their last conversation to memory. He couldn't tell her that she crossed his mind often. He wouldn't chump himself. Miamor had always been out of his league, but the new gift that he was about to give her would level the playing field. "I came to tell you that it's safe to come back. I took care of your problem for you, and I have someone who really wants to see you."

"What are you talking about?" she asked.

Fly Boogie walked up into Miamor's space. He aligned his mouth with her ear and whispered, "That nigga is a fucking memory."

Miamor gasped as she pulled back and looked up at Fly. *You killed Baraka?* she thought in disbelief.

He nodded, confirming the question that her eyes were asking.

"Am I interrupting something?" Murder asked as he entered the bar. "What up, little nigga? I see you still pussy-whipped and ain't even hit that shit yet. Fuck is you doing here?"

Fly Boogie stepped up to Murder coolly, holding out his hand as if it were all love. Murder eased up a bit, but suddenly Fly's demeanor changed and he grabbed Murder's neck and shoved his head into the bar top. "Don't fuck with me. I ain't come here for this, but it can go there if that's how you want to play it," Fly threatened through gritted teeth.

Miamor stood there, in shock. Fly had never been afraid of a challenge, but he had changed. He had bossed all the way up and carried an aura of power that he hadn't possessed before.

Fly mushed Murder's face into the wood hard before releasing him, tossing him.

"Let's go, Miamor," Fly said confidently. He spoke the words as if he knew she was going to comply.

"What you mean, 'let's go, Miamor'?" Murder challenged. "She ain't going nowhere, nigga."

Miamor gripped the broom so tight that her palms hurt. "Miamor can speak for herself," she said. "Fly, can you give us a minute?" she asked.

Fly nodded, but never looked her way. The stare-down between him and Murder was malicious. . . . Their egos were involved. "Fly?" Miamor said again.

Fly looked at her and then stepped off.

Miamor turned to Murder, who was seething in anger. He grabbed her neck roughly, pinning her against the bar as he pointed a chastising finger in her face. "You called that nigga here?"

Miamor hadn't felt this gut instinct in a long time . . . the urge to murk something . . . to bark . . . to attack, but as Murder gripped her neck she felt her old self emerging. Miamor reached her hand beneath the bar where she'd taped her gun. There were weapons planted all around the place. She never knew when she would need one. It was in her nature to stay strapped.

She brought the gun to his temple. "Have you lost your mind?" she asked.

Murder licked his lips in amusement. "My Murder Mama," he whispered. The way he said it sent a chill down her spine. She could never grow with Murder. He obsessed over her being the same young, murderous girl she had always been. There was no room for maturation with him.

Miamor shook her head and lowered her gun. "You have to stop. You have to stop obsessing over me and trying to make me into who I was over ten years ago. I'm not yours, Murder. I haven't been in a long time. I loved you once, but you have terrorized my life . . . stalked me . . . kidnapped me . . . put my back up against the wall, all to make me stay with you. I can't do this anymore. I'm not doing it. It's time we both let go. You are a part of my past, and I appreciate you for showing me how to survive. You and I could have been good friends, but you have ruined that. You have ruined any chance of me ever wanting to keep a connection to you. I'm not yours. I'm not a possession, Murder. Damn! Just let it go. You go your way, I'll go mine. You can have half of the money. It's just time we say good-bye and it's time to move on. You have to accept that."

Miamor spoke with so much passion that tears came to her eyes. It was like she was pleading for her freedom. This relationship had run its course. If she was honest, she would admit that Murder had put a fear in her heart when she was only sixteen years old. He had used that fear to control her ever since. Miamor had always thought that the passion he had for her . . . the obsession . . . would be the thing that killed her. She wasn't doing it anymore, however. She wasn't living this way. Baraka was dead. Fly had come back for her when Carter himself hadn't even bothered to. She was leaving.

Murder lowered his head until their foreheads met. "I love the shit out of you, Miamor. It's always been you," he admitted.

There was just something about Miamor. Murder, Carter, Fly . . . she had connected with them in a way that no other woman could. It wasn't her sex or even her looks, but her mentality that captured their hearts. She was it for them, but there wasn't enough of her to go around. She only wanted one of them . . . Carter. But because of all that had occurred, he no longer wanted her.

"I know," she whispered. She hadn't anticipated this sadness. When she thought of the day they would part ways, she had thought she would feel joy, but she was letting go of her oldest friend. She didn't have family. She didn't have cousins or brothers. Her mother was gone. Her sister was gone. It was just her, and Murder was her oldest connection. "Just let go and take care of yourself. Good-bye, Murder."

"Good-bye, Murder Mama," he replied. She placed the gun on the bar and walked away, breathing a sigh of relief. It was easy. He had let her go. He was letting her walk away. He was . . .

BANG!

The bullet took her breath away and she gripped her stomach as she placed her hands on the blood spot growing on her white sundress. The burning that invaded her back brought tears to her eyes. *He shot me,* she thought in disbelief.

She turned around and looked him in the eyes as Fly Boogie rushed in, hearing the blast.

She fell backward, stumbling into his arms, but her eyes never left Murder's. She knew what he was about to do. She knew him like the back of her hand. He was as connected to her as one of her limbs.

She watched in horror as he turned the gun on himself and put a bullet in his head.

Fly Boogie picked her up. "It's okay. It's okay. I'm going to get you to a hospital, Mia. Just hold on," he said.

"He's dead?" Miamor asked. So many times she had assumed so, only to have him come back to haunt her later.

Fly Boogie turned around and looked at Murder's body. "He's dead, ma."

* * *

Miamor awoke. "I must be in heaven," she whispered as her son's face came into view. He was older, a big boy now, and so close to her that she could reach out and touch him. "Hmm," she whimpered as she shook her head trying to shake off the haze of medication. "Am I dreaming?" she whispered.

Fly Boogie was standing over her now. "Shhh . . . rest, Miamor. I'll explain everything to you when you come to."

* * *

The pain that pierced her abdomen was unbearable as she finally came out of the fog. She struggled to pull herself up as darkness enveloped the room. Fly Boogie was sleeping in the chair next to her, but when he heard her movements he instantly went to her side.

"You're okay," he whispered as he leaned over and rubbed the top of her head. "You're fine. Bitch nigga didn't hit anything major. Bullet went in and out. You just have to rest."

"I had a dream. I saw my son," she whispered.

"You weren't dreaming, Miamor. I came for you because I found him. I found him and Mo when I killed Baraka," he said in a low tone.

He stood up and went to the curtain that separated the beds in the room. He pulled it back and revealed the two boys who were sleeping, cramped in the tiny bed.

Miamor's hands flew to her mouth in disbelief. She was speechless, and her eyes pooled with tears. "How? Is this real?"

She didn't care about the pain now as she swung her legs over the side of the bed. "No, lie down," Fly said.

"C.J.," she whispered. She grabbed the rolling IV stand and willed her legs to hold her up as she hobbled over to the bed. She touched his face and gasped.

"Oh my God! You did this for me?" she asked. She knew that getting to Baraka was nearly impossible. Fly Boogie had risked it all for her. She owed him her life.

Her legs grew weak, and Fly Boogie scooped her in his arms. "It's late. Let them sleep. He's here now. He isn't going anywhere. When you're better, we'll make the trip back and take Mo to his father. I'm in L.A. getting a lot of money now, Miamor. Life is good. Only thing missing is you, but I'm applying no pressure. You have years of catching up to do with your son. I just want to be here for you."

He laid her back in the bed, but she didn't sleep. She didn't want to close her eyes and wake up to find out that this was all a dream. She watched C.J. and Mo all night until they awoke.

"Look who woke up," Fly said, knowing that C.J. had been eager to see his mother.

"Ma!" he yelled in excitement as he hopped out of bed and ran to her, crushing her as he hugged her. She didn't care that he was on her bullet wound. It was the best pain she had ever felt. Tears came. His. Hers. She kissed the top of his forehead. "I am never going to let you go, baby. I missed you so much. I'm so sorry," she whispered.

Mo stood awkwardly. His disappointment was evident. He wanted his mother, but he had witnessed Leena's death for himself. She was gone, and there was no bringing her back. It was the thing that Baraka had used to keep them from running away. He had promised them that he would kill everyone else they loved if they ever disobeyed him. Leena was gone forever, but where was his dad? Miamor looked at him and held out her arms. "Come on, Mo. Don't worry. We're going to take you back to your dad. Everything is going to be okay. You're safe now. I promise."

Fly Boogie flew them all back to L.A. on a private flight a few days later. As they crossed the Atlantic, Miamor turned to Fly. "Thank you," she whispered.

He didn't respond, but instead he pinched her chin softly and brought his face close to hers. He felt her body tense. She was uncomfortable. He paused, thinking twice about kissing her. "You're welcome," he said. Pulling back, ego slightly bruised, he was still full of understanding.

Miamor felt bad. She knew how much he loved her. She just didn't want to mislead him, but she did owe him. *You have to get Carter out of your system. Move on. Fly is a good guy and he did all this for you,* she told herself. Still, she couldn't help how she felt. She had love for Fly. She even found him attractive and loyal, but she was head over heels in love with Carter. *Carter isn't here,* she reminded herself.

Her thoughts consumed her the entire flight. When they landed, a black SUV waited at the clear port and they were driven to Fly's house.

"Wow, you are getting money out here," she whispered when they pulled up to his home. It was beautiful. It was the type of home that was filled with love and laughter, kids, and maybe a dog. "All of this for just you?"

He chuckled. "Yeah. I would only want to share this with one other person, but she bullshitting," he said playfully. "Let me show you around." Miamor blushed, slightly embarrassed. "I think there is a room set up upstairs for each of you," Fly said to them as soon as they got inside. The boys took off, and Miamor looked at him curiously. "I had it put together while we were in the Bahamas. I figured they'd want their own space until you were well enough to track down Monroe and C.J.'s father."

Miamor peeped how Fly didn't speak Carter's name, but she didn't say anything. She smiled. "Thank you," she whispered.

"You don't have to keep thanking me," he replied.

"I can't thank you enough," she answered.

"There's a room upstairs for you, too. If there's something in there that you need that you don't have, let me know and I'll get it for you," he said, pointing to the silver door near the kitchen. "There's an elevator so you don't have to bust your stitches trying to go up and down the stairs."

Miamor made her way slowly to it and up to her room. She sat down on the king-sized bed slowly, wincing as she looked around. She was so grateful that she just let her tears fall. "Thank you, God," she cried. It was time to piece her life back together. This was a second chance to get it right, and no, Fly wasn't the man she thought she would make a life with, but he was a man who loved her. He would do anything for her, and Miamor told herself that it was time to put away her hopes of she and Carter ever reuniting. It was time to live in the present, whether she wanted to or not.

She heard a knock at the door. "Come in," she said.

Fly opened the door. "You like it?" he asked.

She nodded. "I do," she replied.

"There isn't anything that you could ask me that I wouldn't do, ma. You know that, right?" he asked.

Ma, she thought. She closed her eyes briefly. It was what Carter called her.

Her eyes fluttered open. "I know," she replied.

He closed the door and walked over to the bed, getting on his knees in front of her. He spread her legs. "What are you . . ." She paused when she felt him slide her panties to the side. "Oh," she moaned when he sucked her bud into his mouth. It had been three long years since she had been intimate with anyone. She hadn't let Murder touch her. "Oh, wait . . . Fly . . . wait." She threw her head back.

He opened his mouth like a fish and sucked on her entire pussy, pulling her lips into his mouth. He buried his face in her with just the right amount of pressure. She was dripping wet. "You want me to stop?" he asked.

She looked down at him . . . at this young fool in love. She nodded yes, but her lips said, "No." It was all the invitation he needed.

"You taste so good, ma," he whispered while kissing her inner thighs. He licked her with long strokes, like he was trying to clean up a melting ice-cream cone. Her toes curled. "You taste so fucking sweet. Damn, this pussy good." She could feel her womanhood swelling in lust as he stiffened his tongue, targeting her center. Miamor gripped the comforter on the plush bed.

"Oh my God, Fly," she moaned, calling his name. It only added to the fervor. He leaned her back, hurting her gunshot wound slightly, but she took that little bit of pain in exchange for the pleasure he was delivering. He ate her like she was his last meal, licking her passionately. "I'm about to cum," she moaned.

She reached between her legs to place her hands on his head as she melted all over his tongue. He licked her clean and then inserted two fingers as he slid down the crack of her rear. There was no part of Miamor's body that he wouldn't please and he proved it as he brought her to a second orgasm, leaving her spent.

He came up for air and wiped his mouth with a charming smile plastered on his face.

He wanted her. She could see how much by the tent in his jeans, and she wanted it, too. If he tried his hand, she would let him have it, but to her surprise, he turned and headed for the door. He walked out without saying one word and he didn't need to; his actions spoke for themselves.

CHAPTER 10

There was only one place where Money would go after leaving Vegas: Miami. It was his home. It was his city. His father had fed every family in the hood at one point. The Diamond name rang bells in Miami, and he had love. It wasn't hard for him to take over when he returned. After losing Leena and Mo, something had snapped inside of Monroe. He was no longer the levelheaded twin. He was becoming more and more like Mecca as the years passed. Hotheaded, boisterous, ruthless. It was like Mecca's soul had taken over Monroe's body. Now he was all about the lifestyle. He had enough women and jewelry to prove it. Monroe was a kingpin and even the most naïve eye could see that. He didn't care, however. He knew that tomorrow wasn't promised. He had learned that lesson the hard way. He was just trying to live. The sound of his phone ringing was the only reason why he crawled out of bed. The two

Dominican models he had entertained the night before were still sleeping. They had made a Money sandwich last night. He chuckled as he recalled the previous night's events. Even he had to laugh at his outlandish ways. He was a savage. He picked up his cell phone, noticing that it was the gate guard calling.

"Mr. Diamond, you have visitors. Mrs. Miamor Jones is here with three guests," the guard informed him.

Money's blood boiled. He hadn't seen Miamor since Leena's funeral. He hadn't seen anyone since the funeral, actually, but Miamor, he resented. He blamed her for the way that things had unfolded with Baraka. "Let her in," Monroe said. He hung up the phone and slipped on some clothes.

"Get up. Get up. It's time to bounce," he said as he slapped one of the girls on her voluptuous behind. He grabbed the bottle of champagne they had been drinking and tipped it to his lips. He kept it in his hands. *Might as well finish this shit,* he thought.

"Aye, papi, I thought we would have more fun," one of them cooed.

"Fun's over, bitch," Monroe stated. He tossed them their clothes as they dragged themselves out of bed, cursing him out in Spanish.

"I speak that shit, too, bitch. Get out," he said, ushering them to the door.

"You drove us here. How are we supposed to get home?" the other girl asked.

Monroe pulled out a stack of cash and tossed it to the girls. "For your time," he said.

"What do we look like? Prostitutes?" the self-righteous one said, offended.

The other one flipped through the rubber-banded stack and quickly silenced her friend. "Nah, we're square, Money. Call me." She pulled her friend out of the front door as Monroe stepped onto the porch.

He watched as a tinted SUV pulled up and Miamor stepped out of the passenger side. Moments later, Fly Boogie exited the driver's side.

"You've got a lot of nerve showing up here, Miamor," Monroe said, slightly irritated.

Miamor didn't even speak. She simply opened the back door and Mo came running out.

"Daddy!" Mo said as he ran up the steps. The champagne bottle fell from his hands and shattered against the concrete stairs as Mo ran full speed into a stunned Monroe's arms.

C.J. exited the truck and stood in front of Miamor as she placed her hands on his shoulders.

Monroe held out his arms as if he were being hugged by a kid he didn't know. His confusion was written all over his face. He knew this was his son because he looked just like him.

How? He thought as he looked to Miamor for the answers. He picked up his son and hugged him so tight that Mo couldn't breathe.

Miamor, Fly, and C.J. ascended the steps.

Monroe was so emotional that he had to pinch the bridge of his nose to stop himself from crying.

"We'll explain everything," Miamor said as she walked inside. "Boys, why don't you go outside and play while we talk. If I remember right, there's a basketball court in the back," she added.

Monroe nodded, and the boys took off, but before his son could get fully out of the door, Monroe called him: "Mo!"

He stopped and turned to his dad. Mo looked like he was okay. He was back home in one piece. Monroe walked over to him and hugged him tightly. "I love you, son," he said.

"I love you, too," Mo said, before racing out.

He turned to Miamor and Fly. "How are they here? We had a memorial service. Baraka said he killed them."

"He never went through with it," Fly Boogie started. Fly explained the entire story to Monroe, leaving out no detail. By the end of it, Monroe had nothing but respect for him. He would be forever indebted to Fly for bringing his only born back home.

"Did he hurt them? In any way?" Monroe asked, afraid of the answer but having to know anyway.

"No," Miamor said. "They saw Leena be killed and he used that fear to stop them from running or telling anyone else who they really were. But I've asked them hundreds of times and each time they both tell the same story. He treated them well. He wanted us to suffer, not them."

Monroe wiped his face as he took all of this in. Just the day before, he hadn't thought he had anything to live for.

Now he was finding out that he had everything to live for. "We should have looked for them. We should have found Baraka. They were gone for three years. We missed three years with them because we gave up," Monroe said, beating himself up.

"We can't dwell on the time we lost. We just have to make up for the gift that we've been given," Miamor said. She looked at Fly. "The gift that Fly has given us."

She rubbed the top of Fly Boogie's hand, intimately, and Monroe noticed. He was shocked at her display of affection for him. But hell, at that point, Monroe could have kissed him, so he could see how Fly Boogie had won over Miamor after the loyalty he had shown.

"I owe you. Let me pay you for that hit. Show my gratitude," Monroe said.

"Nah. I'm good. I'm not hurting for anything. I've got my own thing going on, my G," Fly said. The fact that he had turned down a huge payday made Monroe respect him more.

"You're a good nigga, Fly Boogie," Monroe said as he stood and slapped hands with him. He pulled him in for an embrace and patted Fly firmly on the back. He turned to Miamor. "Can I rap with you for a second?" he asked.

"Yeah, of course," she said.

"I'll go out and check on the boys," Fly said, dismissing himself.

"Look, Money, I know what you're going to say . . . me

and Fly . . . it just . . ." She searched for the right words. "Happened."

Monroe surprised her when he replied, "I understand. Carter might kill him, but he's good with me."

"I haven't spoken to Carter in three years. Fly came back for me. Carter didn't," she said, her voice cracking in sadness.

Monroe noticed, but didn't say anything. He knew that this strong woman always did have a weakness for his oldest brother. "Does he know? About C.J.?"

"No," she whispered. "I don't know how to find him."

"Yeah, well, that makes two of us," Monroe admitted. "I haven't spoken to Carter, either. I talk to Breeze often. She keeps me connected with Zyir, but Carter doesn't want to be found."

"Well, I have to let him know about this," she said. "C.J. needs him. He's been asking for him. I have to find him."

"You was married to the nigga," Monroe said. "You know him, inside and out. He let you get in more than any of us. You loved him once. . . ."

"Once?" she scoffed. "I will love your brother until the air leaves my lungs. I'm with Fly, but it's because Carter left me alone."

"I'm saying . . . that bond . . . that love . . . if anybody can find Carter, it's you. You know how he thinks. You know his patterns, his habits, his wishes. You'll find him. I can tell you're guarded. You've built up a wall around that subject out of respect for your new nigga. You're going to have to tear that mu'fucka down, though, so you can feel that shit again. That's the only way you're going to locate him."

Miamor nodded.

"And me and you . . ." he said, pointing between the two of them. "We're good. We're family. Thank you for taking care of my son."

CHAPTER 11

Carter stood overlooking the snow-covered woods. The land was covered in so much white that it almost sparkled. What would have normally been a pitch-black night was illuminated by the abundance of snow. It was peaceful. It was a beautiful escape from the evil ways of men, and he never planned to leave. Despite his tranquil surroundings, Carter was haunted. He was tired, emotionally drained, and so full of sadness that it poured out of his eyes. He couldn't stop his soul from revealing his anguish. Any time anyone looked him in the eyes, they could see that he was tormented by memories of the past.

He heard the footsteps behind him and he automatically tensed. He knew who it was. He knew that she meant him no harm, but still, he reacted. He would live the remainder of his life looking over his shoulder, unfortunately. "Why are you awake?" he asked, without turning around.

"I should be asking you that," Sam said as she walked up behind him, caressing his broad, tense shoulders. "The pills aren't working?"

"A man shouldn't have to take sleeping pills to rest at night," Carter replied.

She leaned her head against his strong back and sighed deeply as her arms wrapped around his waist. He was grateful for her. Her presence alone made the seclusion bearable.

"Come on," she said as she walked over to the set of leather chairs that sat adjacent to the fireplace. A notepad was already in place on the small decorative table that separated them. Carter took his seat as she picked up the pen and pad. "Tell me about it."

This was why she was invaluable to him. Sure, she kept his bed warm at night, she cooked for him and kept up the chalet as well, but it was this . . . the therapy sessions . . . that soothed him.

"When I close my eyes at night, I see my son. I see my brother Mecca. I see my father's face," Carter stated in a low, serious tone. "The guilt . . ." He paused and cleared his throat to stop himself from choking up.

"Why do you feel guilty?" Sam asked as she crossed her legs, wrinkles creasing her forehead as she observed him.

"Because of the woman I chose," he said. Sam tensed. Carter's eyes glistened with pools of emotion, but he quickly blinked them away.

"You never talk about her," Sam said. "It's okay for you to talk to me about your son's mother."

Carter shook his head. He gripped the armrests of the

couch so tightly that his fingertips turned white. Although he tried every day, he couldn't forget Miamor. "I can't," he said. He stood and went to the bar to pour himself a glass of cognac. He quickly downed a shot before refilling it.

"You shouldn't drink. It only worsens the depression, Carter. I pulled you from a really dark place. I don't want you to go back there," Sam said.

"It numbs the pain," Carter admitted.

"What did she do to you?" Sam asked, pressing him to talk about things he swore he would never mention. "Why are you so damaged? What could one woman do?"

"She was Helen of Troy," Carter stated. He smirked at the thought of her.

"You went to war for her," Sam replied, a bit envious. "Was she worth it?"

Carter remembered the passion that he felt when he had been with Miamor. He remembered the intensity of their love. Just the thought of their bond made his heart rate increase, but with every good memory there came a bad one. "What I lost because of her . . . nah, she wasn't worth that," Carter stated, finishing his drink.

Sam put down her pen. "When a man finds and loses the love of his life, it's hard for any woman after that to measure up," she whispered.

Carter heard the sentiment in her voice. "Come here," he beckoned. She did as she was told. He pulled her onto his lap as they both watched the burning fire. "I don't want anything close to what I used to have," he assured her. "I'm content here with you."

"I don't want to make you content, Carter," she admitted. "I just want to make you happy." She turned around, straddling him. She was careful not to hurt him. The silk folds of her womanhood were exposed under the button-down shirt she had slept in. His hands caressed her skin as he quickly found her clit, massaging it slowly with his thumb. Her hips began to work as her eyes fluttered and her mouth fell open slightly. He enjoyed seeing her in ecstasy. His desire grew as she reached down, releasing him before she slid down on him. She sucked him in and the feeling of her, the grip she had on him, caused all the tension to leave his body. He cupped her breasts and kissed them gently as she rode him. Her rhythm was slow, his pace was intense, and together their passion filled up the room. Sam leaned back and braced her hands on his thighs while rolling her hips in pleasure. She was caught up . . . in a rapture with this marvelous man. She knew it, as did he. "Oh God, I love you," she moaned.

Carter tensed, and in the blink of an eye, his mood changed. "Wait," he whispered as he grabbed her waist and lifted her off of him.

"What's wrong?" she gasped as she placed a hand over her heart, breathless.

"I haven't been fair to you," Carter said. "I can't give you what you want from me, Sam."

"I don't want anything, Carter. There is no expectation," she said. "I'm a big girl."

"I don't have any love to give," Carter said. "I can appreciate you. I can enjoy you, but I can't love you, Sam."

"I know," she whispered as she cupped his face. "That doesn't stop me from loving you. I hate the woman who wounded you so much. I don't need you to love me, but I won't lie about my feelings for you. I just want you to open up to me. You can trust me with anything. Why do you think I'm here? In the middle of nowhere? You're paying me well, but it isn't about the money. I had family and friends. I'm up here, with you, cut off from the world, and I have never felt more alive. So no, you don't have to love me; just don't shut me out. Don't ask me to go away, and don't hold back."

Carter wished that things could be different. She was good for him. She was a good woman . . . the type any man would love to make his wife. He was just so guarded. He couldn't afford to be vulnerable, not again. After losing his son and exiling Miamor from his life, he didn't think he deserved to feel joy. So instead of allowing himself to connect fully with Sam, he put up guards, blocking her from ever getting too close. They were together in an unconventional way. They talked, the sex was good, and the chemistry was magnetic, but he was no good for her. He knew what kind of karma he had sown. When it came back around, he didn't want to pull Sam into his mess. She could only get hurt being with him. She was too legitimate for him. She didn't know about the wars he had fought, the people he had killed, or the drugs he had sold. She didn't know the kingpin. She knew what he pretended to be now, the simple, secluded persona that he had made up. She had no idea how real things could get in his world.

"Carter, look at me," Sam whispered. Their eyes met. "You're everything to me. Just let me in." She kissed him, and his reluctance melted away as he swept her under him and laid her gently on the bearskin rug.

"Be careful, Carter," she said, concerned. He was fragile. After being shot, he wasn't quite the same. With only one good lung, he moved slower and his pain was not only emotional, or mental, but physical as well. He was broken, but pleasing a woman would always be his expertise. Sam didn't know him outside of Colorado. All she saw was the secluded part of him . . . the man who chopped firewood and played chess against himself. She didn't know his gangster. He was all G, and he handled her body as such. He silenced her worries with a kiss as he entered her, rocking her body. The only sounds that could be heard were the crackling fire and her cries as she called his name over and over again.

* * *

Carter awoke as the rising sun began to sneak past his curtains. They had fallen asleep on the floor, her head resting on his chest. He slid from underneath her, being careful not to awaken her. A chill had settled over the house. The fire had burned out, and the heat alone wasn't enough to battle against the negative-degree temperatures outside. He slipped into his clothes, head spinning from the night before. He pulled on his coat, grabbed his gloves, and stepped into his boots before heading outside. The winter air was biting cold, but he didn't mind. He had grown used to it. He inhaled deeply and then grabbed the ax that sat next to the porch. Never in a million years had he predicted this would be his life, but this was the only place where he could go that didn't remind him of his former life. This had become his refuge.

He headed into the backyard and collected some wood from his stockpile. He then took it to the chopping block and began to break them down. He swung hard, overexerting himself probably, but he didn't care. Since he was no longer in the business of running empires, this was the only way he knew to let off steam. There was no one to punish for the death of his seed. There was no vengeance to be had because he knew that if he even broached the subject, he would be killing himself. Baraka was too powerful a man to wage war against, so he held his rage inside and took it out on the wood every chance he got. By the time he was done, he had worked up a full-body sweat. He picked up an armful of logs and headed back into the house. The piercing scream that cut through the air stopped him midstep. Instinctively he dropped the firewood and headed to one of the guns he had strategically placed around the property. His paranoia never allowed him to be too far away from a pistol, and in three years he hadn't had to use one. It seemed his past had caught up to him. He walked up the back stairs and eased through the back door. He saw Sam, curled up, covering herself with one of the bear rugs as she stared intensely at someone. "Who are you? What do you want?" Sam asked.

Carter rounded the corner with his hand around the trigger, but his heart dropped when he saw who had invaded his home.

"Miamor," he whispered in shock. He didn't know what he felt. Hatred, relief, love, confusion . . . it all plagued him as he squinted in disbelief.

"Hi, Carter," she said. "I haven't met your little friend here. Why don't you introduce us?" Her tone was sarcastic . . . angry, even. Despite the fact that they were no more, she was still sick to her stomach at the thought of him being intimate with another woman.

"Go upstairs," Carter said to Sam without looking at her. He kept his eyes trained on Miamor.

"Carter, who is this?" Sam asked.

"Yeah, Carter, who am I?" Miamor challenged.

"Go upstairs, Sam. Now," Carter repeated, his voice stern.

"No, please stay. I think I deserve to meet the bitch that's fucking my husband," Miamor stated.

"Your husband?" Sam asked in shock. "This is your wife?" Sam gasped.

"In the flesh," Miamor replied. She put the gun she had been pointing at the girl away, tucking it away in her Birkin. "I take it he didn't tell you that I murdered the last bitch I caught him cheating with."

"That's enough, Miamor," Carter said with authority. Miamor shot him a look that could kill, but she didn't say another word as Carter helped Sam from the floor and whispered something in her ear. Sam rushed out of the room, leaving them to their reunion. It had been three years and neither of them had ever made their split official. By law, they were still man and wife.

Carter placed his gun on the counter and stared at her. "Why are you here, ma?" he asked. "Do you know what the sight of you does to me? I was starting to forget how much I resented you until I saw your face."

His words stung, and she cringed as tears accumulated in her eyes. Carter Jones was her man. He was her husband. He had been her everything. *He's still so fucking handsome,* she thought as she took a deep breath to stop her nostalgia. He was different. She could see that he had changed. His beard had grown out fully, and worry had aged his features before his time. He looked tired, burdened, and her heart ached just from his presence. All she really wanted to do was fall into his arms, but she couldn't. He didn't want her. His love had turned to hate for her. She had taken him through too much. Besides, she had moved on. With Fly, none of the bullshit lingered in the air. Fly loved her, and although it didn't feel the same as when Carter had loved her, it was love all the same.

"I hate that you have her here. A part of me was hoping to find that you hadn't moved on," she admitted. "I wanted to kill her when she answered the front door. I wanted to put a bullet through her head."

"Don't speak about her. This is my life now," Carter stated solemnly.

"I never thought you would have a life without me in it. I thought we were soul mates," Miamor said, her lip trembling. She placed her fingers in the corners of her eyes so that her makeup didn't run down her face as the tears emerged. She sniffed, slightly emotional.

"We were," Carter whispered. "But I can't be with you, Miamor. You're reckless. The memories of our baby . . . they haunt me every day."

"I have to tell you something, Carter," Miamor said. "It's about our son." She pulled out her phone and held it out to him, showing him a picture of C.J. "He's alive, Carter."

The news hit him like a ton of bricks, momentarily stunning him as his brow furrowed. He saw her lips moving, but everything after "he's alive," he couldn't fathom. He gripped the edge of the nearby table and bent over it as if pain had spread through his body. Carter was normally so in control, so composed, but when he looked up at her, tears filled his gaze. "How?" he asked. "This is a dream. I'm dreaming right now," he whispered.

"No, it's true. It's real, Carter," Miamor confirmed. "He's alive. Baraka didn't kill him. None of the kids. Monroe's son is okay, too."

Overwhelmed, Carter sat and planted his face in his hands as he cried. He tried his hardest to stifle his feelings and dam his emotions, but it all poured out of him. All of the hurt, the anger, the regret was flooding into his hands as he sobbed. He had never cried like this, not even as a young boy. Not even when he lost his mother or his father or his brother. Not even when he thought he had lost Miamor. She walked over to him and placed her hands on the back of his head as he buried his face into her stomach, pulling her close.

Seeing him this weak moved her. *God, this is such a good man*, she thought. She was mad at herself—livid, in fact—

for messing everything up between them. Now it was too late. Now it was awkward. Forced. Her actions had reduced them to two people with two different lives who shared a child. *This isn't how it is supposed to be. We were supposed to love each other forever.* Her thoughts were filled with sadness, but she was still grateful. Their son was safe, and that was all that mattered.

Carter grunted, slightly embarrassed as he regained composure. Pinching the bridge of his nose, he shook his head. All the nights he had thought of taking his life to rejoin his son when his son had never left him. "I should have gone after Baraka," Carter said. "I should have seen his body with my own eyes before disappearing."

"You didn't know," Miamor said. "Neither did I."

Carter stood to his feet, squaring his shoulders. "How did you get him back? I know Baraka didn't just give him to you."

Miamor sighed. This was the hard part. This was the part where she would have to tell him that she was with Fly.

"Baraka is dead," Miamor revealed. "Fly Boogie killed him and brought our son to me."

Carter's nostrils flared. "Fly Boogie? How the fuck that little nigga get to Baraka? And how you know so much about it? You with that little nigga?"

Miamor lowered her eyes and then took a deep breath as she replied, "Yes."

Carter's jaw clenched as he stared at her. He said nothing, but she could see the disdain and hurt in his expression.

"I—" she started to explain, but he interrupted her.

"Where is my son?" he demanded.

"In Miami, with Monroe. I only left him so that I could come speak to you," she replied. "Come get you."

Sam cleared her throat, announcing her presence. "Is everything okay, Carter?" she asked timidly.

Carter sensed her fear. Miamor had a way of intimidating most men, so he sympathized with Sam. "It's fine." He turned to Miamor. "I'll be in Miami by this evening."

She frowned. "I thought we would go together," she said.

Carter was so angry with her that he could wring her neck. *Fly Boogie? She letting Fly Boogie walk around with my bitch on his arm,* Carter thought. "Nah," he said as he walked over to the front door and held it open. She raised her eyebrows in disbelief. She knew there would be something in the air between them, but she was taken aback all the same. She didn't wear her heart on her sleeve, however. She spotted Sam's notepad and pen, then leaned down to pick them up. She scribbled on the pad and then handed him the note as she walked by him and out the door.

"Here is my number. You can call me when you get to Miami," she stated. She looked at Carter seriously. "You sure this is how you want it to be between us?"

He stepped closer to her and lowered his voice so that he wasn't overheard. "You laying in the bed of the little nigga I used to have watching over my blocks," Carter stated. "A nigga that I used to line up in my army. How did you think it would be?" he asked. "You thought you were going to come in here and we were going to be a big, happy family?" Carter paused and waited for her to answer. "Let me explain something to you, ma. The only reason I'm coming back to Miami is for my son."

Miamor scoffed. "You real bothered for a man who has no interest, but whatever you say," she replied. "See you in Miami, Carter." She walked down the snowy path and back to her rental car. She could have told him that the Fly Boogie he remembered had since graduated in the streets and now had an empire that stretched up and down the West Coast, but she didn't. There was no point in defending Fly because when it came down to it, she would only be doing it out of spite. Her heart would always be in the hands of Carter Jones, but she couldn't force him to open back up to her. Sometimes the past was best left in the past, and although it pained her greatly, she didn't have a choice but to move forward with her life as somebody else's girl.

* * *

Carter's heart thundered in his chest as he watched Miamor pull away. She was his girl. *That's me,* he thought, but his pride kept his feet glued in place. Every fiber in his body had wanted to pull her into him, kiss her, cry with her, rejoice with her over the revelation of their son's survival, but he couldn't. She was poison, and partaking in her would lead to his death. She always had been bad for him and he had always known it, but it wasn't until now that he accepted that fact. He could not allow Miamor to put him or their son in jeopardy ever again. Loving her wasn't worth it. Despite the fact that she was the only person in the world who made him feel whole, he still couldn't take it there. He had to cut it to her rough. He had to make it clear, because she would sniff out any indecision he had. She would recognize his weakness and she would make him love her at the drop of a dime. She had that much power over his emotions. He suffered a silent heartbreak as Miamor disappeared from his view. Some people were just meant to be together. The universe pulled them together, but they were pulling themselves apart and that unnatural separation hurt like hell.

"You neglected to mention that you were still married." Sam's voice caused him to turn around and face her.

"Is that why you don't like to talk about her? Because you didn't want me to know?" she asked.

"It's complicated," he admitted.

"She pointed a gun in my face," Sam said in a low tone. "She said she killed someone over you. Is that true?"

Carter walked right by her without replying.

"Carter!" she cried out. "After three years I think I deserve to know what I'm dealing with . . . who I'm dealing with. You say you own a casino. That you built your empire out West in Las Vegas, but you keep guns hidden in every nook of this house. You have money hidden away under the floorboards, and I'm not talking about a few thousand dollars. You have more than my hands could count," she said. "I know you're not who you say you are. You have scars from bullet holes in your chest and when we have our sessions, you hold back. You can trust me, Carter. You can tell me who you really are. Whatever you've done. It won't change how I look at you."

Carter looked her square in the eyes and said, "I don't know what you're talking about."

"Can I at least go to Miami with you? I'd love to meet your little boy," she said eagerly.

He looked at her sternly.

"I overheard," she admitted. "This will bring out so many new emotions in you, Carter. I can talk you through that . . . help you process it all."

He nodded. "Pack your bags. I'll have a jet waiting at the Denver airport this evening."

She smiled and left the room, leaving him alone with his thoughts. He hadn't been to Miami in eight years. Surely things had changed. So many memories haunted him. Nothing but death and destruction dwelled there, and he hoped that he wasn't making the biggest mistake of his life by going back.

CHAPTER 12

As soon as Breeze stepped off the private jet, she inhaled deeply. The warm sun immediately warmed her face and she smiled. "Miami, I'm home," she whispered as she shed a layer of clothes. She hadn't been back in so long that she had almost forgotten how good it felt. Zyir placed his hand on the small of her back as they made their way across the tarmac to the black SUV that was awaiting them.

"Mr. Rich?" the driver asked.

Zyir nodded as he extended his hand.

"Welcome to Miami, sir," the driver said. He took their bags and then opened the back door for them.

"This feels so much better than that miserable blizzard we just left," Breeze said with a sigh of relief.

Zyir smirked. "I'm Flint-bred, baby. It don't bother me as much," he answered. He reached over and grabbed her hand, squeezing it three times. It was how they said "I love you" without speaking.

She returned the gesture. "I can't wait to see the Diamond estate. It's been so long," she whispered. "Papa would be pleased that we kept it in the family. He was all about family . . . about loyalty. I wish he'd had a chance to meet you. He would have liked you."

Zyir said nothing. Instead, he looked out the window as they pulled away from the jet.

The hour ride to the old Diamond estate was filled with a comfortable silence as memories flooded Breeze. During her teenage years she used to hop all over these streets, shopping and hanging out with her girlfriends. She tried to keep the negative times in the back of her mind because there were so many of them. Her family had reigned over Miami's drug trade, but their power had come at a price and it had been a hefty one.

When they pulled up to the gates of the mansion, there were guards everywhere. They walked on the inside perimeter, earpieces in their ears, black-suited despite the scorching heat. Two men manned the front gate and one sat in a security post off to the side. All were visibly armed.

"Zyir and Breeze Rich here for Mr. Diamond," the driver announced to the men.

Breeze looked at Zyir with a raised brow and said, "It's a bit much, right?" She shook her head, amused, as she cracked a smile. The gates opened and the driver entered, taking them down the long drive to the main house.

"It looks exactly the same," Breeze said, her excitement

growing. As soon as they parked, she was out and up the
steps, walking right in as if she still lived there. When
she stepped inside, her mouth dropped. A woman in six-
inch stilletos and a thong and bra walked right up to her.

"Welcome, beautiful. Mr. Diamond will be right down,"
she greeted them seductively.

"Who the hell are you?" Breeze asked as Zyir walked in.

Another scantily clad woman in hooker heels approached, her sights set directly on Zyir. "Please let me take
your bags. Welcome to the Diamond estate. Can I show you
to your room?"

"Umm, no, miss thing! You can't show my man anywhere," Breeze said, taken aback. "And where is Money's
extra ass?"

Zyir smirked, chuckling slightly. "This nigga is fooling,"
he said to Breeze as he shook his head, amused.

"No disrespect. I'm here to make sure you are well taken
care of. Not just him . . . anything you need as well," the
girl said.

The two women bent down and grabbed the luggage.
"I'll take these upstairs."

"My room is in the east wing," Breeze instructed. The
girls walked away, voluptuous bodies on full display. Even
Breeze had to sneak a peek. She covered Zyir's eyes playfully and nudged him in the ribs, causing him to laugh.

Money walked into the room with two additional women
at his sides.

"What is this? The Playboy mansion?" Breeze asked as
she greeted him. He was as handsome as ever, and on the

outside seemed to have everything together. He was sur-rounded by protection and beautiful girls, but Breeze was his sister. She knew him well. These were all distractions. This was his way of forgetting about Leena.

"Nah, it ain't like that, B," he replied as he kissed her cheek and slapped hands with Zyir. "I'm just living. You never know when somebody will take that privilege away, so until then I'm going at every day like it's my last," he said. "Good to see you, fam," he said to Zyir.

"Likewise," Zyir replied.

"What was so urgent that you and Carter called us all the way down here? I know you couldn't speak over the phone, but I'm curious to know what's brought him out of seclusion," Breeze said.

"Let me show you," Monroe stated as he led the way up-stairs.

He escorted them to the room that he and Mecca used to share as kids and opened the door.

Breeze covered her mouth in absolute shock when she saw two young boys sleeping soundly in each bed. She didn't have to guess their identities. They were the splitting images of their fathers.

"How?" she asked with tear-filled eyes. She had never felt such joy. "This is impossible."

She went to take a step inside the room, but Monroe stopped her. "Let's wait for Carter. Let them sleep. We don't know what they went through when they were with Baraka. They haven't spoken much, only to each other. I want to give Carter a chance to see his son . . . talk to him before we overwhelm them," Monroe said.

"That's best," Zyir said.

Breeze stepped into the room anyway, and bent down over each one of her nephews to kiss their cheeks.

She walked back out of the room and looked at Monroe. "Get rid of the women, Money. I get it. Leena's gone. You're coping, but your son is back now. You don't bring that king-pin shit around him. Papa never did. All we knew was happiness when we were their ages," she said. Monroe knew that it wasn't a request. Breeze didn't boss up often, but when she did, it meant she was serious. He would be sure to honor her wishes.

The doorbell rang.

"That's probably Carter," Breeze said.

They made their way to the front door and pulled it open to find Miamor standing there with Fly Boogie by her side.

"Is he here yet?" she asked, referring to Carter.

"Not yet," Breeze replied, already knowing whom she was speaking of just by the urgent look in her eyes. "It's good to see you."

Breeze and Miamor embraced, genuinely happy to see each other. Their bond had grown naturally over time. They were family, and although Miamor had made mistakes, Breeze didn't believe in turning her back on family.

"Come in," Breeze said.

Zyir looked at Monroe curiously when Fly Boogie stepped inside. "Why is he here again?" He noticed how Fly

Boogie had placed his hand on the small of Miamor's back. "The shit I'm looking at ain't gon' fly."

Zyir had vouched for Fly Boogie years ago. He was the reason why Carter even gave him a position within The Cartel. Now here he was, committing the ultimate act of disrespect. "She's fucking with him like that?" Zyir asked.

"That's not important right now, Zyir," Breeze whispered.

Monroe looked at Zyir seriously and said, "I don't give a fuck about all that. If it wasn't for him, my son wouldn't be at home safe in his bed right now. He would still be with Baraka and I would still think he was dead. He's good money with me. Just let it be. That's Carter's business. He'll handle that."

"Your house, your rules," Zyir stated, but it was clear that he didn't approve.

"Well, we don't have to wait and see. He's here," Breeze said as she looked at the high-tech security screen that showed Carter's arrival. She rushed outside and before he could even emerge from the car, she jumped in his arms.

"Hey, Breeze," he greeted her.

She pulled back from him and looked him in his eyes. His appearance was so different. He was rugged. His big beard was such a huge contrast from the clean-cut, composed boss she remembered. He had withdrawn from everyone when he thought C.J. had died. She hoped this reunion would bring him back to the man he used to be. "I'm glad you're here. I'm glad we're all here. It's been a long time since we've all come together."

Sam emerged from the car behind Carter. Breeze looked at Carter curiously. "You know Mia is here, right?"

"I'm not worried about anything but my son, B. Where is he?" Carter asked.

She nodded her head. "Understandably," she said. "He's upstairs. I'll show your friend around while you handle your business." She turned to Sam. "Welcome to our home, Sam. Thank you for taking such good care of him."

Carter didn't stick around for introductions. He walked into the Diamond estate and bypassed everyone as he headed directly for the stairs.

"Carter," Miamor called as she took a step toward him. Fly Boogie grabbed her elbow, stopping her from following after him. "Give him a moment with his son, ma. It's been three years. He deserves that," he said.

Carter opened every door on his way down the hallway until he found his son, sleeping soundly. Against his will, his face began to contort as he was wrecked with emotion. He was overcome with happiness as the enormity of his son's presence hit him. He knew he was so undeserving of a blessing of this magnitude. He was so grateful, he couldn't stop the tears from flowing. They were endless. They were the most natural expression of love he had ever displayed. In this moment, he wasn't a kingpin, he wasn't a boss, he wasn't a gangster . . . he was simply a father, grateful for the safety of his boy. He had lived the past three years weighed down by the burden of a great sadness . . . a great loss . . . and he had mourned heavily. Today was the first day since he had walked away from The Cartel that he felt like he could breathe. The burden had been lifted and his heart was so exposed that he felt embarrassed by his reaction. No one had ever seen him so weak. Footsteps behind him caused him to straighten his stance and wipe the evidence from his eyes, but when he turned around, Miamor said, "You can cry. I did for almost an hour straight when I first saw him."

Carter tried his hardest to keep his resolve, but he melted again into sobs as Miamor walked into his arms. He cried on her shoulder as she rubbed the back of his head gently. He resented her. His anger toward her was immeasurable, but she was the only person who understood how he felt. He knew that he could trust her with his tears. She was the one person who wouldn't use his weakness against him. Truth was, he hated himself for loving her so much. He rested his forehead against hers.

"It's okay," she whispered supportively as her dainty hands began to wipe his tears away. She used her thumbs to wipe them off of his face and then cupped his cheeks in the palms of her hands. "He's okay," she whispered. "There was nothing you could have done to prevent this. Nothing to save him. I caused this. We missed three years of his life because of my actions, not yours, so don't blame yourself. You cry all of that depression out right now while it's just me and you. Get it out of your system and when you're done, you take back your throne."

He gritted his teeth and calmed himself as they stared into each other's eyes. In her, he saw himself. He knew that he should have looked away. He knew how easily it was for her to pull him in. She could see his love for her blazing within him. It was simmering slowly. He gripped the back of her neck and pulled her into him, kissing her so deeply that she felt it everywhere. He pulled back from her, shaking his head. "I can't."

"Why not, Carter?" she asked. "We have our son back. Why can't we just be a family?"

"It's dangerous being with you. You don't think, Mia. You just react. The last time you popped off, it cost us three years with our son. Next time it might cost him his life. My life. Your life. So let's just not do this. You go your way with your new nigga, and I'll go mine," Carter stated.

"This is about me being with Fly?" she asked. "Just say it, Carter. You're mad because I'm with him. He came back for me! When you walked away and left me, he came back! He gave me my life back. I had a bounty on my head, Carter, and you didn't even try to save me. You just walked away and hid in your cabin on the side of a fucking mountain! He came back. You didn't. So who should really be the one mad here? Me or you?"

Carter squared his shoulders as his jaw flexed in anger. Every time he thought about Fly Boogie and Miamor, he wanted to body something. "That little nigga knows what you feel like, ma, what you taste like . . . and yeah, you said he came back for you after I left, but he was checking for you before any of this shit ever popped off. You had his head gone. Lil' nigga had your name tatted and everything and you expect me to believe you wasn't throwing him no pussy? My pussy? You murked Baraka's daughter because I slept with her. She drugged me that night and you never even gave me the chance to explain that to you. You put her in a grave, Miamor! You buried her alive! What you think I want to do to him? Huh? You think I want to shake his hand? You think I want to thank him? It's taking everything in me not to empty one in his forehead. That's how much I love you. That's how crazy I am over you. I understand now, why you did what you did, but us together? We're dangerous. We aren't rational. Our love is too deadly. I couldn't take you back without murdering that nigga. A point has to be made. And if I do that, I jeopardize my son's future. He loses a father. You see my dilemma?"

Miamor was near tears herself just listening to his internal struggle. "You let him have you, now I got to let him keep you and I'mma do me over here."

"But I love you," she admitted. It was his turn to wipe her tears, but she could tell by the look in his eyes that his word was final.

"It's too late for us, ma," he replied.

The bedroom door opened and their son appeared, causing Miamor to turn away to straighten her face. When she turned back around she was smiling brightly. She bent down. "Hey, C.J., someone wants to see you," she said.

Carter turned around so that his son could see his face. "Dad!" C.J. yelled in excitement as his eyes lit up. Relief flooded Carter as C.J. instantly recognized him. He had been worried that he may not remember him. He had only been five years old when Baraka had taken him, but the time had done nothing to erase his memory. This was his cub, and their bond was instinctive. Carter bent down and picked up his son, noticing instantly that he was no longer a baby.

"Ugh, Dad! I'm not a baby now, put me down!" C.J. said as he kicked his feet. Miamor laughed as Carter placed him on his feet. He was eight and stood before him scrawny but tall. He wore Superman pajamas and had a set of ears on him that made it seem like he could take flight. It was like looking at himself years ago. He was the spitting image of Carter. He held out his hand for his son.

"You're right. You're a young man now." Carter's son shook his hand as he poked out his bird chest proudly. Carter looked at him seriously. "Did anybody hurt you while you were away?"

"No sir," C.J. replied.

"You can tell me anything. You know that, right?" Carter said sincerely.

C.J. nodded.

"I love you, C.J. My word is bond that no one will ever take you away from me again. I promise you that," Carter stated.

"I love you, too, Dad," C.J. said.

Carter nodded toward Lil' Money and said, "Wake your cousin up, get dressed, and come down. It's time to celebrate."

Carter walked past Miamor and back down the steps. When he appeared at the top, he noticed everyone was looking up at him and they all had glasses of champagne in hand.

"Feels good, don't it?" Monroe asked when Carter descended.

"Like nothing I've ever felt, Monroe," Carter replied. Monroe handed Carter a flute.

He then grabbed another off the serving tray that one of the lovely servants was holding and handed it to Miamor once she came down. He held his in the air.

"To family. We are whole again and nothing will break down The Cartel going forth. Family, money, and power," he toasted.

They all drank to that before Monroe added, "Let's break bread. My beautiful, beautiful ladies have set up a champagne brunch on the lawn and a welcome-home party for the boys. The entire city is coming out. Let's have a good time."

* * *

When Monroe mentioned the entire city, he held no punches. When he had come back to Miami, he had built The Cartel back up to prominence. It hadn't ever been so powerful, not even when his father had been alive. He was the king, and every single one of his soldiers came out with their families to celebrate the return of his son. He had hired a full carnival to come out and set up in the vastness of his backyard, but he was careful. Every hood nigga and their baby mama was checked thoroughly before they were granted access to the Diamond estate. Government IDs were taken and photocopied. Monroe would know exactly who came through his gates should he need to reach out and touch somebody after the fact. He had no worries, however. Miami loved him . . . all of Miami. He was the man, and nobody wanted beef with him. He was a living legend.

"Isn't this a bit much?" Carter asked as he and Monroe stood on the expansive deck overlooking the party.

"Nah, it's just right, bro. Relax. Enjoy yourself. Nobody here means us any harm. We're back. Find that pretty little thing, Sam, you brought up in here with you, grab a drink, and enjoy your family," Monroe said. "Where is she, anyway? You know Miamor's ass will have her tied up in a closet somewhere." Monroe laughed jovially as he took a swig of his Heineken.

"Chill out," Carter said with a smirk.

Fly walked up with two beers in his hand and offered one to Carter. "Gentlemen—" he greeted them.

Carter looked down at the beer and smirked as he left the offer lingering in the air. Tension filled the space. Monroe looked back and forth between his brother and Fly, and spoke up in an attempt to de-escalate the situation. "Fly was telling me about this pill shit he into out West. He said it's a lot of money to be made," Monroe said as he accepted the beer from Fly to save him some embarrassment.

"We don't eat at the same table," Carter said squinting as he looked out over the yard, keeping his eye on his son at all times. He was overly aware of his surroundings. He couldn't help but feel like there were too many new niggas around him. Carter wasn't about this life anymore. The status, the attention, the crowd . . . it was all too much for him.

"A lot of things have changed since you've been gone," Fly said.

"Apparently," Carter said sarcastically.

"Look, fam—"

"Kill that fam shit," Carter stated. "The only reason I ain't put your brains on the pavement yet is because of what you did for my son."

A solid-built goon stepped up wearing a black T-shirt and a gaudy diamond crucifix, putting Carter on the defensive. "What nigga? What you gon' do, big man?" Carter grabbed the goon by his collarbone and applied pressure as he smoothly came off his hip with his burner. He discreetly stuck it in the gut of the man. "You got a problem? Fuck is you, nigga? If this yo' team, Fly Boogie, you need to do more recruiting. You know who the fuck you stepping to?" Carter asked through gritted teeth. He was seeing red, but he spoke in low tones so as to not draw attention to the altercation.

"Whoa, whoa," Monroe intervened. "We're all on the same team here. Carter, put the gun away, bro."

Carter calmed down, and Monroe nodded his head at the goon. "Now get your ass out," he said. The dude began to step off, and Monroe lifted his foot, kicking him in the back and causing him to fall down the stairs. "Fuck was you thinking? Stupid ass mu'fucka," Monroe stated. He turned to Fly. "Control your people."

"My apologies," Fly stated.

Out of nowhere C.J. came running up. "Fly!" he called out in excitement. "What's up, man?!"

Hearing his son's excitement caused a pang of jealousy to stab Carter's heart.

"What's good, lil' man? You having a good time at your party? All this is for you. There are a lot of people that are glad that you're home, man."

"Yeah! This is dope! You want to shoot hoops with me and Mo?" C.J. asked.

"Yeah, I'll be right there. Let me finish ironing out a few things with your pops," Fly stated.

"A'ight!" C.J. ran off full speed toward the full-sized basketball court.

Carter was awkward about Fly's relationship with his son, but seeing their interaction softened him a bit. This wasn't about Miamor. This was about what was best for C.J.

"Listen. I realize what you did to get my son back. That alone is enough for me to put the bullshit aside. You respect me, I'll respect you, but I'm good on the business," Carter said.

"There's money on the floor, Carter. Just hear him out," Monroe said. "If he take our coke out West and we bring his pill game here, the shit will be crazy. We stand to make a lot of paper. That pill shit is dry out this way. It's an open market, but he can't come here and get no money without our muscle backing him. I need you on this. You can get Estes on board, too. I've got a plug and it's doing the job, but if I had Estes's product . . . whoo," Monroe said as he shook his head. Just thinking about the profit had him ready to go all in.

"Estes is your grandfather, blood-born, why you can't get to him?" Carter asked.

"He don't want no part of The Cartel if you ain't running it. He's watched everybody around me die. Mecca, Papa, my moms. He said he can't contribute to putting me in the grave. He refuses to play as long as I'm the one calling the shots," Monroe said. "I can do it with this other connect, but it ain't the same. Quality is off. That's why I need you."

Carter chuckled. "Cuz Estes don't give a fuck if a nigga put a bullet in me."

Monroe laughed. "Basically."

Carter shook his head as he looked around the yard. He spotted Miamor, but didn't see Sam anywhere. "I'm good on that. Maybe you can pull Zyir in. I'm about to go find my lady," he said, walking away.

* * *

Zyir stood in the kitchen gripping the countertop as he stood with his head lowered in stress. He pinched the bridge of his nose as he contemplated his loyalties in his head. Sam entered the kitchen and he looked up, straightening his stance as he prepared to walk out. Out of nowhere she grabbed him, pushing him against the wall with force and taking him by surprise.

"I need to talk to you. Right now," she said in a hushed tone. She pulled him into the half bath.

"Not here," Zyir protested as he attempted to get past her.

Sam pulled out a small-caliber handgun and clasped it with both hands, pointing it at him. "Right here, right now," she stated. "Don't forget who you're dealing with, Zyir. We've been trying to build this case for three years. I finally have every member of The Cartel in one place at the same time. I want everybody in cuffs, including Miamor Jones. You get Carter back into the drug business by any means necessary. Monroe will be easy to nab. He's flashy. I want this Fly Boogie character as well and the big fish of the entire operation, Estes. Without Estes, there is no deal for you," Sam threatened. "The district attorney on this case lost to Carter Diamond years ago. We can't afford to leave any loose ends this time around. The Cartel will fall with or without your help. The question is, are you going to fall with it? Now I've been on the inside with Young Carter for three years. Three years up in the mountains and nothing, not even a traffic violation. This case isn't made without him. You need to push him back into the game and speed up the process. You either play this my way or you're finished. Your little wifey is finished. I can make this real bad for you and if I even get a whiff of you having second thoughts, I will ruin you. I wonder what Carter and Monroe would think about a member of their own turning state's evidence?"

Zyir felt like the scum of the Earth. The feds had turned him, and Sam was merely an undercover building the case of her career against the entire Cartel.

"Are you threatening me?" Zyir asked, enraged. "Don't fucking threaten me," he stated through gritted teeth as he pressed his chest against her gun, challenging her. "You better watch who you pull your gun on, Agent."

"You Cartel men really do have a God complex. You,

Carter, Monroe—you're all the same," she chuckled. "But you're not invincible, and I will destroy you. It's time for you to just deliver on your end. I've flipped dozens of street kings like you. The name of the game is self-preservation. Don't you think for one moment that Carter or Monroe wouldn't do it to you if the shoe was on the other foot," she stated. "We're running out of time. I need Carter's hands dirty, and you're going to be a good boy and make that happen for me," she said as she patted his cheek condescendingly before walking out of the bathroom. Her sly smile was infuriating, but what could he do? She had his balls in a vise grip and he had no choice but to do things her way, betraying the ones who had always been loyal to him.

* * *

Zyir started to follow her until he heard Carter's voice. He ducked back into the bathroom and pressed his back against the wall to remain unseen.

"I've been looking for you, you a'ight?" he heard Carter ask.

"Hey, yeah, of course. I'm fine," Sam replied. The sinister tone she had used to threaten Zyir had changed. He shook his head. She was good at playing her role. She deserved an Academy Award for the performance she was putting on for Carter. Everything in him wanted to stand tall and back out on the federal deal he had made, but some things couldn't be undone. He had folded, and no matter what his reasons had been, he would forever be labeled a traitor.

He waited until Carter and Sam went back outside before he emerged from his hiding spot.

In his frustration he punched the wall to blow off some steam, wondering how he had gotten caught up in the first place. Things had spiraled out of control so quickly and now his back was against the wall. He exhaled deeply and then rejoined the party, stepping up to Carter. As soon as he stepped up, Sam dismissed herself, leaving the two with nothing but the opportunity to talk.

Zyir followed Carter's gaze until his own eyes fell upon Miamor, who stood courtside cheering on the game that was going on between Fly Boogie and C.J. "I'm surprised you haven't choked that nigga out yet," Zyir said.

"She's not mine anymore," Carter said.

"Then how come you can't stop looking at her?" Zyir asked knowingly.

"Lil' nigga want to do business. He got the plug on the pills. Monroe is all in. Monroe wants to pull me back in. . . ." Carter let his words drift off. He really couldn't imagine getting back into the streets. They had burned him. He knew the streets had no love for him. The only thing they hadn't done was claim his life. If he kept trying his luck, eventually he would meet an early grave . . . just like his father.

"I ain't gon' lie. Shit in Flint ain't laying like that. Your bro would appreciate if you did decide to come back in for one last run," Zyir stated. "We came up doing this shit. You can run this shit in your sleep. You've been gone for three years, fam, and spent five years locked·up before that. Imagine how good it would feel to have that old thang back. The power. We ran this bitch before everything got hectic and I hate to admit it, but the pill shit is the new crack. Your man might be onto something with that."

Carter was unmoved, but Zyir knew him well enough to know that even if he was contemplating coming out of retirement, it would be a silent brooding. Carter was the type to make moves, not announcements, so only time would tell if he was buying what Zyir was selling. "I'm just saying, give it some thought," Zyir said convincingly. He felt like a piece of shit for going against the grain. Carter was more than an associate; they were brothers. Carter had groomed Zyir. He had taught him everything that he knew. They were family before either of them had ever even uttered the word "cartel," and now it had all been re-duced to this. Zyir realized that they were living their last days. The DEA had a hard-on for all of them, and after they made their move, their lives would never be the same.

* * *

Fly Boogie grabbed his keys from the valet and then waited for Miamor and C.J. as they said their good-byes. He stood patiently at the passenger side of the car as Miamor stood in front of Carter.

"So what's the plan? I guess we need to talk about ar-rangements for C.J.?" Miamor asked.

"I want him with me," Carter said in a low tone.

She sighed because she knew this would be an issue. "Carter, that's not happening. You know that I will never keep him from you, but he's my baby. I need him with me," she said.

"In L.A.?" Carter asked.

She nodded.

Carter sighed. "I want him every weekend. I'll come get him Fridays and drop him off at school on Mondays," he said.

She nodded. "I don't have to tell you to take care of yourself," Carter said, looking at her. They were both aware that everyone's eyes were on them. Sam, Fly, even C.J. was watching them closely.

"Carter, all you have to do is tell me to come home. Forgive me and tell me to leave him," she whispered.

"That's not my place anymore," he stated, his tone cold.

Miamor knew that she had placed layers of hurt onto him. She didn't know if he would ever see her the way that he used to. "It will always be your place," she whispered. She turned. "C.J., come tell Daddy bye."

C.J. ran up and stuck out his balled fist. Carter chuckled. "You dapping it out now, huh?" Carter asked, amused at how much his son had grown up.

"Yeah, all that mushy stuff is for suckers. Fly says it ain't gangster," C.J. said.

"Fly says, huh?" Carter mumbled. He pulled his son in by the hook of his head and gave him a hug. "I'll be there every weekend to get you. Take care of your mama, a'ight?"

C.J. nodded, and Carter kissed the top of his head before he ran to get into the car.

Monroe stepped next to Carter and put a firm hand on his shoulder. "Yo, Fly!" he called.

Fly turned around after helping Miamor into the car. "I put a little something in the trunk for you," Monroe said.

Fly nodded his head and then hopped in the driver's seat and pulled away.

* * *

Fly rubbed his hands together as he popped the trunk. Monroe was about his paper and he was excited about the possibility of getting money together. He hadn't expected Monroe to send him back to Cali with a trunk full of bricks, but he was more than ready for the load . . . even if he had to drive them all the way back to L.A. himself.

He pulled up the trunk in excitement. "Oh, shit!" he shouted as he stumbled backward, in shock at the "package" Monroe had left him. Inside lay one of his goons, specifically the one Carter had checked at the party. His body was cut up in pieces and wrapped in plastic. He had paid a hefty price for his disrespect. Fly slammed the trunk in frustration. He was his own man now. He had power and money, but he would never be on the level of Carter Jones, and he knew that in order to keep Miamor, he would have to be. She had a thing for street kings.

CHAPTER 13

Miamor stepped into her walk-in closet, but instead of shoes and bags, it was filled with handguns and choppers. She felt a presence behind her and turned to see Fly. His lean frame was covered in tattoos, and he gave her a sexy grin as he walked up on her.

"He has a mom who has a closet full of guns," she said. "I'm going to ruin my baby."

"Nah, ma," Fly replied as he pulled her close, pulling her into him. "You're good. He's good. I'mma make sure of that."

Miamor exhaled deeply. She wished that his words held as much weight as he would like them to, but truth was, they didn't. The only man she had ever sought approval from was Carter Jones, and Fly was a far cry in comparison. Every part of her wanted to fly to Colorado and get her man, but Carter had been clear. *He's not fucking with me,* she thought. Carter's rejection stung, but she had a man in front of her who wanted her. He had literally done the impossible just to be with her when he killed Baraka. He had returned C.J. to her, making her feel forever indebted to him. That alone made her feel like she was obligated to give him a chance. He wanted to be her man and in fact he was a good man. He just wasn't Carter. *No one ever will be,* she thought as she halfheartedly hugged Fly.

He noticed her lack of enthusiasm. In fact, he had noticed it ever since she had reconnected with Carter. He stepped back. "You a'ight?"

She nodded. "I'm fine."

"I'm not Carter. All I can do is be me, Miamor," he stated knowingly.

"That's all you need to be," she reassured him.

"I've got the money, the power, but I can't compete with history. If you gon' run back to that man, do that now. Don't be here doing this with me and then one day I look up and you're gone," Fly stated.

"I'm here, I'm with you," she stated.

"A'ight," he said as he kissed her lips.

"I've got to hit the blocks, but I can drop little homie off at school if you want," he offered.

This was why she appreciated him. Fly was great with C.J. He was attentive and went above and beyond to connect with her son. She nodded. "You're good with him," she said with a smile.

"I can be good with another one, too," he said.

Her brow raised in shock.

"I want a baby, Miamor, and I want her to look like you," he said as he boldly palmed the V between her legs.

He had caught her off guard and she didn't know how to respond. She honestly couldn't see herself having children by any other man than Carter. She had never even wanted children. She had made an exception for him. She couldn't commit the same to Fly. Her mouth fell open in satisfaction as Fly Boogie got on his knees and pulled her satin panties to the side, placing his face right in her pleasure. "This is my pussy, Miamor. Can't nobody make it feel as good as me," he mumbled as he ate a full course of her, bringing her to an earth-shattering orgasm right there in her closet.

Fly may not have been her soul mate, but he knew exactly how to please her. *God, that tongue is golden,* she thought as she used her bloodred fingertip to wipe herself off his lips. He wasn't good enough to put a baby in her, but he was good enough to keep making her scream while he tried. She made a mental note to get on birth control. She wouldn't insult him by asking him to strap up, but having another child wasn't on the agenda—at least not for her.

* * *

C.J. rode in the car, silent as he watched the L.A. streets fly by in a blur outside his window. After being away from home for so long, it felt odd to be back.

"You quiet over there, lil' homie, you good?" Fly asked as he maneuvered the car through the busy streets.

"Yeah, I'm good," C.J. said, poking out his bird chest.

He liked riding with Fly. Fly treated him like he was his right-hand man.

"You ready for your first day?" Fly asked.

"Not really," C.J. said. "It's the middle of the year. Everybody already has their crew picked out."

"You worried about fitting in, huh?" Fly said.

Not wanting to seem like he was pressed, the young C.J. said, "Nah, I don't care. I'm just saying. Everybody already got they crew." He kept his chin up, but Fly could tell by the look in his eyes that C.J. was nervous.

"Look, you in what? Third grade, lil' homie? Elementary school is simple. Whoever has the freshest gear gets the most girls and has the most friends," Fly said. "Simple as that."

"Oh, yeah?" C.J. asked, intrigued.

"Most definitely," Fly confirmed. "But first we got to get you out of them button-ups and schoolboy slacks your mama got you in. How about we play hooky today? I'll upgrade your clothes and you can spin through the hood with me today. Sound good?"

"Yeah, that sound good," C.J. said, excited.

Fly turned the car around and headed for Compton. "You ever held a gun, big man?" he asked.

"No," C.J. answered.

"Well, there's a first time for everything," Fly said as he reached under his seat and placed a gun in C.J.'s lap. "Hold on to that for me. That's for you. You riding through the hood with me means you're my right-hand man. Can you handle that?"

C.J. picked up the gun, the weight of it feeling heavy in his hands. He turned it sideways and pointed it at Fly. "Like this?"

Fly snatched the gun from C.J. "Never point a gun at me, C.J. Never," he said. He placed it back in the boy's lap. "Now pick it up, hold it straight, finger off the trigger. Only time you put your finger on the trigger is if you ready to shoot something, you understand?" Fly asked.

"Yes, sir," C.J. replied.

"Chill on that 'sir' shit. Save that for your old-ass daddy," Fly said slyly. "Now wrap your hand around the handle and place your free hand underneath for support."

C.J. did as he was told, but his hand shook, showing that he was intimidated.

"You scared? What you scared of? You the one with the gun. You're the man as long as you got that," Fly said. "You see that red dot on the side?"

C.J. nodded.

"That's the safety. Red means dead . . . that's all you have to remember. You see red and it's ready to fire," Fly said. "Now flip the safety and keep that on you for a little bit. The longer you hold it, the more comfortable you'll get with it."

Fly pulled up to a house in the middle of Compton and parked on the street. "I won't be long. Stay in the car. Keep your eyes open, lil' man."

C.J. watched Fly until he disappeared inside. His eyes scanned the block while gripping the gun in his hands. His heart was beating so fast that it felt like it would beat out of

his chest. Excitement and anxiety had his head on a swivel
as he surveyed everything moving around him. He was so
ready to prove himself that he would have popped off on
anyone who walked by. Luckily it was early morning and
nothing on the block was moving besides the early morning fiends out to score a hit. C.J. had never even been on this
side of town. He was born into privilege. He had no idea
about the way the other side lived. Being in Compton was
like being in a ghost town. He wouldn't admit it, but he
didn't like it. After what felt like forever, Fly came back out,
carrying a book bag. He slid into the driver's seat and passed
the bag to C.J.

"What's inside?" C.J. asked.

"Open it up," Fly said.

C.J. unzipped the book bag and inside lay thousands of
pills. From Xanex to Percocet to Adderall, the colors popped
out at him. Each prescription was in a different clear Zip-
loc bag.

"That's a quarter-million dollars in your hand, lil' homie,"
Fly said.

"Looks like candy," C.J. said.

"It's nothing like candy. You never use the shit you sell.
That shit will fuck your head up," Fly warned.

C.J. was intrigued by the fact that every single pill inside the bag was worth cash money. If there was one thing he
had inherited from his father, it was the love for the flip.
Hustling was in his genes. Fly saw the look in the young
boy's eyes and he grabbed the backpack and placed it in the
backseat. "Now put your seat belt on. Let's get you fresh."

* * *

Fly Boogie pulled in front of the shoe store and parked curbside. He pulled out a wad of money and peeled off ten crispy hundred-dollar bills. He handed them to C.J. "This is enough to buy whatever you want," Fly said casually. "Put your money in your pocket. Never let another nigga count your pockets."

C.J. nodded. He was soaking up every word that Fly said. They hopped out and walked into the store.

"Hey Fly," one of the sales girls greeted him. He was a sneaker head and would come through and easily clear out the store. They knew him well, especially the pretty, young girls in the store. "This your son?" the girl asked.

"This my little homie," Fly introduced. "Tryna get him out of this schoolboy shit." He turned toward C.J. "You see something you like?"

C.J. picked up a retro sneaker. "These?" he suggested.

Fly Boogie nodded while distractedly texting in his phone. "He'll take everything on that wall. Measure his foot and bag us up."

C.J. thought Fly Boogie was the coolest dude he knew. He wasn't old like his father or uncles. He didn't walk around in suits and shiny shoes. Fly Boogie's youthful appearance and casual swag made him more relatable to C.J.

Fly turned around and noticed a police officer approaching his car. He walked outside. "Yo, Officer, that's me," Fly Boogie said. "Is there a problem?"

"You've got some ID?" the officer asked.

Fly Boogie frowned. He wanted to ask why he needed identification, but considering what he had in the car, he wasn't going to cause a scene. "I'm getting ready to reach in my back pocket for my wallet," Fly informed him, not wanting to give this officer any reason to pop off. In his eyes, all cops were the enemy and the LAPD was the dirtiest gang in the game. He moved more carefully around them than around the goons he sold to. He pulled out his license and passed it to the officer. "I'll be right back," the officer said, retreating to his car.

C.J. and the sales girl came out of the store carrying several bags filled with shoes. C.J. went for the car, but Fly Boogie placed a hand on his chest, holding him back.

"Hold up, C.J.," he said, now wishing he had just dropped the kid off at school. Things could be real bad if the officer came back with a hostile agenda. The officer took his time running Fly's plates and checking his name, but Fly didn't budge. For twenty minutes he stood on the curb unmoved, because he knew the cop wanted to rise a reaction out of him. It didn't matter to Fly Boogie. He would play the waiting game all day. He wasn't like most hood dudes who reacted first and thought later. He would remain compliant if that meant he would leave with his life and without his hands in silver cuffs.

The officer came back over and reluctantly gave him his license back. "Move the car. This isn't a parking spot," he grumbled before retreating back to the squad car.

Fly hustled C.J. into the car and hurriedly pulled away

from the block. He wasn't even two blocks away before C.J. said, "Fly, the police are behind us again."

"Shit," Fly said. He peered in his rearview. The cop had let him go only to call in to another patrol and have him harassed again. He wanted to peel off, but with Miamor's son beside him, he decided to play it cool. "Reach in the backseat, C.J. Grab the book bag, put the gun inside," he said as he pulled another burner off his waistline, passing it to C.J. "Put that one in there, too, and put it on your back."

C.J. hurriedly did as he was told.

Fly Boogie pulled over. A coal-sized lump formed in his throat as he gripped the steering wheel nervously. "Just be cool," he said, speaking more to himself than to C.J.

The officer got out of the car and Fly could tell by the way he gripped the pistol on his hip that this wasn't a routine stop. "I need to see your hands!" the cop shouted as he approached the car. He pulled his gun, and Fly Boogie stuck both hands out of his window. "The passenger, too!"

"He's an eight-year-old kid!" Fly Boogie yelled back.

"Out of the vehicle," the officer said, pulling open the driver-side door. Fly Boogie stepped out as the officer roughly slammed him against the car. C.J. wasn't sure what he should do. A crowd began to form as the officer roughhoused Fly Boogie in broad daylight. "What you got on you? Huh? Drugs? Is there anything in the car that I should know about?" the officer asked as he frisked Fly Boogie.

Fly Boogie gave him the grim face and didn't respond. He simply stared straight ahead as he was shaken down.

C.J. eased out of the car with the book bag on his back and assimilated into the growing crowd. The officer noticed and yelled, "Kid! Back in the car! Now!" He twisted Fly Boogie's arms behind his back and slammed him on the hood of the car. The cuffs were so tight on his wrists that they cut into his skin like razors. C.J. watched on in horror. He took a step back into the crowd. "Hey, kid!" The cop started toward C.J., and Fly Boogie rose up, fighting against the officer's force to create a distraction.

C.J. took off down the block, running full speed. His heart pumped, and adrenaline coursed through him as he cut through the bodega. He was running with so much speed that he knocked over a display.

"Hey!" the store clerk shouted, but C.J. was already out the back door. He never looked back to see that he had already shaken the officer. He ran down the alley and came out on the next street. He spotted a bus up ahead. By the time he made it to it, he was out of breath.

He pulled out a pocket full of money. His hands were so shaky, he could barely thumb through the bills that Fly had given him. The bus driver frowned in concern. "This is the wrong side of town to be pulling out so much money," the older black gentleman said. "You in some kind of trouble?"

"No, I'm just trying to get to school," C.J. lied as he stuffed the bills in his jean pockets and then held out a hundred-dollar bill.

"Keep it, kid," the man said. He pointed directly to the seat behind him. "You have a seat right here. What's the name of your school?"

"Brookdale Academy," he answered.

"I'll make sure you get there," the man said.

C.J. sighed in relief as he held on to the book bag for dear life. He had been so terrified that he had to blink away his tears. He had no idea what was going to happen to Fly Boogie. He wanted to call his mother, but if he did, she would know that he had ditched school, so instead he went to school. He would meet her outside afterward like it was just an ordinary day. Only problem was, it wasn't and he had a bag full of pills and guns that he didn't know what to do with.

The bus driver finished his route, letting all of his passengers off until only C.J. remained. It was the first time that C.J. had been to these neighborhoods. The graffiti, the seedy characters, the old school cars and loud music . . . it all intrigued him. Coming up as a son in The Cartel, he only knew about the wealth. He hadn't witnessed the come-up, but riding through the hood made him wish he was from the other side. He had no idea the people trapped in the struggle yearned for the life he had. Miamor and Carter had sold their souls to make sure he didn't live the hard-knock life, and here he was craving a piece of it. The bus driver turned off his service light and then made the hike all the way to the Baldwin Hills, where the bourgeois school was located. C.J. got off at the corner. "Thanks," he said as he passed the old man a hundred-dollar bill and then rushed off.

C.J. headed into school. What he didn't realize was his new school had a no-loitering policy and his presence in the hallways midday made him stand out. The principal spotted him as soon as he stepped inside.

"Mr. Jones, you're late on your very first day."

C.J.'s eyes widened as he stopped walking midstep.

"I'm Mr. Simpson, headmaster here," he introduced himself. He held out his hand for the young boy. C.J. reluctantly shook it as he grasped the straps to the book bag. "Let's get you to class. I'll show you where your locker is. We don't allow book bags to be carried during school hours. You can keep it in your locker and carry your books to class," he informed him.

C.J. nodded and nervously let Mr. Simpson lead him to his locker. He held out his hand. "Book bag?" Mr. Simpson asked. He reached to take the book bag off of C.J.'s back. C.J. snatched it away, shrugging him off, hard.

"I got it," C.J. said.

The principal frowned, but didn't press the young man. They located his locker. "You can pick up a lock from the main office after school. For now, your belongings should be okay without one."

"I need a lock," C.J. pushed as he slid his shoulders out of the straps.

"I assure you," Mr. Simpson said, "no one will go into your locker. We have a zero-tolerance policy for theft." He reached down to grab the book bag from C.J., who snatched it out of his hands. This time, the principal didn't let go. "C.J., let go of the book bag."

"I just need a lock!" C.J. said urgently. He pulled on it, trying to get it out of his principal's grasp, causing the zipper to break. The guns and pills spilled out all over the floor.

Mr. Simpson looked at the contents in shock and quickly

apprehended C.J. "Step back. Over there, sit down on the floor," he said sternly.

Tears welled in C.J.'s eyes and he gritted his teeth, but he did as he was told. He knew he was in trouble and as he watched school security arrive on the scene, he lowered his head, afraid of the consequences to come.

CHAPTER 14

"Where is my son?" Miamor asked the officer sitting at the reception desk inside the precinct. "I've been waiting here for two hours. Where is he?!" Her patience was nonexistent, and anger burned in her eyes.

"He's being processed, miss," the officer said. "When I have more information, I'll provide you with it. Until then, sit down."

Miamor's temper was threatening to boil over, and she had to remind herself that she was standing in the middle of a police precinct. "Listen, you fat, bald, incompetent—"

"Miamor."

Miamor turned around to see Carter standing behind her with his legal bulldog, Einstein, beside him. Carter was clean and dapper as ever in his Tom Ford suit. The beard was gone, and the sadness that had filled his eyes had been replaced by a look of anger. He stood before her strong, shoulders squared, and with an expression that said he wasn't beat for the bullshit. She hadn't seen this version of him in years. He had been holed up in the mountains for so long that she had hardly recognized him before, but this power-ful man in front of her was the Carter she knew. Everything about him signified power. The look of anger that burned in his eyes told her that he would handle this. His presence brought her instant relief.

"Thank God," she whispered as she walked over to him.

"Don't worry. I'll have C.J. out of here within the hour," Einstein said as he left the two standing alone in the lobby to talk.

"What happened?" Carter asked.

Miamor was so flustered that all she could do was shake her head. "I don't know. Fly dropped him off at school this morning and next thing I know, I'm getting calls that he's been arrested and that there were drugs and guns in his book bag," she said.

"Where that nigga at?" Carter asked. He wanted to gather all of the information before he reacted. He could easily piece the day's events together on his own, but he didn't jump to conclusions. He wasn't the assuming type. He would rather hear the facts so that he could handle things accordingly.

"I've been calling him all day. I don't know," Miamor admitted.

"Go home," Carter instructed. "I'll get C.J. and I'll bring him to you."

"I want to stay," she said.

"I said I'll handle it," Carter assured her. His word was law. Even after all this time, when he spoke, she listened. She left the station with the utmost confidence that Carter would get their son out of the sticky predicament.

When Miamor was out of sight, Carter walked up to the same officer at the front reception desk. "How are you?" he asked.

"What can I help you with, sir?" the officer asked without looking up from the computer screen he was working on.

Carter handed the officer his identification. "Run that name through your system," he said.

The officer frowned. "Have a seat, sir." The no-nonsense tone of the officer told Carter that the man had little patience. He was too tired, had worked long hours, and was underpaid. He wasn't going above and beyond for the badge. He was just there for a paycheck.

Carter leaned over the counter and lowered his tone. "You want to know exactly who you're talking to before you open your mouth," Carter said.

The officer wanted to beat his chest and stand behind the authority in his badge, but something told him the man in front of him should be taken seriously. He snatched the driver's license off the counter reluctantly and typed the name into the computer database. Carter's entire rap sheet came up. Even crimes that he hadn't been convicted of lit up the screen.

Murder

Drug trafficking

Intent to distribute

Head of a criminal enterprise

Illegal firearms

Everything that the feds wished they could stick to him illuminated the screen in front of the man.

"Don't fuck with me," Carter stated as he stared at him maliciously, without blinking. "And the woman who just walked out of here . . . next time, you show her more respect. I want my son in my presence in the next ten minutes or you're going to have a problem, Officer Jenson," he said, reading his name tag.

The man's skin turned beet red from sheer intimidation. Carter didn't even blink until the cop lowered his head in submission. Carter turned on his Prada loafers and walked over to the waiting area. "Pussy," he mumbled. Before he could even sit down, Einstein was walking out with C.J. The boy ran over to his father, hugging him. Carter could see the dried tears on his face and the terrified look in his eyes.

"This is bad, Carter. I have lunch with the prosecuting attorney tomorrow. I'll find out how much it's going to cost to make this thing go away. He had two handguns and a shitload of pills in his backpack," Einstein revealed.

"Take care of it," Carter stated. He looked down at C.J. "You know we've got to talk, right?"

"Yes, sir," C.J. answered.

Carter grabbed his son by the back of the neck gently but sternly as he guided him out of the precinct. He didn't speak until they were in his car. Disappointment filled him. He had never even felt this type of letdown before. It was a different kind of feeling. He had done so many bad things in his lifetime that he had lost count, but to witness his son going down a path of destruction broke his heart. He was silent partly because he didn't know what to say.

"I'm trying real hard to keep my anger under control right now, C.J. I provide the very best for you. I've done certain things so that you won't have to. I've lived a certain lifestyle that I never want you to emulate. I want you to know that as long as you tell me the truth, you'll never get in trouble. I'll never punish you as long as you keep it straight up with me. You understand?" Carter asked.

C.J. nodded.

"Nah, you a man. You don't answer me with no head nod. Now I'm going to ask you again. Do you understand?" Carter reiterated.

"Yes, sir," C.J. replied.

"Now what happened? Where did the drugs and guns come from? I think I have an idea, but I want you to tell me," Carter said sternly as they pulled away from the police station.

C.J. was quiet as he thought about lying to Carter. He didn't want to say anything to get Fly Boogie in trouble. "I'm not a snitch," C.J. said as he looked out the window. "So whatever punishment you give me, I'll take."

Carter didn't know if he should be livid or proud. "I

respect that," Carter said. He didn't need C.J. to lay out the story, anyway. The moment his attorney had said C.J. was caught with pills in his book bag, Carter knew who was to blame: Fly Boogie. "Drugs aren't cool, C.J. Guns are dangerous. They don't make you tough. Pulling a trigger is one of the most cowardly things you can do. That takes no thought, no strength. It's stupid. You're my son. You're a future king. No son of mine will use drugs or sell drugs . . . ever."

"I wasn't," C.J. said in a low tone. He looked over at Carter. "Why can't I have a gun if you carry one?"

Carter sighed because he knew that one day he would have to answer for the things he had done. "I know how and when to shoot a gun, C.J. I know the responsibility that comes with carrying one. When you're old enough I'll teach you how to handle a gun and who to and not to aim one at, but that's not for you right now. I don't need you running around L.A. playing cowboy. I want you to enjoy being a kid. You have the rest of your life to be a man; you only have a few short years to enjoy your childhood. You understand?" Carter asked.

C.J. nodded. "Yes, sir."

Carter reached over and pulled his son's head across the seat, kissing the top of it. "I wish I didn't have to carry a gun, C.J. I wish I were the type of man who led the type of lifestyle that didn't require protection. I wish I had the luxury to live by the letter of the law instead of against it. You can grow up to be that type of man. You're supposed to be better than me."

They were silent the entire ride home. Carter had thought he had a few more years before the allure of the street began to entice his son. It was happening too early and it was heartbreaking. Carter didn't want C.J. following in his footsteps. He wanted the streets to be a mystery to his son. His hustle wasn't something he wanted to pass down to his son. Carter knew exactly who had caused this to happen. Fly Boogie was the only person he had words for at the moment. When Carter pulled up to Miamor's home, he could hear an argument brewing on the inside.

"What the fuck were you thinking? Giving my son your shit to hold?" Miamor screamed. She was so loud, her voice carried through the stillness of the suburban neighborhood.

"You think I meant for this to happen? The cops were fucking with me! I was just trying to show him the hood," Fly argued back. "I sat in the fucking bull pen for hours. I ain't feeling this noise right now. All this fucking yapping! It was a mistake! I fucked up! Damn!"

C.J. looked down at his feet. "They never argue. They're arguing because of me," he said, feeling guilty.

Carter shook his head. "They're arguing because Fly Boogie made some bad decisions today. This isn't on you, lil' man," Carter replied. He tried the door. Finding it unlocked, he walked inside. His presence caused an awkward silence to fill the room.

"Niggas don't knock no more?" Fly Boogie asked as he mean-mugged Carter, who scoffed in dismissal.

"Oh baby boy, come here," Miamor said, sighing in relief as she rushed to C.J.'s side.

"Go put him to bed," Carter stated to Miamor as if he had just walked into his own house and not that of another man's.

"Carter . . ." Miamor said, knowing that leaving the two men in the same room alone was not a good idea—not after tonight.

Carter nodded his head, signaling for her to remove their son, and she reluctantly walked out, steering C.J. up the stairs to his bedroom.

"You asked my son to hold your drugs? A hundred thousand dollars' worth of pills in an eight-year-old's school book bag? You put guns in his hands. You got him out here skipping school. I can hear it in his voice that you got him thinking that shit is cool. I'm trying to think of one reason why I shouldn't put you in the dirt," Carter said in a low tone, hands in the pockets of his designer slacks as he walked around the living room, admiring the art that hung on the walls.

"This ain't Nevada and it damn sure ain't Miami, my nigga. L.A. is my city. You can't bury me in my own back-yard," Fly shot back, mugging Carter. He had tried to take him out of the game before, but Carter seemed to have nine lives. Unbeknownst to Carter, he was standing in a room with the man who had shot him. There was larceny in the air. He had no idea the lengths to which Fly Boogie would go to get him out of Miamor's life.

"Let's be clear, little nigga. The only reason I haven't stepped to you yet is because you brought my son back home. That don't give you unlimited passes with me. You want to be me, nigga? You fucking my bitch, trying to play a part for my son, you in these streets trying to build yourself your very own empire just like me . . . so move like me, you unoriginal ass mu'fucka. That woman and that little boy upstairs are my family. They will always be my family. I protected them at all costs."

"That protection was lacking when it came to the Saudis. You wasn't protecting shit. You couldn't stop shit. Baraka took your son and exiled your bitch until I made that shit disappear," Fly Boogie stated arrogantly.

Carter stepped toward Fly Boogie until they were standing toe-to-toe. "You begging me to tag your toes. You better tread lightly," Carter said in a serious tone. "Let's be clear. If you ever put my son in jeopardy again, I will kill you."

"Carter." Miamor stood at the top of the steps looking down at the ego battle between the two men. He looked up at her. "It's been a long day. Maybe you should go."

Carter looked back at Fly Boogie. "We gon' finish this," he said.

"Indeed," Fly Boogie replied arrogantly as Carter headed for the door. Watching him swagger out made Miamor's stomach clench. God knew she just wanted to be with him, but their time had passed. There was no point in forcing something that he had so clearly claimed to not want.

As she watched Carter, Fly Boogie watched her, and he was livid. No matter how much he was there for her, how much love he gave, how much work he put in to being her man . . . she would never look at him with the longing she reserved for Carter. She had a godlike complex when it came to Carter, and Fly Boogie, although a suitable replacement, would never quite measure up. In matters of the heart, you can't compete where you don't compare. Fly Boogie and Carter weren't even in the same league.

"You know how to find me," Carter said as he turned to look at her. "I'll be by in the morning to pick C.J. up."

She nodded and as he walked out the door, her heart sank into her stomach.

Miamor came down the steps. These were the types of problems she didn't know how to fix. The tension that was building between Fly Boogie and Carter would eventually lead to disaster. She didn't know how to remedy that, and she didn't know whose side to pick. Her son was in trouble, her man was jealous of her ex, and she had no idea how to make him feel secure. Carter hated her for things she could not change. These were grown-woman problems. She wished it was something that a bullet could solve. That's where her expertise lay, in the streets. This new level of grown-woman responsibilities overwhelmed her in a way that she had never experienced before.

"You need to remember who the fuck here with you every day holding shit down on a regular. The least you can do is hide the fucking stars in your eyes," Fly Boogie said in a low, menacing tone as he stood directly in her face. "That nigga ain't the only nigga getting money. He ain't the only nigga with muscle. He don't go the juice no more. That's me. It's my time, but you too busy living in the past with that muthafucka to see that I'm trying. Got that nigga coming in my shit, disrespecting me. You lucky I don't slap the shit out of you."

Miamor was taken aback by his aggression. She snaked her neck because she knew that he had to have bumped his head. "You need to remember who you're talking to. I'm going to walk away from you right now because things can get ugly between us real quick. I don't do this arguing thing, so if you can't control your jealousy and check this temper—"

Fly Boogie put his hand around Miamor's neck, stopping her mid-sentence. He pressed her against the wall hard as he pushed his body into her. "I'm not done talking," he said through clenched teeth. "I know who you are, but remember you're not a nigga, Miamor. You're only tough with a pistol in your hands, ma. I'm all man. You can't overpower me," he said as she pushed against him, struggling to get him off of her. He was right. His strength overwhelmed her. "Ain't no pistols in sight. I did everything for you. I murdered Baraka for you. I saved your fucking son and came to get you from that crazy nigga Murder. I knew you wouldn't let that Cartel shit go. Carter got you wrapped around his fucking finger. He cheated on you and then left you to die at Baraka's hands. I saved you. I came back for you. I put a hole in that nigga chest and he didn't die. I should have put one in his head. Next time, I won't miss," Fly Boogie threatened as he curled his fingers in a pretend gun and placed them against her forehead, point-blank range.

Miamor's eyes widened in shock as Fly Boogie revealed

the truth to her. *He shot Carter,* she thought with a gasp. "You shot him? All this time, it was you? You fucking bastard. He fed you!" Miamor whispered in a sharp tone as her temper erupted.

"Don't look surprised, ma. I'll get rid of anyone who stops me from fucking with you. So when I say control those fucking googly eyes, you should check that. I don't want to have to make C.J. a fatherless child. You're either with me or you with him. You can't have both," Fly Boogie said.

This revelation turned all the affection she felt for Fly Boogie into contempt. Miamor had assumed that it had been Baraka who had gunned Carter down in front of the casino years ago, but now she had been smacked with the truth. She had been the cause of that and ever since she had been unknowingly sleeping with the enemy.

"Mama?" C.J. called from the top of the steps.

Fly Boogie immediately loosened his hold on her neck, but he didn't move. He had her cornered against the wall. "Go upstairs, C.J.," Miamor said.

"But, ma," he protested.

"Now!" Miamor roared.

Miamor wasn't the chick to tolerate this change in temperament from Fly Boogie. There wasn't anything to think about. On Carter's worst day, Fly Boogie didn't measure up. She liked him. He had helped her get her head right when everyone else in the world had thrown her away, but she couldn't turn a blind eye to the fact that he had shot Carter. Despite everything, Carter would always be the man she loved. She wasn't doing this Helen of Troy shit. She didn't want to be the woman in the middle . . . there was no middle. She would always be aligned on Carter's side. "I choose him," Miamor said. She head-butted Fly Boogie with all her might, causing stars to appear before her eyes.

"Agh!" he shouted in pain as he grabbed the bridge of his bleeding nose. Miamor stumbled to the kitchen and reached under the sink, pulling out a 9mm pistol. She could never truly leave her past behind her. She had to have guns placed strategically around the house just to feel safe, and today she was grateful for the habit. Revenge was on her mind. Anger pulsed through her. Perhaps she had played the wifey role for too long. Clearly Fly had forgotten how she got down. This was what she did. Committing murder was like riding a bike for her. She would never forget how to do it. "What the fuck, Miamor? Damn!" Fly Boogie said, using hushed tones. "You gon' shoot me? Over a nigga who set you out for the wolves?" She aimed at him. "You pull that trigger, ma, and C.J.'s going to hear the shot. You're going to destroy his entire world. He don't deserve that. He's already been through enough. Now you want him witnessing bodies in the place he lays his head?"

Miamor curled her finger around the trigger. She wanted to dead him where he stood, but he was right. C.J. would hear it and once witnessed, murder was something one never forgot. He had already had his childhood taken away after witnessing Leena's death. Miamor wouldn't let that happen again. She placed the gun on the counter, but never took her hand off of it.

"Fuck!" Fly Boogie grimaced as he snatched a paper

towel off the counter and nursed his face. "You ain't got to go for broke, ma. Damn! Head-butting me and shit." We can fix this. All the shit I've done for you, it ain't good for nothing?" he asked. "I think you broke my shit." He grimaced.

Miamor lowered her head, conflicted. "It counts. It could have meant a lot, Fly. You could have gotten to my heart without shooting Carter. He taught you the game. Him. Zyir. Monroe. They all brought you in, and you put a bullet in his chest," Miamor said with tears forming in her eyes. That bullet had changed the course of Carter's life. "He hasn't been the same since," she whispered. "All because you wanted to, what? Fuck me? Be with me? You could have killed him." The more she spoke, the more she realized how she was to blame. She had allowed Fly Boogie to get close to her. She had even flirted with him, enjoying the attention that he gave her. She had strung him along way before he ever got his shot with her, and it had led to this . . . to deception and disloyalty. *Maybe Carter is right . . . nothing good comes from loving me,* she thought.

Miamor opened the kitchen drawer and she began searching for something.

"He don't deserve you, Miamor. I love you. All of this was for us. You just have to let that nigga go. Ride for me, ma. Nobody knows about what I did but me and you. It doesn't have to go any further than these walls," Fly Boogie tried to convince. "You're not his girl anymore. You owe me."

"You're right. I would never let C.J. hear gunshots thundering through his home," she said. "If Carter was any other nigga, maybe I would be thanking you, but he's not.

Everything you did after shooting him means nothing anymore. Because you brought my son back to me, I'm going to do you a favor and make this quick. You should be thanking me . . . because if I told Carter, it would be much worse."

Fly Boogie's eyes widened when she pulled a silencer out of the drawer and screwed it onto the barrel of the gun. Fly Boogie lunged for her, but before he could even get too close, she let loose.

PSST!

One bullet was all it took to leave him slumped on the kitchen floor. Miamor grabbed her handbag and car keys, then rushed up to C.J.'s room. "Come on, baby boy, let's go," she said as she hustled him out of bed.

"Where are we going?" he asked, confused as she led him toward the back of the house and out the back door.

"We're going to see your dad. He wants you to stay with him tonight," she said as they got into the car and sped off into the night.

CHAPTER 15

When Carter opened the door to see his son standing before him, he frowned. He opened it and pulled him inside. "What's going on?" Carter asked. He stepped out onto the front porch and saw Miamor sitting in her car stoically. She was looking straight ahead as if she were in a trance. Carter immediately knew that something was wrong. "Go in and get comfortable, man. I'll be right back," Carter said as he slipped into his loafers and stepped out into the night. Miamor was the only person who knew exactly where to find him. As soon as he found out his son was still alive and would be living with Miamor in L.A., he had purchased a modest spot in West Hollywood. He spent the majority of his time in Colorado, out of sight, where he could have peace of mind, but he planned to make the trip to Cali every weekend to see his son. He walked out and approached her. He could tell from her body language that something bad had occurred. He opened her door and knelt down beside the car.

"Mia," he said. There was just something about this woman that he found completely endearing. He hated that he had to hate her, because all he really wanted to do was love her.

She gripped the steering wheel as thoughts of indecision, regret, and sadness filled her. Even when she tried to be better, trouble always followed her. "When you got shot in Vegas, we thought it was Baraka's order," Miamor whispered. She looked into Carter's eyes as she finished. "It wasn't. It was Fly."

Carter stood to his feet, looking at her, shocked. "And you fucked with him after the fact? He shot me and you became his bitch? We were going through the divorce. Did you set it up?"

"No!" she shouted as she stepped out of the car. "I don't care what happens between us, I would never want to see you dead! You know me better than that."

"I'm going to murk that nigga," Carter threatened.

Miamor quickly responded, "It's already done."

"What did C.J. see?" Carter asked.

"Nothing," Miamor assured him.

"What did he hear?" Carter shot back.

"Nothing," she responded again.

"Miamor!" Carter said with urgency as if he didn't believe her.

"Nothing, Carter! He saw nothing. He knows nothing," she guaranteed.

"That was your man," Carter said.

"That was a mistake. A desperate attempt to replace a piece of my heart that you still own. You are my man," Miamor replied as she looked at him desperately, her chest heaving up, then down. "You'll always be my man."

Carter knew that living without Miamor at his side could not truly be called living. Without her, his life was calm, settled, ordinary, and safe. He knew he shouldn't want her, but he couldn't deny himself of her presence anymore. If loving her meant allowing danger to creep back into his life, then so be it. No matter how hard he tried to get her out of his system, he could never fully shake her. Miamor was like good dope. He just kept coming back. He rushed her, pushing her against her car, and kissed her passionately. She exhaled in relief as he wrapped his arms around her waist. This was home for her . . . he was home for her. They were each other's compass, and for the past three years they had been lost. Miamor was tired of fighting fate. With him was the only place she wanted to be. "You're going to be the death of me," Carter whispered, knowing that when his time did come, it would be because of something Miamor had done. It was just who she was. She wasn't his strength but his weakness. The euphoria that came from loving her made the inevitable worth it, however. It was easy to love someone when they were doing everything right. He had punished her when he had seen the worst version of her. After killing Yasmine, he had shunned her, blamed her for it all, when in actuality they had all played their part in that disaster. He wanted to love her right or wrong . . . ride with her the way that she had ridden for him tonight.

"Where's the body?" he asked. "At the house still?"

She nodded. He pulled her close and kissed her forehead. "Go inside. I'll have it taken care of." He watched her walk inside and he pulled out his phone to put in the call to his cleanup crew. They would make Miamor's indiscretions disappear. It was reasons like these that he was wary of their reunion. Already she had more blood on her hands. He hadn't been involved in anything illegal in years. He was trying to live his life right so that his son never had to pay for his own bad deeds, but here he was, letting Miamor lead him back to the darkness. Carter just wanted his entire family out of the game. As soon as this one deed was taken care of, he promised himself that he would take Miamor and his son back with him to Colorado, where they could all lead a normal existence.

* * *

"Well, would you look at that?" Sam said as she sat inside the inconspicuous car that was parked curbside up the block from Carter's place.

"Looks like he's cheating on you," her partner, Jacobs, said with a chuckle.

It was a joke, but Sam felt a jealousy stirring inside. It was something about deceiving Carter that made her job feel even more rewarding. She wanted him to love her as much as he possibly could before she finally put her cuffs around his wrists. She couldn't lie: It was hard to not fall for Carter Jones. On paper, he was a ruthless dictator of an infamous drug empire, but in the flesh, he was a king. He was considerate, generous, private, and gentle. She didn't love him, but she didn't hate him, either, and seeing his connection with the infamous leader of the Murder Mamas stirred an animosity within her. It didn't matter that what they had was an act. If it had been real, Carter would be betraying her in this moment.

"That's okay. That girl right there is the key to his downfall. Without her, he's a good man. With her, he's just who I need him to be to build this case. Three years is a lot of time to be in those mountains. I'm ready to be off this case, so however I can get him, I'll take it. I'm going to fry his ass."

* * *

That feeling. Aghh. The amazing feeling that pulsed through Miamor as she rode next to Carter in the backseat of the blacked-out SUV made her smile. He held her hand, intertwining their fingers as if he were afraid she would disappear if he didn't hold on to her.

"We got a lot to work out. We need to sit down and put everything on the table," Carter whispered.

Miamor nodded. "I know, but I don't care how hard it is. We'll work it out. Talk it out. Fight it out. Whatever. I just want this," she said as she stared sincerely at him. C.J. sat in the front seat, bugging the driver with all types of questions as they headed for the airport. This was how it was supposed to be all along. This felt like perfection.

"Do I need to worry about the therapist? How serious is that situation?" Miamor asked.

Carter shook his head. "Once you learn that you don't have any competition when it comes to my heart, you'll be good, ma. That was the problem with Yasmine. You weren't sure. This time you can be. Sam isn't an issue. I'll dead that. You have my word," he promised. He pulled her in for a kiss.

"Uh, Dad?" C.J. called as he pointed straight ahead.

Carter looked forward and frowned when he noticed the caravan of cars pull out in front of them, blocking their path. Instinct kicked in as both Carter and Miamor reached for their guns. Latino goons jumped out of cars. They were outnumbered and outgunned as the men surrounded the car, guns drawn and hanging at their sides.

"Who the fuck are they?" Miamor asked.

One of the men stepped up and shouted, "I'm looking for Carter Jones! We can do this the easy way and have a conversation like gentlemen, or I can sic my dogs on you and get at your wife and kid in the process."

"I don't know," Carter said as he popped open his car door. "Back up. Drive through them if you have to. Take them to the airport."

"What are you doing?!" Miamor shouted as she opened her door as well.

Carter pulled her back inside the car. "I'll meet you at the cabin," he said. "One gun or two, we're still on the losing end of this. Get in the car." His tone of voice left no room for negotiation.

She slammed her door. "You better meet us up there," she said as tears filled her eyes. "If something happens to you . . ."

"It won't," Carter said. He passed Miamor the gun, and their fingers touched. She closed her hand around his, tears forming in her eyes as he pulled away from her and closed the door.

* * *

Sam and Agent Jacobs watched in complete shock as a pillowcase was slipped over Carter's head and he was stuffed into the back of one of the cars.

"Do we want to intervene here? This looks gang affiliated," Jacobs said.

"No. He can handle himself. We'll fall back until I hear from him. He's bringing Miamor Jones and their child to Colorado. I'm sure I'll be receiving a breakup call soon," Sam said.

Sam had no idea what business Carter had with an L.A. street gang, but it was just one more stone to put in the pile that she was building. All incriminating evidence was good. She didn't want to swoop in and blow her cover until the time was just right. By that time, Carter would be in too deep to make a harrowing escape like he did the last time. There will be no missteps, no forgetting to Mirandize him, no hung jury. This time, Carter and the entire Cartel would lose, and justice would be served.

* * *

The smell of weed filled the air, and Carter's Italian shoes echoed against the concrete floor as he was escorted into the warehouse. His face was still covered, but he was unusually calm considering the circumstances. The pillowcase was snatched away and Carter stood in front of a man at a desk. A cigar hung out of the corner of his mouth. He didn't even look up at Carter when he began speaking. "I gave a package worth a hundred grand to a kid named Fly Boogie." He chuckled and shook his head in amusement. "I'll never understand the nicknames your people give themselves," he said. "I'm from the old school. Mexico. We had respectable names back then. Anyway, it disheartens me to find out my package was put in the hands of an eight-year-old boy . . . your eight-year-old boy." He paused to finally look at Carter. "He got caught with it, and my product is now in the hands of the LAPD. This angers me. Somebody owes me a debt, and seeing as how Fly Boogie was stupid enough to put my drugs in the hands of a kid, I can't work with him. Imagine my surprise when I did my research and found out that the little boy who got caught with my drugs is the son of the legendary Carter Jones."

"A hundred thousand is nothing. I'll cover my son's debt," Carter said.

"Of course you will. I've asked around. You have built quite the reputation in this business. I don't want your money," the man said. "I want a partnership. You see, I'm into pills, but with a supplier like you, I can easily take over with the coco."

"If you've done your research, you should know that I

don't take kindly to ultimatums," Carter said, tensing. He felt naked without his gun, but strapped or not, no one was about to railroad him into anything.

"Ultimatum is a strong word spoken by enemies. That's not the direction I'm looking to go with this. I'd rather have your friendship. My name is Josiah, and I'm much more deadly than you think. I own this city. I don't take losses, no matter how minuscule. I prefer to call this a proposition. I will consider your son's debt paid if you agree to supply me with one thousand kilos. A one-time deal," the man said.

Carter was unmoved by the quantity. He had moved ten times that amount in the course of his street tenure.

"I'm out of the game. I don't move that way anymore," Carter resisted. If Fly Boogie was still alive, Carter would have never considered paying the debt. He wasn't the type of man to be bullied into anything. This was inherited debt, and it was being placed on his seed. He would have to make it right just off GP. "Money isn't an object. Whatever is owed, I'll cover, but I don't get my hands dirty like that these days."

"I get it. You're trying to raise your boy . . . trying to steer him from the path that you chose . . . that his mother chose—"

"You don't know his mother," Carter interrupted, tired of the banter. "You don't know my life. My family. Your research didn't tell you that I'll kill every mu'fucka in this building over my wife and my son. You don't want to get into this with me." Carter was always so calm under pressure. He stood in a warehouse full of armed members of Josiah's army, but he was unafraid. Josiah wouldn't kill him, at least not this day, not where he stood. Carter's run in the game had earned him at least that much, but Josiah was politely warning him.

"See, the thing is, Carter, I believe you," Josiah said. "The way you handled the Haitians years ago . . . the way Baraka was killed not by you, but by your flunky, the way your wife and her Murder Mamas almost destroyed your precious Cartel. I believe that a war between us would be hard-fought. But you won't take it there. I have in my possession photos that can do more damage than any bullet." He picked up a manila envelope and pulled out enlarged photos. He held them out to Carter.

Carter didn't take them. Josiah flicked them one by one out of his palm and onto the floor. Carter glanced down and saw Miamor standing with a gun pointed at Fly Boogie. It was pictures of her from just the night before, committing murder.

"We keep a close eye on people we do business with," Josiah said. "You do this for me . . . get me the thousand kilos, and I make those pictures disappear. If not, the LAPD will have a warrant for her arrest by morning."

There it was. Miamor. She was his Achilles' heel. Carter smirked and then turned around and strolled out the way he had come in. "I'll be in touch," he said just before making his exit.

"Damn," he uttered as soon as he stepped foot outside. He immediately pulled out his phone and sent Monroe a text.

I'm coming to Miami. Be ready for me.

Carter looked around, unaware of where the hell they had taken him. He gritted his teeth in frustration as he began to walk. He wanted to put as much distance between himself and his enemy as he could. He had walked away from all of this three years ago. Now here he was, deeper in the streets than ever before. It was such a tangled web and he suddenly realized why they called the dope game "the trap" . . . because once you stepped in, there was only one true exit: the grave. Carter only hoped he wasn't dancing on his.

CHAPTER 16

The sound of the waves whispered loudly as Zyir sat on the fifty-foot yacht in the middle of the Atlantic. He was anchored twenty-five miles off the coast of Miami. It was the only place where he could find solace. Zyir hadn't slept in months. The closer the feds got to closing their case, the more he was plagued by insomnia. When his body absolutely couldn't take any more, his eyes would close against his will only to pop back open from the nightmares of his betrayal. He had never thought he would be the man he had become. He had put a bullet in Ace's head years before for the very same act of deceit. He was ashamed of himself. Zyir Rich . . . a federal informant. It didn't even make sense in his own mind. His love for Breeze had changed him. He was most loyal to her, but by being so, he was giving the middle finger to the very man who had saved him. He knew that Breeze wasn't to blame. Her love was the purest thing he had ever felt, but he still faulted her. They had become distant. He couldn't even look at her without feeling a bit of disdain. He hated that he loved her so much. The conflictions that tortured his psyche made him wish he had never met her, but at the same time he couldn't see himself without her. It was the mystery of falling in love with a girl like Breeze. The depth of his commitment to her knew no limits. He was sacrificing his character by protecting her.

The sun blazed down over him as he sat, hunched over, elbows on his knees in deep contemplation. He gripped his phone in his hands. *I should just tell him,* Zyir thought. *Give him a heads-up that the feds are on him. Tell him about Sam.*

Zyir knew that once he admitted to Carter what he had done, their friendship would never recover. There was no gray with a man like Carter. Only black and white. You were either a stand-up guy or you weren't. Friend or foe. Ally or enemy. Zyir had crossed the line that led to the other side. He would have to remain there. His heart felt empty . . . raw . . . and as he sat there he knew that what he had done was unforgivable. He had single-handedly destroyed a bond that had taken a lifetime to build. As long as Zyir could remember, Carter had been his friend, his brother, his mentor. He pinched the bridge of his nose to stop the emotions from welling in his eyes. He couldn't remember the last time he had shed tears, but the gut-wrenching battle being waged on his conscience was enough to cause a lone tear to escape.

Fuck this shit, Zyir thought to himself as he located Carter's contact information in his phone. *I've got to warn him.*

Before he could press call, Breeze's face illuminated on his screen.

He gritted his teeth at her timing. It was like she'd sensed him. They were so connected; despite the fact that they weren't even together, she knew that he needed to hear her voice.

Zyir knew the lovely melody of her tone would talk him out of warning Carter, so he declined the call, sending her to voice mail.

This was an impossible choice to make. His best friend or his wife. His wife or the nigga who had taught him everything. Breeze or Carter. Carter or Breeze. He loved them both dearly. They were probably the only two people he had ever loved, and now he had to destroy one to save the other. The pressure was eating him alive.

Breeze called right back, probably shocked at the fact that he hadn't answered. No matter what he was doing or where he was, he always made time for her. She was his priority. Still, he silenced the call. He knew the texts would come next.

Breeze
Zy. What's up babe? Why aren't you
answering for me?

Zyir couldn't take this type of guilt. He made his way to the aft of the yacht and stood out on the extended deck that hung into the water.

I can't take this shit. This shit is too much. No matter what

I do, somebody gets hurt. This ain't for me. None of this is for me anymore, he thought. He wanted to say that his thoughts weren't his own . . . that he wasn't thinking clearly . . . but he was as sharp as they came. Not a thought crossed his mind that he hadn't pondered for some time. He prided himself on remaining focused, free of inebriation, of narcotic . . . to always be on point. It was a lesson Carter had taught him . . . one of many, in fact. The deep blue, rolling waves enticed him. *All you got to do is step off,* he told himself.

His phone chimed again.

Breeze
I hate that you're out on the yacht by yourself.
Be careful. You can't swim. You know I worry.

Zyir closed the text. It was like she could feel he was on the brink. The cold water on his feet caused goose bumps to pop up onto his forearms. It was a beautiful day to die. His death wouldn't erase all that he had done, but at least he wouldn't feel it. He couldn't live with this. He had tried for three years, but the secret was too much to bear. How he wished he had been the one the police pulled over in his car that day. He would have taken his punishment like a G without a second thought. He knew that should-haves, could-haves, would-haves didn't matter at this point. Life hadn't served up the circumstance that way.

Zyir
I love you so much, B. Even when
I'm not with you.

It was the last message he would send. He wanted her to know that, because once he stepped into this ocean, she would question it. She would question everything. She would blame herself for his death, and that was the last thing he wanted her to do. He just needed the madness inside his head to stop. He would rather be dead than continue to be a pawn that the feds manipulated.

Breeze
I was going to wait until you came back from
Miami to tell you this, but it seems like
you need a pick-me-up.

She sent a photo to him, and Zyir's breath caught in his throat. It was an ultrasound image. Zyir couldn't contain the sobs that erupted from him. He couldn't help it. The liquid rolled effortlessly down his face onto the screen of his phone. This time when she called, he answered.

"Hey, Daddy," she greeted him playfully, but when she heard him crying, her tone changed. "Zyir. What's wrong?"

She had no idea what that one picture had just stopped him from doing.

"You're pregnant?" he asked as he sniffed loudly and regained his composure. "You're pregnant, B."

"I am," she said with joy. "We are!" She laughed.

"But I thought . . . ? After the damage from Ma'tee's rape, I never thought we could . . ." Zyir paused as he wiped his face in disbelief. "Wow, ma. I'm so happy. You just saved me, ma. You saved me," he whispered.

She didn't know what he meant, but she could hear the happiness in his tone.

She was over the moon. She had waited, just like last time, to tell him because she wanted to be sure. Breeze had agonized over the secret for months because she was fearful that it would end in tragedy like the first time. Every time she sat down to pee she checked her panties for blood, but when she had felt the first flutter inside of her, she knew: Everything would be all right. The sound of the baby's heartbeat had been music to her skeptical ears, but she still didn't tell Zyir. Not until she was past the twelve-week mark. Not until it was safe. "We're having a baby," she said.

"Aww man," Zyir said. He was on an emotional roller coaster. It was instinctive for his next words to be "I've got to tell Carter."

The mention of Carter's name made Zyir solemn, but he shook it off. He had to cooperate now. Breeze was carrying his child. She had just upped the ante.

"Okay. I love you, Zyir Rich," she said. "Be safe out there."

"I will, B. I love you, too."

Zyir climbed back up onto the main deck of the boat and lifted the anchor before turning the boat around. As he headed back toward the Miami shore, he couldn't help but think of his betrayal. Carter didn't deserve it. Not after all he had done for him. But it was happening. As he sailed back toward the marina, he couldn't help but think of the way Carter had entered his life.

* * *

Zyir hid under his bed as tears flowed down his face. Timidly, he was balled up in a fetal position, with both hands over his ears in pure terror. He had soiled pajamas and his body was sweaty because of the hot summer night. Pure fear had pushed him to urinate on himself involuntarily. He heard the screams coming from his mother's bedroom and was anticipating the moment that it would stop. His mother's alcoholic boyfriend had yet again gone on a drinking binge and was in the process of beating his mother. Zyir, only seven years old, couldn't understand why the man his mother loved so much would become such a monster. He didn't understand the effects of alcohol and the inner demons that it usually exposed. Zyir tried to press his hands against his ears to muffle the horrific sounds, but the screams were too loud to drown out.

After a few minutes of the arguing and beating, Zyir couldn't take it anymore. He crawled from underneath his bed and tip-toed out of the apartment. After slowly unlocking the door, he then stuck his head out and scoped the apartment's hallway. After see-ing that the coast was clear, he ran across the hallway to the door of his older friend, Carter Jones. Zyir, with a blanket in hand, knocked on the door with tears in his eyes. He waited patiently with his head down, hoping that Carter would answer the door. He knocked again and waited. After a minute had passed and he got no response, he turned on his heel and headed back to the hell that he called his home. Just as he reached his door, he heard a chain being slid off the lock and Carter's door cracked open. Carter stepped out, wiping the sleep out of his eyes and wearing nothing but boxers.

Carter squinted to see Zyir and noticed that his friend had been crying.

"Come on, lil' homie," Carter said as he waved Zyir into his mother's apartment. Zyir wiped his tears from his eyes, headed across the hall and through the door. Carter was a few years older than Zyir, and Zyir looked up to Carter. He felt a sense of relief when he was around Carter. Carter was home alone since his mother worked the third shift.

Zyir looked around the apartment and wished that his mother kept their apartment this nice. Carter had everything. The latest television, leather furniture, and custom carpet that melted in between Zyir's toes every time he walked. Although they were in the projects, while inside Carter's place, it didn't feel like it. Zyir slowly walked in with tears in his eyes. Carter threw his arm around him and guided him to the couch. Zyir always felt safer around Carter, and the horror he'd felt just moments before slowly began to fade.

"That nigga over there again?" Carter asked.

Zyir only nodded.

"A'ight," Carter said as he nodded. "It's all good. You can stay

the night over here." He tossed Zyir a pillow and a spare cover. He then turned on the television, knowing that Zyir was afraid of the dark but would never admit it. "Good night, Zy."

"Good night," Zyir replied.

Carter was halfway to his room when he doubled back. "Yo, do that nigga ever hit you, Zy?" Carter asked.

"No, just my mama," Zyir said. He didn't want to admit that he, too, was a victim of the abuse. He didn't want to look weak in front of his friend. Carter left it alone, but he had a feeling Zyir was lying.

"Come here," Carter said. "Let me show you something."

Zyir climbed out from beneath the cover and followed Carter to his room. He watched curiously as Carter pulled a shoe box from under his bed.

"You ever held a gun before, lil' homie?" Carter asked.

Zyir shook his head and looked with wide eyes as Carter pulled out an old .38. It was raggedy, but it worked.

"You got to protect your mama, Zyir. A man protects his family," Carter said as he handed the gun to Zyir. "It's yours."

"For real?" Zyir exclaimed as he wrapped his hand around it. It barely fit in his palm and it was heavier than it looked. He had never shot a gun a day in his life, but just having it made him feel like he was sitting on top of the world.

"Yeah, it's yours," Carter said.

"Thanks, man," Zyir replied.

Carter nodded. "Now tell me the truth. That nigga be hitting on you, too?"

Zyir pulled his shirt off, feeling comfortable enough with

Carter to reveal his secret. He turned around and showed Carter his scar-covered back. It looked like someone had used him as a human ashtray. It was so bad that Carter's eyes filled with tears of anger.

"He burned you with cigarettes?" Carter asked.

Zyir threw his shirt back on over his head. "Not in a while. He just been getting into it with my mama," Zyir said.

"The next time that nigga even look at you funny, you shoot him," Carter said.

Zyir nodded as he aimed the gun at the wall.

"BOOM!" Carter yelled, scaring Zyir so bad that he dropped the gun. Carter burst into laughter.

"First you got to learn how to shoot it," Carter said. "We can set up some cans on the roof after school tomorrow. I got some bullets."

* * *

The next day, Zyir awoke early and crept out of Carter's apartment. He was always too embarrassed to stay for breakfast with Carter and his mom, so instead he woke up at the crack of dawn to make his escape. When he entered his apartment, his mood instantly changed. He walked quietly to his mother's door, lifting his tiny hands to knock. He pressed his ear against the door. He knew her boyfriend was gone because he didn't hear his drunken snores. He opened the door and reached for the light switch, but as he flipped it, nothing happened.

"Ma?" Zyir called. "Ma, you okay?" he asked. He walked into the dark room, stepping over empty liquor bottles and empty fast-food bags. "Ma!" he said as he shook her.

It wasn't until he got right up on her that he saw why she wasn't responding. Her face was bashed in. Blood covered the pillow and the sheets. "Ma!" Zyir screamed as he shook her. "Ma, wake up!"

Zyir was sure she was dead and tears welled in his eyes. Her face was so badly beaten that he didn't recognize her. Zyir ran out. He needed help. His heart beat out of his chest as terror seized him.

"Where you think you going, little nigga?"

His mother's boyfriend stood between Zyir and the door. He had a large hunting knife in his hand and a huge sack in the other.

Zyir was frozen. His eyes went from the knife to the bag to the devilish look on the man's face. Was he going to cut his mother up? If not, what was the knife and bag for? He wanted to run, but his feet wouldn't move and he had left the gun at Carter's.

Zyir had a feeling he wasn't going to make it out of the apartment. He had seen too much.

"Please, I won't say nothing," he said.

The man stalked over to him and grabbed him by the neck, using so much force that Zyir thought he would snap it. "Get your little ass in here," the man barked. "I told that bitch about her mouth. I told her. Now look what the fuck she made me do."

He tossed Zyir onto the floor, hard, causing his head to hit the corner of the wall. The man climbed on top of him and put his hands around Zyir's neck. Zyir's eyes bulged out of his head as he kicked his legs frantically. He couldn't breathe. His lungs burned so bad as tears rolled out the sides of his eyes onto the dirty carpet beneath him. He was about to die all because his mother had chosen the wrong man. Zyir felt the blood vessels in his eyes bursting. Seconds felt torturously long, until he slowly began to not feel anything at all. Then . . .

BOOM!

The weight of the grown man collapsing on top of his body crushed him. Zyir was too weak to even push him off. He just lay there only half-conscious, on the edge of death.

"Zy! Zyir!"

That was Carter's voice.

"Zyir! Wake up!" Carter screamed. "Mama!!!!"

Carter pushed the man off of Zyir and pulled Zyir's limp body toward the front door. "Mama!"

The gunshot had lured nosy neighbors into the hall, but none dared go inside.

Finally his mother emerged from their apartment. "Carter! What did I tell you about . . ."

When she saw her twelve-year-old son struggling to carry Zyir to the door, she put her hands over her mouth in disbelief.

"Call 911! Don't just stand there! Call somebody!" she shouted as she rushed inside. "Oh my God! What happened?" she cried.

She heard the groans of the man in the hallway and watched in horror as Carter stood to his feet, walked over to the man, and stood over his body.

BOOM!

Without remorse, he put a bullet in the man's head just as the cops came swarming in.

"Put your hands where I can see them!" the police yelled.

"No!" Tonya yelled. "No!" She left Zyir lying there as she ran to Carter. "No! You will not arrest my son! He was protecting his friend! Help him!" She pointed toward Zyir, who had slipped into unconsciousness.

Her screams fell on deaf ears as they pushed her son against the wall forcefully before placing him in cuffs.

"Stay with Zyir, ma," Carter said as they escorted him out.

"We've got another body back here," another officer called out. Tonya stood as she watched the paramedics tend to Zyir.

"We've barely got a pulse. Let's get him in the bus," an EMT yelled. She stood horrified as she watched them load Zyir's small body onto a stretcher while working to save his life. Zyir's eyes fluttered open and he saw Carter being escorted out. He couldn't keep his eyes open long enough to see anything more. The last thing he remembered hearing was someone say, "I'm losing him."

* * *

Zyir remembered the day as if it had happened just yesterday. If Carter had walked in a minute later, Zyir would be dead. Carter had saved his life. He had killed for him. Due to the evidence against his mother's boyfriend, Carter never served a day in lockup. He was put on probation until the age of eighteen and walked away without a felony conviction. Zyir had lost his mother that day, but he had gained a brother. From that day forward, Zyir and Carter were inseparable. They had always had each other's back . . . until now. Zyir picked up his phone and sent Carter a text.

Zyir
I love you, fam.

Carter
Fuck you being all sensitive for little nigga?

Zyir
Ha!

Carter
I love you, too, my G.

They hadn't spoken the words to each other since they were young kids. Ego often caused men to mask their emotions, but Zyir felt it necessary to say. They were family, and Zyir didn't know how long he had before Carter's love transformed to hate. He reminded himself that he was doing this for Breeze as he stepped off the boat where two federal agents were waiting to wire him up.

CHAPTER 17

The rolling hills of the golf course were the perfect shade of leprechaun green. The country club was full on this Saturday afternoon, and the mild temperatures accompanied by a cloudless day made the perfect combination for tee time. Carter and Zyir stepped into the ritzy building. Their black skin immediately made them the focal point of the many club members. It was a members-only type of club. This may have been Miami, but it was still the South. It was clear they didn't belong, but they still walked in like they owned the place. Both dressed in designer, tailored suits it was evident they weren't there to step and fetch. They screamed money . . . real money . . . long money . . . not the gold-chain-wearing, flamboyant, hood-rich type, either. They were made men. They had acquired their riches their way, playing by their own rules. Bosses. That's what they were.

Black kings and they knew it. Carter bypassed the reception area and walked right onto the fairway, where he knew Estes would be. It was so routine that even the most unworthy adversary could catch him slipping. Nine a.m. tee time every Saturday. It never changed. For over thirty years, he had come like clockwork.

Carter and Zyir waited patiently, keeping a respectable distance as he watched Estes swing.

Estes turned and noticed them waiting. He took his time before calling them over. Carter smirked. Even in old age, Estes kept it G. They were on his time. He respected it. Finally he motioned for them to approach.

He held out his hand to Carter to shake. He ignored Zyir. He didn't talk to the help, only the man who wore the crown.

"You going to sit back and watch or you going to pick up a club?" Estes said as he patted his head with a handkerchief that he retrieved from his pocket. "This one will do just fine," he said as he handed his own club over to Carter. Carter stepped up to the tee, and to Estes's surprise, swung the iron like a pro. Estes wagged a finger at him as Carter came back by his side. "There is more to you than meets the eye, young man."

"Lucky shot," Carter said, smiling. Carter looked around and said, "You're a little too relaxed, aren't you? You slipping in your old age?" he asked, only half-jokingly. "You're too accessible out here."

Estes huffed as he shined his club. "The men at par two are my men. The fat fella over there reading the newspaper, fifty yards out, on that bench—that's Bruno, my hench-man. The field hands, fixing the lawn, have guns on their waists. They are my men as well. I don't go anywhere without protection."

Damn, Carter thought. *He has goons everywhere.*

"Well, you're not here to make me look bad, so speak your piece." Estes was straight to the point.

Carter tucked his hands in his pockets. "I have a friend who wants to open a bakery, but they don't have access to enough sugar," Carter said discreetly.

"Too much of a sweet tooth is a bad thing," Estes said. "I've told Monroe. He thinks that if he sends you, I will change my position."

"I assure you, Estes, Monroe has nothing to do with this deal. This is all me," Carter guaranteed.

"How much sugar do you need?" Estes asked.

"A thousand squares," Carter answered.

"Must have a lot of goods ready to bake?" Estes replied.

"Can't bake without sugar," Carter confirmed.

"I suppose not," Estes agreed.

"I'm buying in bulk, so I'll need a good price," Carter said.

Zyir smirked, somewhat glad that Carter wasn't incrim-inating himself. The wire he wore beneath his clothes was picking up the entire conversation. Carter hadn't said any-thing that could be used against him. He hoped it stayed that way. He was doing his part. He was cooperating. It wouldn't be his fault if Carter never gave the feds the evi-dence they wanted.

"Doesn't need to be said. I can get a shipment out to you as early as Tuesday," Estes said.

There it was. A date for the exchange. It was the exact information that Zyir didn't want Carter to disclose.

"My man," Carter replied, extending his hand. They shook before Carter and Zyir departed.

Zyir was silent and deep in thought as they made their way back to Carter's car. Carter unlocked the doors and then looked over at Zyir. "You good, Zy?" Carter asked.

Zyir realized he was wearing his heart on his sleeve. Carter had sensed his moody disposition. "Yeah, fam, yeah, I'm good," Zyir replied, but the fact was, he had never felt worse. He had turned into the type of nigga he swore he would never be: a snitch.

* * *

"Get rid of this, throw this tacky shit out, toss this cheap shit," Miamor said to herself as she cleaned out the room that Sam had once occupied. Miamor was thoroughly enjoying tossing out her things. It had killed her to see another woman with Carter. It had hurt her even more that she couldn't snatch the bitch out of her starter-pack Louboutins. She was trying to grow and be a better woman this time around, so instead she took pleasure in packing up the cardboard box.

"Basic ass bitch," Miamor mumbled with a frown as she tossed a cheap collar shirt into the box with the rest of the worthless items.

When she opened the top drawer she pulled out a shirt

and a cell phone fell onto the floor. Miamor picked it up curiously. "Why would she leave her phone?" she whispered. It was an old-school flip phone and Miamor opened it nosily. Before she could snoop, the doorbell rang.

"Magda!" Miamor called out to her nanny. She was so grateful that the woman had agreed to resume her employment after so many years. Miamor didn't trust anyone with her son, so when deciding to hire someone to help with the day-to-day, her original nanny was the only one who had come to mind. She'd paid her a year's salary in advance just to get her to relocate to Colorado. "Can you get the door, please?!" she shouted. "And tell C.J. that you are his nanny, not his maid. He can clean his own room!"

"*Sí*, Señora," Magda called back. A few moments later Magda's voice broke through the air again. "Señora! It is for you!"

Miamor snapped the cell phone shut and placed it in her back pocket as she made her way to see who the hell was at her door. She didn't know anyone out here, so this random guest was unexpected.

When she rounded the corner, she saw Sam was standing there.

"Thank you, Magda. Please keep C.J. in his room," Miamor said, not wanting her son to see her fly off the handle should it come to that. "You are just asking me to slap the shit out of you right now. Why are you here?"

"I came for my things," Sam said.

"Yeah well, you're a little late. They've been disposed of," Miamor replied.

Sam wanted to get inside the house to retrieve the phone. It was her only reason for coming. The feds were close to bringing Carter up on charges. On Tuesday they would have all the evidence they needed when they intercepted the exchange between Estes and Carter. If Miamor discovered the phone, it may arouse suspicion. Sam was anxious to get it back.

"Call Carter. He won't mind me coming in to make sure I didn't leave anything," Sam pushed.

"You don't need to speak with Carter. You're speaking with me," Miamor said firmly. "You don't have any more business with him."

Sam chuckled, infuriating Miamor. "Actually, I'll see him soon. We've got a date that neither one of us can avoid," Sam said slyly. She couldn't help but antagonize Miamor. She turned to walk away, knowing that she would have the last laugh. Soon she would have Miamor in handcuffs and all of her tough talk would be used as evidence to convict her.

CHAPTER 18

"Alright, people, look alive," Sam said as she strapped on her bulletproof vest and addressed the men and women before her. "Today is the day we bring down the most deadly criminal enterprise in Miami. The plane will be here at six a.m. We'll have a bird in the sky in case Carter tries to flee, and we'll have men on the ground, hiding behind the trees in these woods next to the clear port strip." Sam had a map of the area spread out over a large table as she gave out the directions. "These men are ruthless. I want you to be sharp today. Stay focused. I want every agent in this division to make it home to their families tonight. I don't want any casualties. We haven't come this far to have it end with dead suspects. Let's try to keep this thing clean, by the book. We don't want to give them any room to get off on a technicality. Let's load up." She grabbed her gun off the table and holstered as she made her way through the Miami field office. Today was the day her career would be made.

She walked briskly through the halls and as her partner, Agent Jacobs, rounded the corner, he aligned by her side. He handed her a vanilla latte as they exited the building. "You ready to be Agent Tiffani Gamble again?" he asked.

"I've been undercover so long that I forgot that was my real name," Sam said as they entered their unmarked SUV. "I can't wait to see the look on Carter's face when he has my cuffs around his wrists or that pretty little bitch of a wife he chose."

Agent Jacobs pulled away from the field office with SWAT and a twenty-person DEA team following them. It was time to take down The Cartel.

* * *

Zyir stood in the bathroom, gripping both sides of the sink as his head hung low. He was ashamed of himself. He was about to lose a brother today. Zyir had tossed and turned all night, thinking about his betrayal to Carter. Their bond was more than friendship. They couldn't be closer even if they shared the same bloodline. Carter had fed Zyir when he was starving; he had protected him; nurtured him. Carter had been the single force in his life that had molded him into the man he had become. He owed Carter everything, but instead he was showing him the ultimate form of disloyalty. Zyir looked up at himself and rage took over him. How he had been so stupid to get himself in this position in the first place was beyond him. He should have never allowed himself to love Breeze. It was his affection for her that forced him to put her well-being before his honor. The feds knew that. They banked on that. Either he got them to Carter, or they arrested her on drug charges. Sacrificing what he stood for was the only choice he could make. He couldn't let his wife go through that, so it was Carter who had to take the fall. Zyir told himself that Carter would do the same if it were Miamor, but even as the thoughts entered his mind, he knew they were false. There was no question about Carter's character. He was real, through and through; a real street nigga with *je ne sais quoi*. Carter was a rare breed.

Zyir's rage caused his chest to feel empty. He felt queasy. In his frustration he reached up and pulled the entire medicine cabinet off the hotel wall. The mirror shattered as it hit the floor. He couldn't even look at his reflection without feeling overwhelming disgust.

KNOCK! KNOCK!

Zyir took his time answering because he knew who stood on the other side. He walked over to it, wearing nothing but his Calvin Klein boxer briefs, and opened the door.

"Today's the day," Sam said.

Zyir said nothing as he turned and walked back into the room. She entered along with Agent Jacobs. "I've done my part," he said as he flopped down on the bed. "I'm done. I don't need to be there to watch it all go down."

"Actually, you're not done. There is still one more thing left to do. Since Estes refuses to do direct business with Monroe, we don't have anything on him that will stick. I need you to wear a wire and go to the Diamond estate. Get him talking about today's exchange," Sam instructed.

"I said I'm done," Zyir stated.

Sam nodded. "Okay," she said. She picked up her walkie-talkie and said, "Send local PD to Flint, Michigan, to retrieve Breeze Rich. Conspiracy to distribute a controlled substance, possession of a controlled—"

"Wait!" Zyir shouted. He was between a rock and a hard place. "I'll do it."

"I thought so," Sam said smugly.

She turned to Jacobs. "Wire him up."

* * *

Sam hid behind the large tree and looked down at the members of her team awaiting the plane's arrival. Even in the early morning, the Florida heat was suffocating. Sweat covered her entire body under her clothes and vest. "Where are they?" Jacobs's voice came through her earpiece, asking the same question she had just been asking herself.

"Patience is a virtue, Jacobs," Sam replied, keeping her eyes straight forward. The sound of an approaching aircraft could be heard before it ever came into view. Sam held her breath in anticipation until she finally saw a small aircraft descending from the sky.

"Hold steady. Move on my mark," she whispered into her headset. She held up a closed fist to the other agents, keeping them at bay. She wanted the aircraft to be turned completely off before they made their move. She waited. Five minutes, then ten, then fifteen. "Where are they?" she whispered.

"Where is Jones?" Jacobs's voice came through her earpiece again. "Isn't he supposed to meet the plane to pick up the shipment?" Sam didn't answer because she didn't know what the hell was going on. She knew Carter. She had spent the past three years getting to know him. He executed plans with precision. Something was awry.

"Let's take the plane and find out where Carter is later," Sam said. When she heard the pilot cut the engine and saw the staircase lower to the ground, she opened her fist. "Move, move."

They swarmed the plane, running full speed with guns drawn. Sam's adrenaline pumped as she shouted, "DEA! On the ground, now!" The pilot came off the plane, alarmed and with hands raised.

"This is a search warrant to search this aircraft," she said, handing him the papers.

Sam rushed up the steps and into the cockpit to find an empty plane. "Where are the drugs?" she asked, confused.

She rushed down the steps and confronted the pilot. "Where are they?" she shouted, enraged.

"Where is who?" the pilot asked. "I don't know what you're talking about."

"Take him in," Sam said. "And tear this plane apart until you find something." She turned to Agent Jacobs, frantic. "Are we picking anything up on the wire from Zyir?" she asked. She was flabbergasted.

"Yeah, he's walking into the Diamond estate as we speak," Jacobs said. "This wasn't his doing. He hasn't tipped anyone off."

"Damn it!" Sam said as she threw up her arms. "I'm making this arrest today! Carter ordered the shipment. We just have to figure out the real location for the exchange. Get me to the surveillance van now. I need to be on the other end of that wire."

* * *

When Monroe's guards saw Zyir's face, they let him into the gates without second-guessing. It only made the pit in the bottom of his stomach deepen. He was a snake and he knew it. Monroe and Carter trusted him with their lives. They gave no one this much access to them, but he had earned the privilege. He drove down the long driveway and exited the car. Taking the steps two at a time, he approached Monroe's front door. He hesitated on knocking. He stood there, conflicted, but he knew it was too late to turn back. *The exchange is done. Carter's probably already in handcuffs,* Zyir thought, an extreme sadness filling him. *I might as well finish this.*

He rang the bell.

Moments later, Monroe opened the door.

"What's good, bro?" Monroe greeted him. It wasn't even a question as to why Zyir was at his door before noon. Zyir was family and was always welcome. "Come on in. I've got the chef whipping up breakfast."

Zyir stepped inside and followed Monroe into the dining room. "I was just telling Carter to call you. It's been a minute since we've sat down and broke bread together. Perfect timing," Monroe stated. "We were just discussing the shipment that's coming in today."

Zyir couldn't hide his shock when he saw Carter sitting coolly at the table, sipping coffee, while reading *The Wall Street Journal*.

"I thought you had that business to take care of this morning, bro?" Zyir asked.

Carter nodded. "It's still on."

Monroe took his seat and added, "This paranoid nigga and his extra security measures. He switched the shit up. He doubled back to Estes after y'all left the golf course and had him put the bricks on a sixteen-wheeler the same day. They'll be there this afternoon."

"I'll fly out to meet the driver and store the bricks in our warehouse," Carter said.

Zyir cringed because he knew the wire had picked all of that up.

"What's wrong, Zy? You look like you've seen a ghost," Monroe observed.

"I'm good. I'm good. Drank a little too much last night. I need to get some food in me," he said.

Carter frowned. "Since when you drink to get faded?" he asked.

Feeling the need to change the focus, he said, "Breeze is pregnant. Got me thinking if I'm going to be a good father and all that. This life . . . this game . . . the treachery," he said, feeling like scum. "I needed to take the edge off."

Carter stood. "My man a hunnid grand," he said jovially. He walked around and embraced Zyir, giving him a firm pat on the back. "Congrats."

"That's dope, Zy," Monroe added. "That's love right there. I can't believe B didn't tell me. We're going to have to celebrate. Throw a huge party."

"Yeah, well, before you bring the entire city out, let me go back West and handle this business," Carter stated. "After this, we are all out. We're done with the street shit. We got babies. We're fathers. It's time we hang this shit up. It's only so long we're going to run this game before it destroys us. We have a responsibility to know when enough is enough. Let's not make the same mistake as our father. Let's learn from that and leave gracefully."

Zyir was crushed. The magnitude of Carter's words and the timing of it all was so ironic, Zyir knew he would never forgive himself for the chain of events that were about to occur.

"You need help out there with the shipment? You good?" Monroe asked.

"Nah, I got it. One last flip," Carter said.

"One last flip," Monroe confirmed.

* * *

Miamor stood, gazing out of the window, chuckling as Magda and C.J. built a snowman in the front yard. She was so far removed from the streets in the isolation of these mountains, and it was comforting. She felt so lucky to have survived everything she had been through. To have another chance at real love and to have her son safe felt so good. Miamor had come out of the fire molded instead of burned and she was grateful.

"Let me tackle this laundry," she whispered to herself. She knew that Magdalena would have done it, but she was trying to settle into this domestic routine. If she kept herself busy, she could never mess up the good thing she had going. She planned to fill her days with dutiful wife and mom work so that she would never fall back into her habits as a Murder Mama. She was done with that. Everything she needed was right here. Carter would be home later that evening and he had assured her that after this last run, he would step away from the game as well.

Miamor went to the massive laundry room and began to sort through the dirty clothes. She picked up a pair of her jeans and shook them out. Her eyes widened when the cell phone she had found in Sam's drawer fell to the floor. Her heart skipped a beat. She didn't know how she had forgotten to go through it the other day, but today she knew she wouldn't be able to fight the curiosity. She picked it up, flipping it open. *Damn it, it's dead,* she thought. She rushed to the kitchen and pulled open one of the drawers. Inside were all kinds of electronic cords and extras. None of them fit. She knew that her phone wasn't compatible. *Magda has an older-model phone,* Miamor thought as she rushed out the back door. An in-law apartment sat above the main house. It was where Magda retreated to after her shift was over. Miamor crept inside and quickly located her charger. She took it and went back to the main cabin. She didn't know why she was so pressed to go through Sam's phone. She was confident that Carter had ended things, but something still gnawed at her. Call it women's intuition, but Miamor had always been able to sniff out a snake. After waiting a few minutes, the phone finally powered on and Miamor went through the text messages. They had all been erased. She then went through the call log.

202-555-0931	1:45 a.m.	7 minutes
202-555-0931	2:10 a.m.	7 minutes
202-555-0931	2:22 a.m.	7 minutes
202-555-0931	3:16 a.m.	7 minutes
202-555-0931	4:00 a.m.	7 minutes

What the hell? Miamor thought, finding the call log extremely odd. All of the calls took place during the middle of the night, probably while Carter was asleep. *Who was she talking to? What area code is 202?* Miamor pulled out her own phone and looked it up. *Washington, D.C.* Her gut screamed.

Miamor's heart pounded in her chest as she pressed the call button. She bit her lip as the ringing filled her ear.

"You have reached the Drug Enforcement Administration. Please enter the access code to the agent you are trying to reach," an automated voice filled the phone.

Miamor gasped as she dropped the phone. Her hand covered her mouth in disbelief. *She's a fed. Oh my God. She's an undercover fed,* Miamor thought as tears filled her eyes. There was no telling how much information Sam had gathered on Carter, but Miamor knew that she had been around long enough to build a successful case. Miamor immediately called Carter. "Come on, answer . . . answer," she urged frantically. His voice mail picked up. She knew he was probably at the airport. He always turned off his phone as soon as he stepped foot inside. She checked the clock. His flight didn't board for another two hours. She called Monroe. Again, she received the voice mail. "What the fuck!" she shouted. Zyir was her next try. Voice mail. Miamor felt like she was losing her mind. She stormed into the room Sam had occupied. She had never finished taking all of her things out. She went through the entire room, tracing her hands around the baseboards, looking for microphones and cameras. She emptied drawers, opened envelopes—all to come up with nothing. In frustration, she swept everything off of the nightstand, knocking it over accidentally.

A large yellow envelope was taped to the bottom of it. Miamor pulled it off and emptied its contents on the bed.

A USB drive fell out. Miamor rushed to her laptop and inserted the drive. "Oh my God," she whispered. Over a thousand documents and pictures were on the file. She opened them, one after another. There was enough material to put Carter in jail. Miamor opened an untitled document and read it.

I have concluded there is a criminal enterprise happening around Mr. Jones; however, I am unable to link him directly to it. It is imperative I catch him exchanging massive quantities of narcotics in order to seal this case. Whoever is arrested at this type of exchange will be brought up on kingpin charges. I will continue my investigation until I can find out when the next shipment will be.

Agent Tiffani Gamble

"The next shipment is today," Miamor whispered, tears coming to her eyes. How had this happened? How had Carter let the feds get so close? Miamor felt like her world was crumbling, and sobs seeped from her lips. *With this much evidence, somebody has to take the fall. Whoever shows up to the exchange, the charges will fall on that one person. That can't be Carter,* she thought. Miamor wiped her eyes, grabbed her handbag, and rushed out of the house.

"C.J.!" she shouted as she approached him. "C.J., come here," she said.

He could see the tears that she had tried to hide. "You okay, ma?" he asked.

Magdalena stopped and looked at her in concern. "Señora?"

Miamor nodded. "Mommy's fine, baby. I need you to listen to me. I love you. I love you more than life itself. You are the best thing that has ever happened to me. You're the best part of me. I'm with you even when we aren't near each other. You hear me, my prince? I'm in here," Miamor said as she touched his chest. "And I love you. I want you to know that. I love you more than anyone else in the world. You be a king, okay?"

C.J. looked unsurely and felt his own tears forming in

his eyes. This felt too much like good-bye. "I have to do something and you won't understand it until you're older, but just know I did it for you and your father . . . for our family."

"You're coming back, right?" C.J. asked.

"Yeah, baby. One day," she answered. "But until then, I'm always close, because love crosses all distance. Where will I be until you see me again?"

"In here," C.J. answered as he pointed to his chest.

Miamor pulled him into her for a long hug and she kissed the top of his head. "You're a king, Carter Jones, Jr., and I love you."

She turned to Magdalena. "Take care of him. Carter will be by to get him soon."

Miamor hopped into the car and took off down the mountain. She picked up her phone and dialed the number to the driver who was scheduled to pick Carter up at LAX. Carter didn't trust many people, but he always kept an ally in cities he frequented.

"Hello?" a man answered.

"Hi, Iman. This is Miamor, Carter's wife," she said.

"How you doing?" the guy replied.

"I'm fine. I'm calling to let you know you don't need to pick Carter up today. I'll be in town. I'll scoop him up myself," she said. She had no intentions of getting Carter. She would be in town, all right. She needed Carter's schedule thrown off to delay his arrival at the warehouse.

"Sounds good. Tell him to hit me when he touches down," the man said.

"Will do," Miamor replied before hanging up.

Miamor raced to the airport. She had to board the quickest flight and get to the warehouse before Carter. She would take the fall for him. She knew he would be better on the outside, with their son. Carter was too good of a man to shoulder the weight of the entire Cartel. This wasn't supposed to be his karma. *Me, on the other hand, this is exactly what I deserve.* She wasn't a good person; she was only good for Carter, and this would be her last gift to him: his freedom.

* * *

Carter arrived at LAX and walked out of the airport. He had no luggage to retrieve, so he was making good time. He still had an hour to make it across town. To his surprise, his man wasn't waiting for him as anticipated. He picked up his phone to call his ride when he noticed that Miamor had called him more than ten times. Before he could press her name to call her back, Zyir's name flashed across the screen.

"I just touched down, fam, let me hit you back. This nigga late. I'm out here waiting . . ."

"Don't go to the warehouse, Carter," Zyir said.

Carter heard the stress in Zyir's voice. In all of their years working together, he had never felt an inkling of distrust toward Zyir.

"You got to say something after that, Zyir, because I don't like the direction my imagination is taking me," Carter said sternly.

"Switch up the plans," Zyir said. "Just whatever you do, don't go to that meeting."

Carter felt his temperature rise as anger overtook him. "Nigga, be clear. You talking around the shit. Spit that shit out, Zyir. I raised you, homie. So I know you not saying what I think you saying," Carter said. His volume was low, but the tone of his voice was threatening. He had never come at Zyir sideways. Zyir had never given him a reason to, but today, on this sunny L.A. day, he felt the tides of their friendship changing. Their brotherhood was turning sinister because Carter knew what Zyir's next words would be. He hoped and prayed Zyir said something different.

Come on, Zy. Say something, homie. Say anything other than what I'm thinking, Carter thought. His eyes watered from a mixture of hurt and anger. Zyir's silence was admission enough. "Say that shit, Zyir. Tell me you ain't been laying down with pigs," Carter said. He held his tone steady, but in person he was breaking down. This was his little man; his right hand. Zyir had been a brother to him before he had ever discovered he had a family in Miami. They say soul mates can come in the form of many things— not only between a man and a woman. Zyir and Carter had forged a friendship on something deeper, and this new revelation of deceit was ripping a hole straight through Carter's chest.

"Be clear, Zyir. Be the nigga I taught you to be. What the fuck is you saying to me?" Carter demanded.

"DEA is waiting at the warehouse. It's a setup," Zyir finally said. "I fucked up."

"Yeah, you did," Carter answered.

CLICK.

Carter felt like he couldn't breathe. He loosened his silk Gucci tie and bent over, placing his hands on his knees. The pain in his gut, the empty feeling, the nausea. He was sick from grief because although Zyir wasn't dead, he was dead to Carter.

Carter couldn't think clearly. He had never had an adversary of this kind . . . the kind that he loved too much to kill, but hated too much to let live. It was a conundrum. He gritted his teeth as his fingers stabbed Miamor's name on his phone's screen.

"Carter!" she answered frantically.

"He fucked me, ma. Zyir is talking," Carter said. He could reveal his hurt to Miamor. She was his rib, his wife. She knew exactly how much this had hurt him.

"Sam is a federal agent, Carter," Miamor revealed, further unraveling the puzzle. Zyir had introduced him to Sam. He had been setting him up for the past three years.

"We've got to go, ma. Pack up some things. You and C.J. meet me—"

"It's too late for that," Miamor replied sadly. "I found Sam's evidence. The Cartel is going to fall. She doesn't have the kingpin yet. She suspects it's you, but she doesn't know for sure. She needs you to make the exchange you set up today to pin it all on you. She won't find a kingpin. She's getting a queen pin instead. I got it, Carter. I'm pulling up to the warehouse now. Take care of my son. I love you."

Her words echoed in his mind. *She's getting a queen pin instead. She's getting a queen pin instead.*

"Mia! Miamor!" his voice boomed through the phone, and he could hear her breathing, but she refused to respond. She didn't need him to talk her out of this. Somebody had to fall from grace. The government had a hard-on for their empire. Carter couldn't take that fall, Monroe had Mo to think about, Breeze was the most innocent of them all. That only left her. She would pay for all their sins.

"I love you so much. You've taught me how to love someone other than myself. This is me loving you . . . just let me do this," Miamor said.

"If you love me, turn around, ma," Carter said. "I can take care of this. We've got lawyers for shit like this. Don't be stupid, Miamor. There's no me without you, ma. This can't happen. What I work so hard for, if I couldn't make this shit go away with a little paper? Turn your ass around, Miamor. Now!"

He was losing it. The universe was working against him today, throwing more at him than he could take. He had never pleaded for anything in his life, but he was begging her to not do this because once done, it couldn't be taken back.

"Good-bye, Carter."

Carter grabbed the first taxi he saw and threw every dollar he had in his pocket through the passenger window.

"Hey, man! What the hell?" the cabbie asked, throwing up his hands as the money slapped him in the face.

"I need a driver for the day. All that's yours if you take me where I need to go," Carter said.

The driver looked at the hundred-dollar bills scattered across his front seat.

"Hop in," he said.

Carter climbed inside and leaned his head against the back of the seat. He knew that he wouldn't make it in time, but he had to try. He couldn't let Miamor do this, but what he didn't know was that it was already done.

FINAL CHAPTER

Miamor sat drumming her bloodred nails against the long table that sat in the middle of the warehouse. Bricks on top of bricks sat on the table in front of her. A single tear fell down her cheek as the door to the warehouse began to rise and the DEA agents rushed in. They were fully suited, badges in plain view, and guns drawn as they filtered inside.

"Let me see your hands! Hands up!" they shouted as they stood in front of her.

She sat, legs crossed, in a Carolina Herrera tailored pantsuit. Her makeup was flawless, and not a hair was out of place on her pretty little head. This day had been a long time coming. Her downfall. She had always wondered how it would go down and who would have the balls to take her out of the game. She began to chuckle right in the face of law enforcement. "I've gone up against some of the biggest gangsters in the world and you muthafuckas are the ones to take me out," she said as she fell into hysterics. Sam came through the crowd, and Miamor's laugh simmered to a sinister smirk. She began to clap, slowly, exaggeratedly, as she leaned back comfortably. Miamor eyed Sam with malice. "Bravo, bitch, you deserve a fucking Oscar," Miamor said. "You played your part really well . . . a little too well for a fed, don't you think?" she asked, knowing the agent had fucked her man.

"Where are the rest of them?" Sam asked. "Where is Carter? Money? Estes?"

"It's just me. I'm all you get," Miamor said calmly.

Sam turned to the agents behind her. "Tear this place apart. Everything in here is evidence."

There had been no time to clear the bricks from the warehouse. There was enough cocaine to put Miamor away for the rest of her life. There was no way that The Cartel could get out of this unscathed. Someone had to take the fall, and Miamor made the decision that it should be her. It was the least she could do for Carter after all he had done for her. He had loved her when she was unlovable, forgiven her for things that were unforgivable. He had crowned her when he should have killed her. Carter was a king and he deserved to sit on his throne, not rot in a jail cell. Miamor knew there was a special place in hell for her, and she accepted that. She would miss Carter and C.J. every day, but she honestly believed that this was for the best. Carter would take better care of C.J. than she could. She loved them so dearly that she was willing to be the sacrificial lamb in order to save their family. Living without them would be the hardest thing she ever had to do, but at least they would be living. With her around, there was no telling which of her past skeletons would threaten their existence. Carter could make his exit from the game and raise their son without her. They were better off that way.

Sam drew her weapon and approached Miamor cautiously. Miamor got on her feet, causing Sam to stop momentarily. Even unarmed, Miamor's reputation implanted fear into others. "Miamor Jones, you have the right to remain silent. Anything you say can and will be used against you in a court of law. . . ."

Miamor didn't resist as Sam cuffed her. She simply accepted that it was the end of an era. It had been a hell of a ride. She had loved, lost, cried tears of joy and pain. This was it. She always thought she would go out in a hail of gunfire, but she didn't want that. She had lived her entire life that way. She wanted her son to be able to come and see her face should he choose to visit. He couldn't do that if she was lying in a grave somewhere, so instead of going out like a G, she simply complied. She tuned Sam out as she read off her rights and then stuffed her into the back of the squad car. She was sure that Carter would do his best to get her off. There would be lawyers, bribes, a lengthy trial . . . he would spare no expense on her behalf, but the confident look in Sam's eyes let Miamor know that the government's case was airtight. She wasn't being prosecuted for just her crimes; she would have the entire Cartel's history of violence on her back. They were going to fry her and she would let them, because as long as they convicted her, they couldn't convict Carter. It was a great sacrifice for a great man who had shown her the greatest love of all. She owed him this.

* * *

By the time Carter arrived, Miamor was gone. He climbed out of the car, among the crowd of reporters who were questioning the agents about what was being dubbed "The Drug Bust of the Century." The feds had *his* bricks of cocaine lined up, showboating the arrest. Carter scanned the place desperately looking for Miamor, but in his heart he knew it was too late. She was gone, and there was nothing he could do about it. Carter gritted his teeth and slid back into the cab, conceding defeat. In the blink of an eye, his entire world had changed. Just yesterday he had felt on top of the world. He had had everything, their entire futures mapped out in his head. He had just learned a vital lesson: Tomorrow wasn't promised, and loyalty among men was scarce. After this day, for him, life would never be the same.

* * *

Monroe heard the sirens first. They were in the distance, probably held up at his armed gate, but he knew they wouldn't be stalled for long. They had come to arrest him . . . to crumble the empire that had started with his father.

"Daddy, that's the police," Mo said.

"Yeah, son, come here," Monroe said as he got down on one knee in front of his child. "I want you to always remember that I love you, son. I love you more than the air in my lungs. You're a Diamond, and Diamonds are forever. You

keep that in your mind. We don't fold, son. We don't follow. You're a king. You're bred from kings. Don't cry. Stay
strong. Be a man of your word. Be smart. Trust no one but
family, and always know that I'm with you. I'm with you
even when I'm not with you because I'm in here," Monroe
said as he pointed to his son's heart. The sirens drew closer,
and Monroe had to pinch the bridge of his nose in order to
stop himself from becoming emotional. "You understand?"

"Yes, sir," Mo answered, sticking his chest out slightly
in pride.

"I love you, son."

"I love you, too, Daddy," Mo replied.

"Now go into my bedroom. Put the code into the panic
room and stay inside. Don't come out until your auntie
Breeze comes for you and don't look at the screens on the
walls, Mo. You a man of your word, right?" Monroe asked.

His son nodded. His eyes teared.

"Don't cry, son. I'm in there . . . always," Monroe
stressed, pointing at his son's chest. He pulled his son in for
a hug and then kissed the top of his head before pushing
him toward the room. He pulled out his cell phone and
speed-dialed Breeze. She answered on the first ring.

"B, I don't have much time. The feds are here. I need you
to come get Mo. He's in the panic room. He's not coming
out until you get here," Monroe said.

"Money, wait, you're talking too fast . . . the feds? What
are you—?"

"Just come get my son, B!" he said urgently. "Take care
of him. I love you." Money ended the call and then rushed

into his office. He loosened his tie and paced nervously, placing his hands on his head in distress. He wished he could
lie down and take the time that they were trying to throw
at him, but he refused to let them take away more years of
his life. They had done that once before. He had told himself once he got out that he was never going back inside.
Street legends always died on the throne. His father had
died that way. Now, he would, too. He rushed to his safe
and pulled out an AK–47 with the hundred-round drum.
He was a one-man army. Money wished this didn't have to
play out in front of his son, but it was now or never. The
feds were at his front door. If they took him into custody,
he knew he would never see another free day in his life. He
refused to live on his knees. He would die on his throne
before he allowed himself to become a slave to the system.
He gritted his teeth as he fought the feelings of anxiety that
filled his belly. He made sure he was locked and loaded before walking slowly down the steps. He looked around,
knowing that it would be the last time he would see this
home. It was the place where he had grown up. The Diamond estate. It was the castle that Carter Diamond had
built for his children. Monroe wouldn't disrespect it by having a gunfight inside. He stepped outside on the front
porch and walked out into the middle of the circular drive.
Flashing red and blue lights approached. As many agents
as they sent, you would think they were coming to take
down a giant. In a sense, they were. Monroe was a street
king. He would not be defeated easily. His ego wouldn't al-

low it to happen that way. They pulled up a hundred yards away from him and filtered out of their cars.

"Monroe Diamond! I have a warrant for your arrest!" one of them shouted.

He didn't hesitate. He sprayed.

RAT TAT TAT TAT TAT TAT TAT.

The AK–47 thundered as he rained bullets down on them. The kickback from the powerful weapon was so strong that he had to brace himself as he gritted his teeth while curling his finger on the trigger. Glass shattered as he shot out the agents' car windows. They cowered under gunfire and quickly returned with some of their own. Even with the high-powered weapon, he was outgunned. There was only one of him; there were a couple dozen of them and they were firing at him from all directions.

The first bullet that hit him took his breath away as a burning sensation spread through his chest. The impact of the bullet knocked him to his knees, but he never let go of the gun. He gritted his teeth as the taste of blood filled his mouth.

"Put down the weapon! Put it down!" the feds shouted as they aimed their weapons at him. He spit the blood out of his mouth, but it was futile. It only filled up more.

"Agh!!!" Monroe screamed in anger. He stood to his feet. "You can't kill me! I'm the king of Miami! This is my shit!"

He staggered to his feet and hugged the trigger, spraying bullets everywhere. "Muthafuckas!" Bullets riddled the police cars that sat on the front lawn. The federal agents tried to show restraint as they cowered behind their cars, but Monroe wasn't letting up. He had a chopper and if they wanted to come for him, he wasn't going peacefully. Eventually they returned fire. It was like the Wild Wild West in his front yard.

"Daddy!"

Monroe heard Mo's voice and he turned around, bloody, wounded, as he stared into his son's eyes. He held his head high as he watched tears slide down his son's face. "Diamonds are forever. I'm in here," he said as he hit his chest proudly with his free hand. The fear that registered on Mo's face broke Monroe's heart. He never wanted his son to see this part of the game. This was the part that tainted young boys . . . this was the ugly part of it all, but it was too late. Mo was witnessing that gangster shit.

The agents used this distraction and fired relentlessly as Monroe's body jerked left, then right from the impact of the bullets. They shot Monroe down as if he were a rabid dog, right in front of his seed, who stood watching it all, in horrified shock.

Monroe felt his life slipping. It felt as if he were drowning, but his eyes never left his son's. He saw himself in Mo. His life played out like a movie in front of him. He saw his parents. He remembered how he had looked up to his father. He had wanted to be just like him, and now, in the last moments of his life, he realized he was. He had died because of the game . . . a game where there were no wins for anyone. It wasn't what Big Carter had wanted for his children, especially one as intelligent as Monroe. It was then that

Monroe realized he had played the game of life incorrectly. Big Carter took to the streets so that his children would never have to, but instead, they had all followed in his fated footsteps. It was a tragic cycle that had led to the demise of an entire bloodline. The pain began to overwhelm Monroe as he gritted his teeth while gurgling on his own blood. He had never felt anything like this slow burn. All he wanted to do was take a deep breath . . . to just inhale . . . but he couldn't, and as he fell face-forward into the pavement, he heard a familiar voice.

"Its okay, bro. Just let go. It all goes away once you just let the streets go."

Monroe blinked slowly because he knew that his mind had to be playing tricks on him. Mecca was in front of him as clear as day, talking to him . . . urging him to let go. He choked and he struggled, trying to fight the grim reaper as long as he could. It hurt so bad. He couldn't breathe. He couldn't. He couldn't. He wanted to just get air to his lungs, but he . . . just . . . couldn't. *I'm dying*, he thought.

"Just let go, Money. I'm right here," Mecca's voice said. "It won't hurt anymore once you let go."

Monroe finally listened as the struggle stopped and he just lay there as the last shallow breaths seeped from his body. *Damn, he's right. It doesn't hurt,* he thought. A calm passed over him in his final moments. A euphoric feeling swept over him, removing all pain. His crying son was the last thing he saw before permanently closing his eyes. Monroe "Money" Diamond was no more. With him, the legacy of The Cartel would be buried six feet under.

* * *

Sam walked into her apartment feeling victorious. She flipped the light switch. "Damn it," she said as she sucked her teeth, realizing her light had blown. She had been undercover for so long that she hadn't darted these doors in months. "I'll be surprised if anything works at all." She wiggled the light switch up and down again, to no avail. It had been a long day. Hell, it had been a long three years. All she wanted to do was come home to her own place and wrap her mind around what she had just achieved. Her investigation had finally come to an end and she had closed her case. It wasn't the conclusion she had in mind, but it would be enough to land her a promotion. Taking down The Cartel that had duped the federal government years ago would put her on the fast track. It was what they called "the case of a lifetime." Most agents were lucky to even get one. It was the case that Supreme Court justices were made of, which was her ultimate goal. The arrest of the leader of the infamous Murder Mamas and the death of Monroe Diamond was an accomplishment. She hadn't nailed Carter, but she had done enough to make her career a long and fruitful one. She took off her holster and placed her weapon near the table that sat near the front door. The tension that had been building in her body left her with one long sigh. "God, I need a beer," she said to herself before heading to the kitchen. She ran her hands through her hair and pulled it back into a sloppy ponytail before opening her fridge. The interior light came on and she grabbed a beer from the top shelf. Popping the top, she took a long swig before turning to head to her room.

The silhouette of the person sitting in the chair before her sent her into a panic as terror struck her. "Shit!" she shouted in alarm as she dropped her beer.

"Sit down," Aries demanded in a calm tone.

Sam's eyes shot to her holstered gun that she had placed by the door, but before she could even make a move, Aries fired on her.

PSST!

"Agh!!!" Sam screamed in excruciation as she fell to the floor.

Everyone had always pegged Miamor as the most deadly Murder Mama, but Aries was highly underrated. She pulled triggers with less remorse than any of them. She had just blown off Sam's knee without thinking twice. "I asked you nicely the first time. Now you don't have a choice but to sit," Aries said.

Sam writhed as blood soaked through her pants and she grabbed her knee in pain. Aries stood and walked over to the federal agent. She bent down in front of her. "We wouldn't want anyone hearing you scream now, would we? They might interrupt our fun," she sneered. She snatched the kitchen towel off of the stove and stuffed it into Sam's mouth, then pulled a roll of duct tape from the messenger bag she wore across her body. She wrapped the tape tightly around Sam's entire head. Anger flickered in Aries's eyes as Sam tried to scream through the tape. "See, Miamor knew there was something fishy about you," Aries said. "She just couldn't place her finger on it. Turns out you're a fucking fed." Aries grabbed Sam's long hair and wrapped it around her fist until she had a tight hold on her. She dragged the woman across the floor mercilessly, leaving a bloody trail along the way. "Get in the chair," she said. Her voice was so calm that it sent a chill up Sam's spine. The look in Aries's eyes was sociopathic. She had no remorse. No emotion. This routine was automatic for her. No matter how much she tried to keep the beast in her dormant, it always surfaced . . . eventually. Sam struggled to climb into the chair. Aries grabbed Sam's wrist and forced her hand to lie flat on the kitchen table. She pulled out a hunting knife from her bag.

"Agh!" Aries shouted as she jammed it through Sam's hand. She used so much force that the knife went through Sam's hand and through a good portion of the table, keeping Sam in place. Sam hollered in agony. Aries was unaffected by her screams.

"The problem with taking out a Murder Mama is that there is always another one you have to worry about. We just keep coming and coming for your head. Miamor is my sister. We have been at this thing together for a long time. You took her away and for that, you have to answer to me. My murder game is worth six figures. I don't do this for free, but the minute you put shackles around Miamor's wrists, you made this personal. You are on my bad side, and that's not a very safe place to be."

Sam screamed. She cried, but her sounds were inaudible behind the tape. No amount of pleading would get her out of this predicament. She had destroyed an empire. She had dismantled a family. She deserved every bit of pain Aries wanted to inflict, and Aries was in the mood for punishment.

"Go ahead. Me hear screaming dulls de pain. Releases endorphins or something in de brain," Aries said as she circled Sam like a predator sizing up prey. "Although it doesn't look like you are feeling any relief." Aries chuckled. She wanted to make Sam's death as slow as those years that Miamor was about to endure, but she knew that the longer this took, the more her chances of getting caught increased.

It was one of the rules of the Murder Mamas. "Get in and out," Miamor had always said. "Don't let your rage become a distraction. When you get distracted, you get sloppy; when you get sloppy, you get caught." Tears came to Aries's eyes because she knew she would never see her beloved friend again. It would be too big of a risk for Aries to ever walk into a prison for a visit. They would be forever parted by the steel and concrete that would serve as a cage to Miamor for the rest of her life. That fact made Aries sick to her stomach. She had felt it before when Robyn had been executed, and before that when Anisa had been killed, and even before that when Beatrice had lost her life. She was the last one standing, and it was a heavy burden to bear.

"You took away me family," Aries said as she stopped directly behind Sam. She bent down to whisper in her ear. "You're a fucking pig . . . a fucking filthy fed pig. You deserve to be slaughtered like one." Sam's eyes widened in panic. "Tell me . . . is it true that your life flashes before your eyes before you die?" She quickly pulled the knife out of the table and slid it across Sam's neck in one smooth movement. She walked around Sam's body and stood in front of her, watching as blood streamed from her throat. Sam gurgled as she struggled to breathe. The sound was music to Aries's ears. "You fucked with de wrong one," she said. Aries didn't move until all of the life had drained from Sam's body. She then walked to the sink, rinsed off the hunting knife, and then placed it back in her messenger bag. She wasn't worried about fingerprints because she had never taken off her gloves. She wasn't new to covering her tracks. There wasn't a forensics team in the world that could pin a murder on her. Aries walked out the door, disappearing as if she had never even been there at all. Miamor had been avenged. Fuck Karma . . . that bitch worked too slowly. Aries's method was much quicker and much harsher than the winds of life could have ever been. Sam would never get a chance to reap the rewards of taking down The Cartel. She was being promoted, all right. She was going up into the heavens. Aries had made sure of it.

* * *

"Where are my keys?" Breeze whispered to herself as she opened up her kitchen drawers. Monroe was in trouble. She had heard it in his voice that he planned on doing something stupid. Her nephew needed her. Monroe needed her, and as she frantically ripped her home apart, she could feel tears building in her eyes. "Damn it!" she screamed. She rushed into the master bedroom and opened her nightstand to no avail. She sighed and then hurriedly went to Zyir's side of the bed. She opened the drawer. She rummaged through his belongings, and relief flooded her when she located her Benz fob in the mess. Just as she was about to close the drawer, a picture caught her eye. She frowned as she stared at her own mug shot. Flipping it around, she read the inscription on the back.

Just a friendly reminder of what's at stake. Get my evidence. Either bring down The Cartel, or you fall with them.

Evidence? Breeze thought. She dropped the photo as if suddenly it were hot to the touch. She went back into the drawer. Breeze had never snooped on Zyir. She had never felt the need to invade his privacy. She trusted him, but now her antennas were up. Monroe was in trouble, and now Breeze suspected Zyir was the reason behind it.

"Hmm, hmm."

The sound of Zyir clearing his throat made her freeze.

"What are you doing?" Zyir asked.

"What did you do?" she shot back, accusatory, as she stared at him with disappointment in her eyes.

He didn't even have to respond for her to know the answer. The look of guilt and sorrow that spread on his face told it all. She bent down and snatched the picture off the floor. She read the back aloud. " 'Either bring down The Cartel, or you fall with them'?" She had been shouting and she hadn't even realized it.

"I can explain," he stated.

"You're talking to the feds," Breeze surmised as a quea-siness settled into her stomach. She didn't know if it was the pregnancy or the revelation that had come to light, but all of a sudden she felt sick.

"I had to, B. They were closing in on—"

"They're coming for Monroe right now! While I'm stand-ing here arguing with you, they're storming my parents' estate!" Breeze shouted in disbelief. "I trusted you! We all trusted you!"

"Let me explain it to you. I did this for you," he said. The way she was looking at him was breaking his heart. "You know me. Just hear me out."

"I don't know anything about you," she said. She turned around and rushed to the bathroom, locking the door behind her. She barely made it to the toilet before vomit erupted. She was hot, literally and figuratively. Sweat beads built on her forehead as her anger pulsed.

"B, you have to calm down . . . this stress ain't good for the baby. Just let me in. Let me tell you how it came to this," Zyir pleaded.

She didn't respond. Her heart was so wounded that it felt like it had lost its beat. She climbed to her feet and turned on the faucet. She cupped her hands under the water and took some into her mouth, gargling. She then splashed water over her face, completely overwhelmed.

"Breeze, open this door! Let me talk to you, B. I love you. It was all for you. Just hear me out."

She heard him, but she had no response. Breeze couldn't even develop the right words to say. She couldn't stop shaking her head in disgust. This was a betrayal that she could have never seen coming.

Breeze stood in front of the bathroom mirror, her head bowed as she gripped the sides of the sink. The knot in her stomach was so big that it felt like someone had stabbed her. She squeezed her eyes tightly while gritting her teeth. Betrayal burned. It seared through her soul as the lies she had been told replayed in her mind. All this time she had been sleeping with the enemy. The deception that she had discovered stung. It ate away at every memory that she and Zyir shared. She thought she knew him. She had thought they were soul mates, but if that were true, how had he so easily fooled her. He had been working with the feds and she had known nothing about it. Every day he had hidden it from her, which made her ask the inevitable question: *What else is he hiding?* It felt like someone had punched her in the gut. The wind had been knocked out of her. Zyir, a man who had shown her nothing but exemplary character and loyalty . . . a man who had saved her life . . . a man she had given 100 percent of herself to had turned snitch. It felt like a bad dream. Zyir was nothing like the man she'd thought him to be. In her family's book, there was nothing lower than a nigga who didn't stand tall when his back was against the wall. Even Breeze, with her privilege and spoiled ways, knew that to cooperate was to betray every moral that had been drilled into her since birth. He had dishonored his name and there was no excuse. Breeze felt like she didn't know the man she had lain next to for years.

Breeze gathered herself. She didn't have time to do this

right now. Her brother was in trouble. Her nephew needed her. There was no doubt in her mind about what had to be done. Her father would have killed Zyir for the trespass. Mecca would have tortured him slowly. Monroe would have cut him off. Carter would have mourned the betrayal. All of these things would have been a well-deserving consequence to the choice that Zyir had made, but no punishment would hurt as much as the one Breeze was about to deliver. She opened the door to the bathroom and Zyir stood, hands on either side of the door, blocking her exit as he stared at her with regret-filled eyes.

"Let me be clear. You and I are over. I won't give birth to the seed of a snitch. I'm aborting this baby and I never want to see you again. My family meant everything to me, and you destroyed it," she said. She pushed past him and headed for the door.

"It was either them or you. If I didn't do it, they were going to indict you for the bricks that were in the back of the trunk from the traffic stop a while back. I cooperated to make sure that didn't happen," Zyir admitted.

His words halted her midstep and her heart sank. "What?" she said as she turned toward him. Tears moistened her cheeks as it all began to make sense. She could fathom this. She knew that his love for her outweighed all. It overrode his loyalty to even his oldest friend, Carter.

"I couldn't let you do a day in prison, Breeze. You're my wife . . . my rib . . . if I have to choose between my character and your freedom, you're going to win that battle every time. It ain't right," Zyir said, growing emotional as she saw pools of anguish build in his eyes. He quickly blinked away the tears and composed himself. "But it was my only option. I came up with Carter. He is my family, just as much as he is yours. You think I wanted to do this? You think this shit hasn't eaten away at me every day? You can't leave me, B. You can't kill my seed," Zyir said as he got on his knees and wrapped his arms around her waist. He kissed her stomach, and Breeze closed her eyes. So many feelings coursed through her body. She loved and hated this man all at the same time. "You're all I have left."

"You shouldn't have made this decision for me," Breeze whispered. "My family isn't built on disloyalty, Zy. I would have done twenty years before I would have given up my brothers. I'm not the strongest Diamond. I'm not the bravest or the most gangster, but I am the most loyal. They are my brothers. We share the same blood. You have ruined them. You have ruined me. You should have said something—if not to me, then to Carter at least. Snitching is never an option. So now what? They get jammed up and you walk away free for dirt that you all did together. You were supposed to be family. What future could we ever have now?"

Zyir stood to his feet and cradled her face in his hands, his face frowning in inner agony. "We can have the rest of our lives, Breeze. Don't leave me, B. I just wanted to protect you," he said.

Breeze took a step back. Her heart was shattered because she no longer trusted him. She had no idea that there was even a side to him that could do something so foul. She wanted to be his wife, to be the mother of his child, and the ride-or-die on his arm, but she couldn't.

"I can't be with you and I can't have this baby. I don't want any piece of you inside of me. I never thought the day would come where I would see you as my enemy," she said. Her words weren't malicious, but they were sad because they both knew that she meant them. He deserved them, and they pierced his heart like tiny daggers. "Good-bye, Zyir." It pained her to walk away from him. She knew his intentions were good, but she just couldn't look him in the eyes. Zyir had been her king. Her superman. She had looked up to him, placing him on a throne so far up that no one could ever touch him. By cooperating with the feds, she had lost all respect for him. Once she no longer held a man in high regard, he would be deemed unworthy of her forever.

She thought that he would come after her. She was sure that he would plead his case over and over again, but he didn't. She was grateful for that much. Breeze didn't want him to see her break down as she rushed out of the house. This was the last conversation they would have. She had no words. There was nothing left to say. She climbed in her car and pressed the button to start the ignition. Before she could even pull away . . .

BANG!

The sound of a single gunshot echoed through the air. Breeze jumped, and her head snapped in the direction of their home.

"No," she whispered. She fumbled with the door handle and exited the car, but before she could even take a step, she stopped herself. She bit down on her bottom lip and sobbed. She hit the roof of the car. "Damn it, Zyir!" she screamed. She already knew what had gone down. She didn't want to see it. Seeing him with a bullet in his head at his own hand would alter who she was. She would be haunted by it for the rest of her life. It was the punishment for the act of betrayal he had committed. If he hadn't done it, eventually someone would have. Instead of running from the inevitable, Zyir had welcomed it. He hadn't done all of this to end up alone. Without Breeze, life wasn't worth living.

Breeze climbed back in her car and beat her steering wheel in frustration as she cried and cried and cried. This was not how things were supposed to be, but it was her reality. In the blink of an eye, Zyir had changed the game for everyone. She picked up her cell and dialed 911.

"911. What is your emergency?"

"I'm worried about my husband. I think he may have hurt himself, and I'm not home. Could you please send an officer out to 707 Susan Lane?"

She hung up and put her car in drive as she pulled away from their mansion, wrecked with plenty of regret.

She was headed back to Miami, where The Cartel had begun and where it would now end—all because of the man she had chosen to love.

Epilogue

Loneliness. That's what Carter felt as he walked the streets of Barcelona while looking at pictures of his son, Mo, and Breeze. He was grateful for those images. They made his days a little bit easier, giving him temporary relief from the anguish that was a constant weight on his heart.

His narrow escape hadn't given him time to take C.J. with him. He had been forced once again by the law to leave his son behind. Not being with him was torture, and Carter was biding his time until he could return. He vowed to walk back into C.J.'s life one day. Until then, a phone call once a month to a burner phone and postcards would have to be enough.

He ducked down an obscure alleyway, pulling the collar of his Burberry trench coat up over his neck as he kept his head low. Whenever he went to public places, he kept a low profile. He was wanted in the States. If he was ever caught, there wasn't a doubt in his mind that he would spend the rest of his days in a federal prison. He vowed not to meet that fate.

He entered the building where he had been holing up. It was a one-bedroom flat that sat on the top floor, overlooking the busy city. The feds had seized his accounts, but luckily he'd had the foresight to stash half of his money in a Swiss account. He could live the rest of his days luxuriously if he chose, but right now he just wanted to restore a sense of normalcy to his life. Things had spiraled so far out of control that he no longer knew how to rein in his problems. They overwhelmed him. Burdened him. Destroyed his inner peace. He entered the flat and quickly locked the door behind him. He had only the necessities. He didn't want to acquire anything that he would regret having to leave behind. Living the life of a wanted man, there was no way to know when he would have to up and leave. He had to move carefully if he wanted to remain free. Carter sat down and flicked on the television, turning to CNN.

It was the only way he could see her face. Miamor was awaiting trial, and her story had been plastered all over the news for months. The feds were portraying her as a murderous queen pin. The new-age Griselda, they had dubbed her. Carter knew that the description was accurate. Miamor was a villain. She wasn't the good girl in anyone's story except his own, but she wasn't being prosecuted for her crimes. She was taking the fall for his, and that fact tortured him daily. She was a good woman. The most real that a man in his position could ever dream of, but she was still a woman. She shouldn't have to carry this for him. She was facing life in prison while he was hiding in the shadows in Spain. It didn't feel right, and every day he was compelled to go back.

He picked up the burner cell phone and speed-dialed Breeze.

"What's wrong? You're not supposed to call until next week?" Breeze asked as soon as she answered the phone.

"I miss my son, Breeze. My wife's face is on the TV screen. She has nobody, B. She's fighting these charges by herself. I'm a man. I can't let her take this for me," Carter said as he sat down on his couch while staring at the news.

"This is how she wanted it, Carter. You can't come back here. Not right now. Probably not for a while," Breeze said. "And you can't call here too often. This is risky. You said once a month," she reminded him.

"I know. I'm losing it over here, Breeze," Carter said. It wasn't often that he revealed his vulnerability but Breeze was his sister and she was the only one who could relate to the type of loss he was suffering from.

"I know. I'm losing it here, too. Being in Miami won't make the pain go away, Carter. I live through it every minute of everyday," she whispered. "Zyir—"

"Was a good nigga," Carter said, interrupting her before she could defame Zyir's character. "He was a good nigga in a bad situation, Breeze."

They both grew silent. They hadn't spoken of Zyir since everything had fallen apart. Carter's eyes grew misty and he quickly blinked them away. "Remind yourself of that when you're rubbing your belly. That baby's father was a real nigga. He held me down for a lot of years. You can't fault a man for doing the unthinkable to protect the woman he loves. He wasn't trying to get himself out of trouble with the law, B. He was trying to save you. It's fucked up and his actions hurt us all, but I understand it. The love of a woman will make you step out of character. I just wish he had come to me."

He could hear Breeze's sniffles through the phone and he knew he had brought her to tears. "Thank you for talking me into keeping this baby, Carter," Breeze whispered. "It's all of him that I have left. I just drove away that day. I didn't look back when I heard the shot. I just drove away. I'll never forgive myself for that."

"We all have things we wish we could go back and do differently, B," Carter replied solemnly. "Go see him. The fact that he took one to the head and didn't die is reason enough to check on him," Carter said.

"I just can't," she replied.

His heart was fractured. Without Miamor and C.J., he felt empty . . . soulless. He was incomplete. Despite the fact that Zyir had broken the code, he didn't want Breeze to feel the loneliness that he lived with.

"You want to speak to him? We've already been on the phone too long," Breeze said, changing the subject to C.J. They always restricted their communication. The last thing they needed was for Carter to be caught.

"Just for a moment," Carter said. "I'll be brief."

Carter heard the rustling on the other end as Breeze called his son to the phone.

"Hello?" C.J. greeted him.

"Hey, big man," Carter said.

"Daddy!" C.J. replied. "What's up! Where are you? You on your way back yet?"

"Nah, not yet, C.J. Dad is handling some business right now, but I'll be back one day. It might take me a while, but remember that I love you. Your mother—she loves you. Until I get back, your aunt B is gonna take care of you, a'ight? Don't give her a hard time. Keep your head on straight and stay out of trouble," Carter said, clearing his throat to make sure his torment wasn't reflected in his tone.

"Yeah, a'ight, Dad," C.J. said. "I love you, too. I've got to go. Me and Mo about to go hoop."

Carter chuckled. His son was getting older by the day. He was only eight, but each time he spoke to him, he seemed to have matured. "Take care of each other, C.J. That's family, and family is—"

"All you got," C.J. finished. "I know, Dad. Got to go. Later!" he shouted as he dropped the phone. Carter was amazed at the resiliency of children. He wished that he could bounce back as easily as C.J. did, but life hadn't burned his son yet. He knew nothing about the woes that Carter suffered from.

Breeze got back on the phone. "Carter, I've got to go. The police are pulling into my driveway," she whispered.

He could hear panic in her voice. "Stay on the phone,

B," Carter replied. "How many of them?" he asked. He stood to his feet. This was the problem. He was too far away.

"Three squad cars and a SWAT truck," Breeze replied.

"Boys, get in here!" she shouted, her voice shaking. "Carter, what the hell are they doing here? What could they possibly want now?"

Carter's jaw tensed, and he gritted his teeth while pinching the bridge of his nose. Stress invaded his entire body. "I don't know. Call Einstein on your house phone. Hurry," Carter instructed.

Before she could even respond, Carter heard a loud . . . BOOM!

The sound of the door being rammed off the hinges echoed through the phone as Carter heard yelling on the other end of the phone.

"On the ground, now! On the ground! Who else is in the house?"

Carter heard the phone drop, and his stomach went hollow.

"Nobody! Just my kids! Two boys, but they're just kids!" Breeze shouted.

"Breeze Rich, you are under arrest . . ."

Carter went deaf as he heard the officers reading his pregnant sister her rights. He gripped the phone as the screams of his son and his nephew shouted at the officers.

"Who do we have here?" a voice said, finally picking up the cell phone. Carter was livid. The fact that he couldn't do anything had him heated. It took everything in him not to say anything. He clenched his teeth so tight that the pressure made his jaw ache. Carter sat on the phone, listening, as did the officer who had picked up the line. They were at a standoff, waiting for each other to speak.

"Who is this?" Carter finally spoke.

"Agent Rivard, with the IRS. Who is this?" the man asked.

"You know who this is," Carter responded pompously. Carter knew this game. The DEA couldn't pin a narcotics case against Breeze, so in came the money police, the IRS. They would slap her with tax evasion, fraud, and any other monetary crime that they could make stick. The feds were out for blood, his blood. Breeze's arrest was a sure way to smoke him out of his hole. "Agent Rivard. You should have left well enough alone. I'll see you soon."

"Is that a threat?" the agent shouted. "Are you threatening me, you son of a bitch?"

"Absolutely," Carter replied. He ended the call and rushed over to the small safe he kept beneath the bed. In it were numerous passports with different aliases. He grabbed one and then stormed out of the door.

His anger overwhelmed him. His heart beat as if there were thoroughbred racehorses inside of his chest. He couldn't sit in Europe tucked away safely while his family was taking hits that were meant for him. First Miamor, now Breeze. Breeze was the most innocent of them all. If she went down, his son, Money's son—they would have nowhere to go. No, this couldn't happen, and he wasn't going to let it. He hailed a cab, knowing that it would be damn near impossible for him to catch one easily. To his surprise, one pulled up quickly. Carter hopped inside. "El Prat," he said, telling the driver to head to the airport.

His brow was wrinkled in stress and concern as he stared out of his window. "My man, why aren't we moving? I don't have all day," Carter said.

The door across from him opened, and a woman slid into the cab. "This cab is taken—"

Before he could even finish his sentence, the woman pulled out a syringe and injected it into the side of his neck. Carter gripped her wrist as his eyes bulged in fear. Suddenly his hold on her loosened and his body went limp against his will. He watched helplessly as a smirk of satisfaction crossed her face. He tried to place her face. Who was she? Was this one of Baraka's hitters? Ma'tee's? He couldn't help but wonder which part of his past had come back to haunt him. As he tried to figure it out, the world around him faded. His heart burned as sweat beads appeared on his forehead. *Damn*, he thought. This was not the way he thought he would go out. The fear in his eyes made the woman burst into laughter. "Relax, baby, you're not dying. I just need you to go to sleep for a little while. Night, night," she said. No matter how hard he tried to keep his eyes open, they slowly closed. The last image he saw was her red, pouty lips mocking him. Once he was out, the woman slyly leaned Carter against his door.

"Everything all set?" the driver asked.

"All set. It's about time the opportunity presented itself. We've been waiting for this moment. Let's head to the clear port," she replied.

* * *

Carter groaned as he came to. He felt the fabric of a pillowcase over his head. It stifled his breaths as the fabric covered his nose, slightly suffocating him as he sucked in his own recycled air. There were others in the room. He could hear them, struggling, questioning, demanding the same answers to questions he pondered himself. Carter sat stoically as he realized his hands and legs were bound to the chair he had been planted in. Everything was fuzzy. Voices sounded far away. He was still groggy from the effects of being drugged, and he had no idea where he had been taken. He shook his head, trying to clear his thoughts from the heavy fog that was weighing down his mental. He couldn't think straight. His senses were dulled, but his heart sensed very well that danger was near.

The sounds of other people chatting became more coherent as he came to. He heard at least three different voices. He couldn't pinpoint exactly whom they belonged to. *Where am I?* he thought. Apparently it was the exact same thought running through the minds of the others in the room. It was complete chaos as everyone tried to figure out what was going on.

"Where the fuck am I?" a female voice asked.

"I can't see anything! What's going on?" asked a man.

"Whoever is behind this—untie me right now!" a man said with a heavy Spanish accent.

"Please help!" someone screamed. The screams only made things worse. It was the unknown that haunted Carter. *Am*

I in police custody? he thought. The absolute darkness beneath the pillowcase was causing paranoia to creep into his bones.

Suddenly, a man's voice broke through all of the chaos: "Listen! We can't figure this thing out if everyone is talking. So let's all relax and talk this out."

Who is that? Carter thought. The man's words settled the room. Carter listened as the man continued.

"I was driving and I got ambushed. Guys in masks jumped out on me and then I remember everything going black," the man said as everyone listened.

"That's exactly what happened to me, Baron," a female voice said as she also tried to relieve herself from the bondage.

Baron? Carter thought, catching the name that the woman had thrown out. He ran it through his mental Rolodex, but drew blanks. This was getting more odd by the minute.

"It's me, Anari," the woman said, announcing herself.

Again, Carter was drawing blanks. He had never heard of Anari but her name was legend in the streets. She was the woman who could make it snow. She was heavy in the game and was a member of the supreme Clientele drug syndicate.

Carter was tired of playing guessing games, so he made his presence known. "My name is Carter . . . Carter Jones," he announced. He also was bound and blindfolded. "The last thing I remember is being ambushed out of the blue in Spain."

"I'm Dahlia," another woman spoke up, "and the last thing I remember . . ."

The sound of metal doors clanging open caused everyone to freeze. Carter didn't know what to expect. Some of the most powerful people in the underworld were in that room, but ironically none of them had control over what was about to occur. The sounds of shoes clicking on the floor echoed throughout the room. Every single soul in the room was on edge, and the anticipation was thick. It was as if they could hear each other's heartbeats. The sound of the clicks got louder and louder and eventually they stopped. The hairs on the back of Carter's neck stood up as his imagination got away from him. He wasn't used to being in a position like this. He was the play-caller, but someone else was pushing the buttons in this situation. One thing was for sure: This wasn't the feds.

Carter's pillowcase was pulled from his head, and the bright lights of the room blinded him. He squinted as he looked around and saw that he was in a spacious room with marble floors. The artwork on the ceiling was incredible, something like he had never seen before. The hand-painted ceilings were beautiful and so high that it looked like he was staring into the heavens. They were all seated around an oak table that had a gloss that shined like no other. There were six of them in total. Carter recognized no one. A man walked around the room, freeing them one by one.

"Who are you?" Carter asked.

He was tall, slender, with salt-and-pepper hair. His brown skin was fair, and he wore his hair in a low cut.

Carter's apprehensions eased as he stared intently at the man. There was something about his eyes. They were warm, showing no malice.

"I apologize for having to bring you all here in this fashion, but it was the only way. Please do not be alarmed. I am not your enemy. I have no bad intentions here." He had a smooth, relaxing voice. He spoke loud and clear. Most of all, he spoke with confidence.

Once he had uncovered everyone, there was complete silence. Everyone looked around the gigantic room and admired the black-and-white checkered floors and stunning paintings on the walls and ceiling. It was something none of them had ever seen before. It was simply amazing.

Everyone wanted to say something, but no one did. Carter's mind raced.

"Every single one of you has been handpicked to help me and my organization. All of you are considered to be the best at moving narcotics. The best drug dealers in the world are at this table, and we felt that you could help us move a new product," the man said, looking each one of them in the eyes as he talked. He moved his hands elegantly as he spoke clearly. He grabbed everyone's attention, and they were itching to find out more. "If anyone wants to walk out the door, you have the right. A car will be waiting outside and will take you to a private jet. That private jet will take you anywhere you want to go, and you will never hear from my people or me again. The choice is yours," the man said. He paused for a second and waited to see if anyone wanted to leave.

"Keep talking," the woman named Anari said as she clasped her hands. She set them on the table and leaned forward, obviously very interested in what the charming man had to offer. Carter sized her up. Her beauty was unmatched, but the cunning look in her eyes told Carter that she was ruthless. She carried herself like a boss, and her power was evident at first glance.

"My organization is a society that works together to achieve a common goal. We have seen others do this on a massive scale and control the country . . . the world, even. It's time to tip the scales and restore the order," he said with conviction. He placed both of his hands behind his back and slowly began to circle the table.

"My organization has created a drug that provides the high of cocaine and yet when the drug fades, it gives the euphoria of heroin. It is taken orally and, get this . . . it's not a health risk. There is no downside to the drug. It doesn't affect your health, organs, or burn cells in the brain. It is a drug that gives you the high that so many desire without consequence. It also gives you the libido and desire of a twenty-one-year-old spring break student—all in one pill. Of course, we could take this public, but once the USDA gets ahold of it, the generic knockoffs will be on the streets in literally weeks. This will crumble our market and destroy our purpose. There is an exotic plant in India called the 'rebe' flower. This particular flower is the only strand in the world . . . and we are the only ones who have access to it," the slim man said just as he stopped at the opposite end of the table.

"I want to take the time to introduce everyone here. To my left is Baron Montgomery. We've been looking for him for months now. He was one of the biggest drug distributors in the Midwest and is known for his business savvy.

"To the right of him is Carter Jones, head of The Cartel of Miami. Son of the late Carter Diamond. He is young, aggressive, and has the leadership qualities that the youth flock to.

"Next we have the one and only Anari Simpson. I have to be honest with you, I am impressed. She single-handedly entered the ranks of the elite and is believed to be worth over a billion dollars . . . and her empire was built on dirty money."

"You better believe it," Anari confirmed as she looked down at her manicured French tips cockily. The whole room burst into laughter and lightened up.

"I told you she's a keeper," the slim man said while smiling and giving her a wink.

"Next we have the Dahlia. Our African connect, and our way to the five families in Africa. We want to use your connections to expand to your homeland."

Dahlia rolled her eyes and crossed her arms, not sold on the idea. "What can you do for me? Why do I need to help you? I'm doing just fine on my own. I have the African mob behind me. I am above this," Dahlia said, letting her greed and power trip take over.

"Like I said before, this is optional and we are not begging you to be a part of this thing of ours. It was just an invitation," the slim man said calmly. "With all due respect, of course," he added, not wanting to offend anyone.

"I'll pass. With respect, of course," Dahlia said sarcastically as she slowly stood up.

"Well, thank you for your time, Dahlia. Sorry to have inconvenienced you with the sudden abduction. I wish you nothing but the best. The door is just to your rear," he said as he politely waved his hand toward the exit door.

Everyone watched as Dahlia made her exit.

"Well, now that we have handled that, shall I continue?" the man asked. After getting a head nod from the group, he proceeded.

"Everyone, meet Millie," he said as he pointed to one of the two ladies in the room. "We have been watching her for years. Her game is heroin, and she has established a great track record in moving street product. We need that. We want to put this drug in the high society of America, but also on the street level.

"Last but not least, we have Brick. He has a following like no other. He has the manpower to help distribute," the man said as he looked over at the well-built man who remained quiet and observant. He had a real intense look, and his stature and strong facial features made him intimidating. "He owns the streets and has the muscle to handle whatever needs to be handled if a problem arises. His connections with the GDs and bloods will be instrumental. We need his followers to follow us. With that, we will be strong and have a street presence."

The room was quiet, and everyone looked at one another,

trying to feel one another out. They all had one thing in common: They knew the game. They couldn't believe what was happening, but they all wanted in. One by one, each of them began smiling and slowly nodding in agreement.

Carter cleared his throat and spoke up. This sounded like the opportunity of a lifetime, but he had situations back in Miami that couldn't be put on hold. "I can't commit to this at the moment. Sounds good, but I have some loose ends to tie back home." He was vague, but the man looked at him knowingly.

"I'm aware of your conflicts, Carter. If you are a part of this movement, once we are done, I will make those problems you're having in Miami disappear," the man assured him.

"Just like that?" Carter asked, wondering who this man was to yield such power.

"I'm a man of my word, if nothing else," the man answered.

Carter reluctantly nodded.

"Well, I guess there is nothing more to say. Anybody up for a trip?" the slim man asked as he rubbed his hands together while smiling.

"Absolutely," Anari said as she looked at him with her piercing eyes. "One more thing. Where are we? It's beautiful," she said as she looked around the gigantic room and its artwork.

"We are in Rome. This is inside the Vatican," the man said.

"You've got to be kidding me," she said. She couldn't

believe what she was hearing. They were talking business inside one of the world's most sacred places. This institution was more powerful than all of them combined. It was eerie.

"No lie. I will let you guys catch up and mingle. I will be outside waiting. Everyone has a car waiting for him or her outside. From here, we will go to the jet strip and head out. I will explain everything you need to know on the way to India.

"White men have been doing this for years. It's our turn. We don't even have to name this thing of ours. The public has already done that for us. Welcome to the Illuminati. . . ."

ABOUT THE AUTHORS

ASHLEY AND JAQUAVIS are the *New York Times* best-selling authors of more than thirty novels. They are the youngest black writers to ever debut on the prestigious *New York Times* list. The duo is responsible for breathing life back into black fiction and was recognized by *Ebony* when they made the Power 100 list in 2012. The duo has also signed their first movie deal for their bestselling novel *The Cartel*.

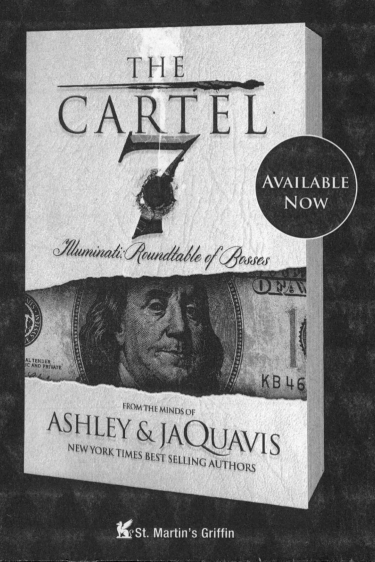

Now Available from

JaQUAVIS COLEMAN

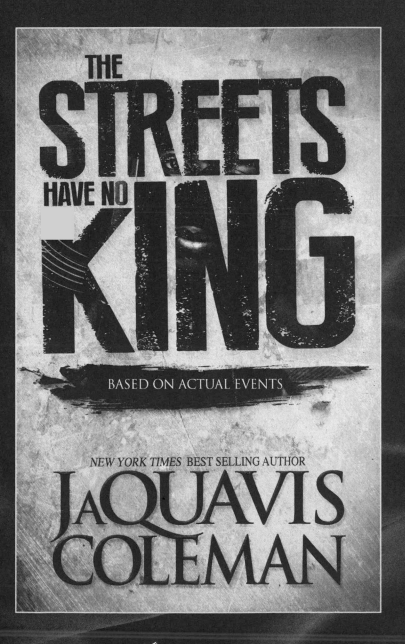

THE STREETS HAVE NO KING

BASED ON ACTUAL EVENTS

NEW YORK TIMES BEST SELLING AUTHOR

JaQUAVIS COLEMAN

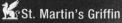 St. Martin's Griffin

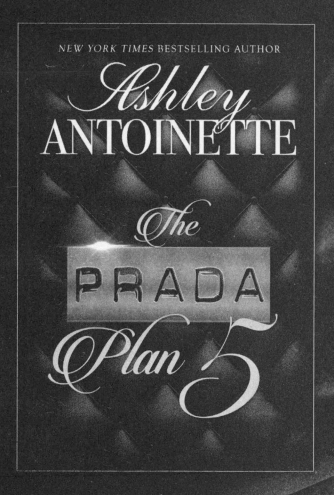